TESSA DUDER TRAINED AS a journalist and has published more than forty works of fiction, non-fiction and anthologies for both children and adults. Her debut novel *Night Race to Kawau* (1982), recently re-issued in a 40th anniversary edition, was followed by the classic young adult novel *Alex* (1987), which was published in five languages and adapted for a 1993 movie. Recent works include biographies of Margaret Mahy, Sir Peter Blake and Auckland's pioneering 'First Lady' Sarah Mathew. Her latest is about the charting of New Zealand by James Cook, and in 2019 the four *Alex* books were published as *Alex the Quartet*.

Her awards include a number of children's fiction prizes, the Storylines Margaret Mahy Medal, the Katherine Mansfield Fellowship to Menton, an Artists to Antarctica award, the OBE and in 2021 the CNZM. She holds an honorary doctorate from the University of Waikato and won the 2020 Prime Minister's Award for Literary Achievement (Fiction). Tessa also serves on the board of the Storylines Children's Literature Trust of New Zealand Te Whare Waituhi Tamariki o Aotearoa and was for twenty years a Trustee of the Spirit of Adventure Trust. She has four daughters and two grandchildren and lives in Devonport, Auckland.

WWW.TESSADUDER.CO.NZ

Auckland showing Point Britomart, 1840.

Mount Eden
Mechanics Bay

Official Bay

Point Britomart Commercial Bay

The Sparrow

Tessa
Duder

PENGUIN BOOKS

PENGUIN

UK | USA | Canada | Ireland | Australia
India | New Zealand | South Africa | China

Penguin is an imprint of the Penguin Random House group of companies, whose addresses can be found at global.penguinrandomhouse.com.

First published by Penguin Random House New Zealand, 2023

10 9 8 7 6 5 4 3 2 1

Design and cover illustration by Carla Sy © Penguin Random House New Zealand
Author photograph courtesy *Channel* magazine
Image on pages 2–3 (H Y, Auckland Showing Point Britomart, 1840, sepia wash, 166 x 230 mm) courtesy Auckland Art Gallery Toi o Tāmaki (gift of Sir Henry Brett, 1915)
Prepress by Soar Communications Group
Printed and bound in Australia by Griffin Press, an Accredited ISO AS/NZS 14001 Environmental Management Systems Printer

A catalogue record for this book is available from the National Library of New Zealand.

ISBN 978-1-76104-767-1
eISBN 978-1-76104-768-8

penguin.co.nz

Dedicated to the memory of the women and girls cruelly and unjustly convicted, transported and imprisoned 12,000 miles from their homeland, to those who died and those who, against all odds, survived.

Contents

1. Arrival

THEY GAVE US NO WARNING.

Not one single person on that ship told us to brace ourselves for the shock or cover our ears. No one yelled out 'Harry, quick! Help get the little ones down below.' Though I'm not surprised: I learned thousands of miles ago that your average sailor hates human cargo — convicts the worst, of course, but poor emigrants not much better. We complain and get sick and have to be fed.

Besides, we're all much too interested in the two native canoes paddling at speed towards us, also with what's happening up on the headland. Earlier we saw two boats being lowered from the government ship anchored nearby and a party rowed ashore. One of them, judging from the skirts, was a woman.

An important ceremony is happening today, apparently.

So, with all eyes turned towards the land, no one notices what the crew of the other ship, the *Anna Watson*, are getting ready to do.

One minute the harbour is calm and peaceful, the sun high in the sky. Barely a sound, just the cries of a few seagulls and voices from the canoes being carried across the water by a cool breeze. I'm leaning over the railings, the sun warm on the back of my neck, but longing with all my being to get off this ship and stand on dry land that doesn't move. I have a whole new life to start living.

We've been at anchor seven long days, confined below when

it rains, which is often. And before that was the incident coming into the Waitemata, when we ran aground on an unseen rock in the middle of the harbour. I was on the main deck, and the horrid jolt as we hit threw us all right off our feet. Then, apart from a few sailors yelling at each other, an ominous silence. A skinny crewman was ordered to strip to his waist and dive down to assess any damage. We watched as he climbed back over the railings, to report to the captain no damage that he could see. Other sailors came panting up from below to report no damage to the hull, no water rushing in, so far.

We passengers waited, and waited, some in tears, others calming their children, all fearful for our lives until at last the tide turned and after several hours the ship floated free.

To have come so far, endured so much . . . Oh please Lord, let not my short life end in this godforsaken place. Let those native people in the canoes be the friendly sort, not those we've heard about who throw spears and rocks and stinking fish. Who do fierce war dances and are still thought to feast on human—

'Look! Look over there!' Children beside me along the railings are pointing at the headland, where a large flag is now fluttering cheerfully atop a tall pole. Red and blue, of course British. We can hear cheering.

Next minute, a thunderous, ear-splitting, bone-shattering BOOOOOM!

It comes from the nearby government ship, the *Anna Watson*. We stare at her, shocked to the core. White smoke is pouring from the stern. Is she firing at us? At the canoes getting ever closer? At the natives seen gathering around the flagpole, outnumbering our people?

Are they firing at the flag itself? Why would they do that? Has a war started?

Every one of the little children aboard our ship is shrieking in terror, running round the deck in distressed circles or burying their snotty noses in their mothers' skirts. I scoop up one fallen baby aged about two, only to find she has soiled both her clothes and my own breeches, already frayed and grubby.

The mother comes rushing across the deck. 'Harry, oh forgive us, I'm so *sorry*!' The spoil is solid enough for me to scrape most of it off and toss over the side.

Near me a crewman bellows ''Tis only a salute! Twenty-one guns and nowt to fear! Be calm, folks, be calm!' But no one else hears him over the din, since very soon a second shot is fired.

And then not only do the children redouble their howling, along with the animals housed on the decks of both ships — bleating sheep and goats, moaning cattle, outraged chickens — but from inlets on both sides of the harbour about a million birds have risen in great clouds, shrieking and squawking loud enough to wake the dead. Within seconds they've disappeared down harbour to a safer place. Ducks, maybe? Or nesting seagulls? Swans? Some unknown species befitting this alien place?

Then there is a third boom, and a fourth and a fifth, regular as a town clock striking the hour. A couple of boys known for their mischief are now gleefully pounding their small fists against the railings.

'Six! Seven! Eight! Nine!' The rest of the children are still wailing or having their noses wiped, or have been swiftly handed down to safety below deck.

'Nineteen! Twenty! Twenty-one!'

It is over. But by this time some of us have realised worse is to come. Our own cannon at the stern is being readied and the sailors are standing alert for the mate's order to fire.

'Another twenty-one?' I ask Paddy, a grey-haired sailor who since Hobart has become something of a kindly uncle to me.

'Fifteen for us, boyo,' he says. '*She's* official, see?' His voice is heavy with sarcasm, as he nods towards the other vessel. 'Her Majesty's loyal toffs on gov'mint busy-ness.'

With all the families taking refuge below, away from the thunder and the drifting smoke, only the two mischiefs, the terrified animals, Paddy and myself are left on deck to count off the fifteen.

With each firing, the cannon recoils and the whole ship is felt to shudder. Gun drill is feckin' rusty, Paddy mutters, the gun never fired in anger or even as a warning. But I admire how each sailor does his particular job smartly, like a clockwork toy.

At last our fifteen are done. The smoky smell of gunpowder settles on the ship. The animal chorus dies down. But that isn't the end of the shooting: the *Anna Watson* must reply with yet another seven! The delighted mischiefs scamper round the deck, mimicking soldiers firing muskets. Pow! Pow! Pow! They take turns to drop dead. One trains his pretend firearm on me, and I obligingly stagger across the deck and fall against the coiled ropes, mortally injured and dramatically expiring like Nelson at Trafalgar, to their great amusement.

I humour them because I'm expected to, in the role I'm playing. Though I'm some years older, and taller, they still see me as one of them. Little idiots, who will grow up to be great idiots. No one on the ship — I'm confident — has reason to suspect that young Harry, travelling alone from Port Nicholson, isn't quite who he appears to be. Not even Pigtail Paddy.

The smoke has cleared and the harbour is again silent, except for an occasional shout from the two canoes, now quite close. They must be thinking it very strange, for these ships that supposedly come in peace to be firing off their cannons, so many times, at a completely empty sea.

No one would have warned them, either.

It will be a while before the birds know it's safe enough to return. And for our younger children and their parents to come back up on deck without fear of the guns.

After weeks of tedium, that spring day, September the eighteenth, I'll remember for three things: the cannons going off, the boat races, and seeing my first Maoris up close, one especially.

During our short time in Port Nicholson we'd seen very few native people, and then only at a distance. Here, apart from the two canoes, and that one village we passed off to port, near the harbour entrance, there's no other sign of life. Although the breeze is nippy, I stay on deck to watch the shore party being rowed back to the *Anna Watson*. Another bigger boat is lowered, and one launched also from our ship, and the next thing — glory be — they're lining up to have a race! With nothing else in the harbour to use as markers, they're heading our way. Paddy, leaning beside me on the railings, is in the mood for talking.

'See those folks,' he points as the two boats round our stern with much shouting about keeping clear. 'They be the toffs, the gov'mint officials and p'haps some gentlemen passengers. Their smart clobber 'tis dead give-aways. Some not too handy with oars! Now those,' he says when a second race sets off, 'they look like mechanics. I heard tell they're down from Kororareka, desperate for work.'

'Mechanics?' I ask.

'Carpenters, sawyers, bricklayers, all for buildin' houses. Stonemasons for walls, blacksmiths, boatmen, too. Honest labourin' men.'

He waves a hand at the low hills, covered with a kind of scrub, on either side of the harbour.

'Sure and plenty of land hereabouts, when it's cleared. Soon good work for all. That headland with yon flag, first thing they'll put up, a feckin' church. Always do. Fat priests flush with Popish money, or hard-faced London clerics — they'll see to it.'

He clears his throat lustily and spits into the water below.

'And those wee bays, soon enough there'll be houses built for the toffs and a wharf for the low tides so they don't get their dainty feet wet. You poor folk with the hungry children get leaky tents somewhere, well away from the toffs— Now will ye look at that! The savages have come out to play.'

'You shouldn't call them that.'

'That so, boy? Well, you just remember me, yer shipmate Paddy, when big black men with tattoos creep round your camp, scarin' folks to death.'

'They're not black, they're brown.'

'Brown or black, no different. They're savages!'

Though sickened, I let that pass. I didn't want an argument, not today. The two native canoes, up until now watching the racing with their paddles idle, are lining themselves up side-by-side. At a shout, paddles flash and the canoes quickly gather speed.

On the streets of Hobart the few native people I'd seen were dark-coloured, black almost, dressed in rags, sad and wretched. These paddlers, maybe twenty in each canoe, look fit and strong, their naked chests and muscles glistening with sweat, or maybe oil. The idea of racing against white settlers' boats must be a novelty, as they're grinning, enjoying themselves. The paddles flash perfectly in time. Two men in long cloaks stand proud, one at the stern steering, and the other in the middle, I guess to be the captain. Some paddlers are grey-haired, several just boys.

One, a youth in his prime, gazes up at us along the railings, clearly fascinated by us and our strange vessel, but not missing a beat as the canoe turns in a graceful curve around our stern. His hair is caught in a knot on the top of his head, a large piece of carved bone lies on his chest. There's only one way to describe him: beautiful — beautiful, beyond imagining.

'I heard o' war canoes bein' two times as long,' says Paddy as the race finishes amid much shouting and cheering from the *Anna Watson*. One native from the winning canoe climbs on board the ship, perhaps to get their prize. 'Wi' paddlers hundred or more,' he goes on. 'Flesh-eaters all. Best steer clear, when you get ashore with nowhere to run. Give 'em wide berth, boyo. Don't want to find yourself stuffed like a chicken into a cookin' pot.'

It's getting cold and this conversation unwelcome. Among the passengers who'd come aboard in Port Nicholson, all much disgusted with the mud and rain and broken promises of that settlement, was a young priest who'd assured us that eating human flesh was no longer practised. Cannibalism was a tradition associated with tribal warfare. We newcomers, he urged, must put aside our fears, and endeavour to establish good relationships with the local people.

Well, today is probably a reasonable start, I think, as the canoes head back to that bay we'd sailed by earlier, the one with the village and people walking around, and, behind, green slopes that looked like gardens. And above them a prominent small mountain, one of a number we can see from the ship.

One day soon, I'll go exploring. No one will notice a mere boy scrambling up these lumpy green hills, maybe ten or fifteen of them on both sides of the harbour. Paddy thinks they might be the remains of ancient volcanoes.

For most of that last night on the ship, I lie on the hard boards of my allotted space, restless, my mind churning. Nocturnal noises in the men's quarters have become familiar: snores, heavy breathing, farts, coughing, throats being cleared, howls as spasms of cramp take hold. Rats squeaking and scurrying, water slapping against the sides of the ship, timbers creaking. Thumping footfalls and bells signalling the change of watch interrupt what sleep I do get.

Now I've reached the end of my long journey from Sussex, the reality of my situation is becoming all too evident. From tomorrow, I'll no longer have even the *Platina* to call home.

It's not only that I'm nearly penniless, without family or friend. Back in Hobart, in my desperation to escape, I'd given no thought as to how long I could keep up this charade.

It's not just the boys' clothes, or the boy's clumsiness I've feigned since I fled from the hellhole that was Cascades. I know that some events will take place, sooner or later. My hair will grow again, long enough to plait. My breasts are still small rosebuds, but won't remain so. And as the women at Cascades told me, sometime soon I'll start to bleed from 'down there'. I'm fourteen and probably overdue for this to happen, but happen it will, they say, and every four weeks thereafter.

And going ashore, sooner or later, I must take from the canvas bag I use as a pillow that plain brown skirt stolen from outside a tavern in Hobart. If I'm careful, I will manage the changeover myself, at the right time, in my own way.

But if Harry becomes careless, he might find himself unmasked, to general disbelief and contempt. The women will be shocked, the men angry, the children mocking. I'll be that girl 'who took us for fools', be shunned as an outsider, a bad egg. It will be some time before my deception is forgotten or forgiven.

I lie on the *Platina*'s wooden slats, shivering with cold in my grimy, stinking boys' clothes. I scratch at rashes in my armpits caused by lack of washing and bites, from lice or fleas or both.

In the night a wind gets up, and the slapping of waves against the hull wakes me from a dream of my brother Jesse polishing a rosy apple to a high sheen on his sleeve. He hands it to me with a smile. But when I take a bite, the skin is tough and the soft flesh is floury and tastes of . . . nothing.

September 1836

WE WERE SENT TO the market that fateful morning to buy fresh cheeses and cooking apples. A message had come that the next day my father's sister, Aunt Dorothy, would be visiting us with her husband and daughter. Mother was determined to bake them a tender pie of new season's apples, the best she had ever made. It would be served with clotted cream and the treat of cinnamon, to cries of joy and wonder.

As we set out, my brother Jesse was in a sullen mood, following yet another disagreement with Father. I would much rather have gone on my own, but this was declared impossible for a girl not yet eleven. Father was busy finishing off a saddle, so Jesse was directed to stop sulking and accompany his sister. His mood darkened further; normally he avoided me as much as possible.

He wanted to take the narrow country lane, about two miles to the nearby market town, but there was a shorter way across the fields and up to a height for a fine view of the sea. I had lifted up my skirts and run easily up the slope, but Jesse arrived puffing, flushed and dripping sweat, to immediately throw himself down onto the grass to recover.

I felt no sympathy or love for my brother, tall for thirteen but already portly, short-tempered both with his family and with the customers who came into the saddlery to talk about a new saddle or other tack, despite all my father's entreaties for him to be, at the very least, civil. I suspected some returned only because they appreciated the fine quality of my father's work.

It was a misty early autumn day, warm and still. Beyond the sloping fields and hedgerows lay the blue sea, with the white sails of three ships slowly making their way, I supposed, to the London docks or leaving England to take cotton goods to India or even convicts to Australia.

I knew this through listening to a naval captain, who'd lost an arm, he said, 'on the West Africa Station chasing down slavers', and had retired to our village to breed horses. He often talked with Father of majestic tall ships carrying full sail through white-capped seas, of tyrannical captains and of visiting tropical islands like Jamaica and Tahiti and St Helena. And I also remembered the three village boys of Jesse's age who one day were seen talking to some roughly dressed strangers, and the next were nowhere to be found and their mothers weeping, inconsolable. They had heard tales from their own mothers of how captains ordered press-gangs to find crews for their ships and the bloody battles that were fought at sea.

Our path dropped us down into the river valley, past haystacks, apple orchards and through copses of old chestnuts and oaks. Once over the stone bridge, past the town clock, there was the familiar marketplace, bustling and noisy.

I knew many of the stallholders, and where to find the goods like flour, meat, rice and potatoes. Of course we kept hens, and a milk cow, and churned our own butter and cheese, but tomorrow for Aunt Dorothy there would be special Cheshire, blue Stilton and round soft cheeses, a roast of mutton and that special apple pie. It had been a good apple harvest: fruit all shades of pink, gold and bright shining red were piled into barrows and wicker baskets. I chose six rosy cooking apples, but Jesse ignored my request to buy two bright-red beauties to eat on the way home.

He had been given the coins for our purchases, which we made briskly and without the usual friendly chatter with stallholders. His mood improved only when he saw a boy I knew to be apprenticed to our village blacksmith, a boy I always avoided, and who my father regarded as a 'bad influence'. Of all Jesse's friends, Tom was the one I disliked the most, his whining voice and insolent stare.

I watched their hearty greetings until I recognised the piping tune and drum-roll that announced a Punch 'n' Judy show was about to begin. How fortunate that the show was here today to lift my spirits! Jesse agreed I could go, clearly glad to be shot of me, but adding tersely that I should meet him outside the tavern by the town clock when it was over. I ran off, determined not to let Jesse spoil my day.

2. Ashore at last

FROM DAYBREAK, I QUICKLY learn how hard and long a boy without family is expected to work, now that our journey is over and a new life beginning. I'm alone, a skinny boy at everybody's beck and call, dawn to dusk.

In skirts, I would have been told to mind the little children, make sure they didn't wander away around the rocks or stumble into a cooking fire or the tug of an outgoing tide. That's easy, yet surely is just as important as 'boys' work'. All our luggage and gear will get heaved ashore eventually, but you can't bring a drowned child back to life or magic away a terrible burn or broken bone.

We are put ashore to a little bay at low tide, so there's a distance of wet, sticky mud to cover before reaching dry sand. Stepping through the sludge is hard work. You don't want to lose your balance and fall over. One babe-in-arms, being handed from the boat to a sailor, gets dropped, earning the father's wrath. Several wives are carried on their husband's backs, their combined weights sinking them ever further down.

Other women, the older girls, rather than ruin a precious pair of boots, choose to abandon modesty, pulling up their skirts and wading ashore up to their bare calves in muck. The mischiefs make a game of it, kicking brown water at each other.

I'm not complaining, like most around me. I welcome the feel of soft mud squelching between my toes, the sight ahead of pale grey sand rising to low, grassy banks, and, behind, the green hills covered with bracken. No matter the biting wind, threadbare clothing, the dread of all the discomfort and uncertainty that lies ahead. The ground is real and solid and, glory be, does not move. I'm a little unsteady on my feet.

And word is getting around: we're being housed on this beach, part of the land bought peaceably yesterday by government officials from those friendly Maori chiefs seen up on the headland. That explained the flag and the cheering, the small crowd of Maoris watching, and the singing heard after nightfall from the *Anna Watson*. Someone there had a guitar.

If any one person is actually in charge of the rabble gathering on the beach, this official is nowhere apparent. As well as the boatloads of passengers being ferried back and forth from the *Platina*, there is similar activity from the *Anna Watson*, maybe a hundred of us all told, not counting the sailors manning the oars and helping to load and unload the boats. The incoming tide, slowly covering the wide expanse of wet mud, is helping to make the journey shorter and quicker.

Not only are bodies to be got ashore: boatload after boatload, too, of bags and cases and chests of all shapes and sizes, boxes of food, bundles of tools, tents, tarpaulins, chairs, tables, camp beds and other furniture. Bags of coal and bricks, sawn timber for houses, two handcarts.

And all the animals! From both ships come several cows, chickens in cages, sheep and milk goats. From the government ship, two very restless horses! Late in the day, even a small square piano that, like the horses, belongs, I hear tell, to a Mrs Mathew, wife of one of the officials. Watched over by her, four sailors add it to the piles heaped along the beach.

Rain threatens, so it's all hands to put up tents before sundown, unfolding the stiff canvas and hammering pegs into the ground. Parents leave older children to look after howling babies while they search desperately for their luggage. A distraught mother, seven children clustered around her and husband nowhere to be seen, pleads for me to bring over their family box of food. It's heavy, and I stumble over the uneven ground, but I'm a boy and boys manage.

For yet more stony-faced mothers cradling babies or soothing bewildered children, I take their pails and fetch water from a stream running down through the bracken. That little creek is about the only pretty thing on this windswept shore.

One facility is quickly established. A mate from the *Anna Watson* rounds up men who've unpacked their shovels and spades and instructs them to dig a hole further along the foreshore, well above the sand.

'Listen up! That there . . .' he shouts to the crowd, as dirt flies from the hole now deep enough for the diggers to have reached below their own height, '*that there 'ole* is the communal privy. For sake o' hygiene it'll be used for toileting by all the people. Young and old, *without exception*. D'ya hear me now? Anyone seen soiling the beach or the foreshore, even pissing under bushes, *will be censured and fined*.'

This announcement is met with a dour silence, so he adds: 'And when that there latrine is full, which won't take long, we'll seal it up and dig another!'

Above the hole the carpenters have placed boards where you put your feet to squat, and a couple of wobbling handrails to hold onto. Around it stands a screen of leafy branches cut from shrubs. Very soon I hear mothers complaining that even the older children must not use it alone; they will need to be held safely over the hole to prevent the unthinkable. Whatever the sailor man says, they'll not stop their littlest ones pissing in the shallows.

By sunset and many small miracles, most families have found

their boxes of food, utensils and billy-cans. As the light fades, the orange glow of flames casts ghostly shadows on the faces huddled around the cooking fires. Lanterns light up the tents where younger children have already been bedded down. The rain has mercifully held off.

And one fear has been put to rest. It's our childhood game of whispers, started when one wife is heard to ask if this grassy flat area might house snakes or poisonous spiders or even scorpions that can kill you or leeches that suck your blood or centipedes as long as your forearm. Within minutes the word is travelling swiftly between tents that there probably are snakes and venomous spiders and scorpions and leeches and centipedes. Everyone must remain vigilant at all times, must protect the children from harm. Many folk have come from New South Wales, and if snakes are present and dangerous to human life over there, why not here?

The young priest is sufficiently prompted by crying women and pale, wide-eyed children to stand up and reassure the throng that they should have no fear. This is a land without snakes. The missionaries up in Paihia, who have been resident there some twenty years, believe this to be so. They say the colony is akin to Ireland, blessedly free of serpents, adders, vipers, pythons or any other form of snakes. No scorpions or leeches that they know of.

But as I move around the encampment I can hear many are not convinced.

I never thought that here I would yet again be reduced to begging.

With the last of the light, not one kindly adult has offered a morsel or two to a homeless boy now faint with hunger. Begging means pity, or refusal, neither to be endured. Thieving can be under cover of darkness, when all the families are asleep in their tents and the fires and lanterns doused. Taking just what I can find, I tell myself, a little from each, so none will notice or be deprived.

It seems a long time before all the lanterns and fires are put out. My stomach is rumbling. A baby wails for its mother's milk, men with cramp groan. No moon rises from anywhere, so that only on the two anchored ships are there lights, one apiece on the foremast.

But there are big fluffy clouds, silvery against the blackness, casting enough of a glow for me to be able to make my way between the tents and not disturb a sleeping animal or tread on the last embers of a fire.

Grunting noises alert me to someone stumbling down to the foreshore: from trickling sounds, a man pissing, then with muffled curses finding his way back.

Judging it safe, I scavenge like a wild animal. I find a half-eaten biscuit discarded in the sand, and a billy-can with enough stew to feed two or three, but from which I use two fingers to take only a few scoops. Beside another spent fire is a pot with a meagre scraping of salty porridge, and at a third they've left some sticky lumps of burnt rice in a tin bowl. Another two morsels of half-chewed biscuit — a feast!

Fetching water so often during the day means I know the way along the foreshore to the little stream. The water is cold and sweet, and I drink greedily. Squatting low on some rocks soon to be covered by the tide and without fear of discovery, I pull down my boys' breeches and piss luxuriantly.

In time, I fall into a fitful sleep, burrowed into a sandy nook between some tree roots and grateful the rain has held off. I try,

I really try, to bury my lingering resentment that not one family has thought to offer that shy, gawky boy Harry, all on his own, just a little food or the corner of a tent where he can curl up. He could repay their kindness by fetching driftwood for fires, say, or even child-minding. He could even pay some money.

The soft trickle of the nearby stream is soothing, but every time I'm half-woken by the distant bells for the change of watch, one ship after another, I'm reminded of the Cascades bell jolting us awake before dawn for another fourteen-hour day, the hunchback old warden who marched through the long prison dormitory, swinging the hand bell to and fro . . .

September 1836

MR PUNCH HADN'T YET appeared when I found the little stage with its gaudy striped curtains and a crowd of eager children. They all cheered his arrival in his jester's red and green, that hooked nose and jutting chin so prominent and curved they nearly met as a circle. Between them was painted a scarlet smile with a fearsome row of white teeth. In truth, though I laughed along with the crowd, I started to hate Mr Punch, his silly hat and shrill, squeaky voice.

I used to find this show in the market amusing, but that day, older and irritated by Jesse's churlish manners, it puzzled me. Why was Mr Punch so mean and cruel to the Baby and to his wife Judy when she tried to protect the child? Why did the children laugh so when he ended the scolding by hitting both Judy and the Baby with that wooden slapstick nearly as big as himself? Why did we laugh even more when all the other characters also got hit: Joey the Clown, the Doctor, the Policeman? Mr Punch was such a bully, yet we laughed.

Did we like seeing even puppets get hurt, or, just as bad, didn't care? Today's show finished with Mr Punch being confronted by an angry Crocodile, who gobbled him up. We all cheered at that, and clapped the grey-haired puppeteer when he came out to take his bow, but I came away feeling that the day had been spoiled.

And there was still the walk home with Jesse. As I threaded my way through the crowds towards the tavern, I hoped that a jug of ale might have improved his mood. Or that two jugs had not made him quarrelsome. I definitely didn't want to see Tom the blacksmith boy again.

Enjoying my freedom, I dawdled between the stalls, admiring the wares of the woodworkers, the toy-makers and the fishmongers. Beneath the bakers' stalls, cheeky sparrows pecked at crumbs and crusts dropped from above; I loved them for their persistence, their quickness and curiosity.

Sweet smells drew me to the flower stalls, and equally bright colours to the barrows of the vegetable growers, and, of course, those joyful displays of new apples, shining like jewels. My mouth watered for a taste, but I had no money. I stopped to watch a tall constable deal firmly with a disturbance at one of the stalls, settled without anyone getting hit.

By the time I reached the tavern my spirits had risen, and more so when I saw that Jesse was alone, even greeting me with a smile. No, I hadn't kept him waiting, Tom had just gone, to meet someone.

Perhaps I would like an apple? The one that he was polishing on his sleeve and held out to me was bright shiny red.

3. Needing work

AS THE DAWN SKY turns a deep apricot, I stand up, stretch my legs, brush off the sand and face the grim reality that lies ahead. It's clear I can't expect or ask for charity from any of the families, and so will need to work for my food. The mechanics won't have spare money for whatever a desperate lad might do for a few coins, but the government officials from the *Anna Watson* might.

I'd noticed a group of them, conspicuously smart in their black frock coats, raising a large tent on flat ground not far from where I spent the night, pitched suitably distant from the common herd. Crouched behind a bush, I watch them emerge into the daylight, blinking and stretching, and hear scraps of conversation about lost bags and ruined boots and a noisy rooster whose neck deserved to be wrung.

The more I see and hear, the less I fancy my chances of employment, of being taken seriously. To them, I'm just an urchin, not strong or useful, probably cunning and untrustworthy, more than likely a pickpocket.

And I also realise, enviously watching them light a fire and prepare a breakfast, that the past four years have left me bashful and clumsy, fearful to approach and ask a favour from respectable people like these.

Paddy would have smiled to hear one with a particularly loud voice proclaiming that the tidal mud of this supposedly vaunted harbour is absolutely *intolerable* and the *first* task ashore must be putting in a wharf, *before anything else*, even before starting the erection of the government house — they're bringing the timbers ashore from the *Platina* today — a *wharf*, gentlemen, should be the *absolute priority* . . . these boots acquired from Regent Street have been absolutely *ruined* . . .

Talk of the *Platina* turns my thoughts in a new direction. I remember Paddy telling me that Cap'n Wycherley, as ships' captains go, was one of the better ones. The worst, God rot their black souls, were drunkards, brutes or madmen. Or phantoms rarely seen except to gaze down expressionless from the poop onto the flogging of some poor bastard as his back gets covered with blood. But Pigtail Paddy had been with this Old Man seven months, all the way from Gravesend round the Cape of Good Hope and through the Southern Ocean.

To be sure, Cap'n Wycherley was a rare un, a true gentleman. There'd been no floggings or even lesser punishments. That didn't happen often.

As I watch the officials eating their breakfast, complaining all the while, a solution to my problem comes to mind. Of course, good Cap'n Wycherley is the key! But first, I must get back to the ship. Happily I see a longboat approaching the beach with the first load of the day. The sailors tramp ashore through the mud to dump their boxes on the sand, grumbling and cursing, but they don't raise any objection when I politely ask for a ride back out to the ship. One family of mechanics, I tell them, is much distressed about a mislaid box of food, probably left aboard.

So I trail them back over the mud out to the boat. Directed to sit quiet in the bow, I'm then ignored. The only talk is about the weather turning miserable cold, and, from the looks of it up there to the north, worse is coming. Short, choppy waves make rowing difficult, and the risk of being swamped is high.

The wind bites through my mean clothing, and occasionally an oar sends a shower of spray over me. I clutch the modest bag containing all my worldly belongings to my chest to keep it halfway dry.

There's no sign of Paddy on deck, but I'm told by a sailor that Cap'n Wycherley can be found below, in the crew's mess. I'm nervous: since Port Nicholson he'd been a remote figure beside the wheel, alert to the set of the sails, the far horizon and the activity on the deck before him.

Up close he's less forbidding, even grandfatherly, with piercing blue eyes, weather-beaten cheeks and neatly trimmed whiskers. Within ten minutes he's learned from me that I'm unattached to any family. In Hobart I'd been put on the *Platina* by a rich uncle paying my passage to Port Nicholson to rid himself of a troublemaker. (How easily these stories come!) But being a miserly old skinflint, I say, this uncle has given me no money. So now, being disembarked ashore, I need to earn my crust.

Perhaps, I say far more boldly than I feel, I can be useful carrying the smaller timbers of the government house up from the hold. That will free up the proper crew who could look after the big pieces too heavy for me.

'Ah yes, the Manning frame house for the esteemed Lieutenant-Governor,' he smiles. 'Quite a story attached to that unusual cargo.'

From Paddy, I know most of it already, but the captain, now all his passengers have gone ashore, seems inclined to chat.

'You probably heard: down in Port Nicholson they tried every trick in the book to have us unload the timbers and all the furniture right then and there.'

'Yes, I heard.'

'They assured me, in the region were nearly a thousand settlers — reason enough for the new governor to put his capital and his grand house in that thriving township. The harbour is central to the colony, it offers deep water, the chosen site is flat. And not so many Maoris thereabouts to be a worry. What did the Waitemata offer? Next to nothing!'

We look out the porthole at the gloomy scene on the beach, empty of people and signs of life. Heavy rain is now falling on the sad little collection of tents, obscuring the hills and volcanoes behind.

'In Hobart I received orders from London that left no doubt: I am to unload the governor's house where the capital will be sited, and nowhere else. That's why we're here in the Waitemata and not in Colonel Wakefield's windy little settlement.'

He sighs and lights up a pipe. 'Though I don't envy those young families who chose to sail on north with us,' he murmurs. 'It's going to be tough-going for a few months, years even. But snow doesn't fall here, the wind is less fierce. And the local people are friendly, as we saw yesterday.'

I must have shivered, for he turns his gaze on me. 'You're cold, young man, and no doubt hungry, too?'

I nod, because I'm indeed ravenous.

'I'll employ you while we remain at anchor. You work hard for a shilling a day, you get food from the galley, a hammock, a Guernsey and a decent waterproof jacket you can keep when the job's done. How does that sound?'

Boys do not burst into tears of gratitude, I tell myself sternly, as I manage to look suitably solemn while muttering some thanks. It's been a long time since — other than Paddy — I'd heard any words of kindness or been made any helpful offers. A shilling a day!

'Have you eaten anything at all, since going ashore yesterday?' he asks.

'Not much, sir.'

'No family held out a crumb?'

'No, sir.'

He grunts, his expression sad. 'Then get ye down to the cook. There'll be some porridge left from breakfast.'

'Yessir.' Would a boy salute? I decide not. The immediate prospect of food, even lumpy ship's porridge, is making me smile stupidly.

'After that, report for duty to the mate. As you know, we start unloading Governor Hobson's mansion this morning. But it'll take a couple of weeks to get it off. All sixteen rooms of it. Marble fireplaces! And a deal of furniture besides.'

He takes a deep puff and blows smoke at the ceiling of the cabin. 'I hope the new governor's more frugal with government money here than he's been up north. I'm told, money squandered on carpenters and new furniture, even after he knew — beyond doubt — that he'd be shifting the whole circus away to the south.'

'How do you know this, sir?'

'Port Nicholson gossip. News travels. They're no great admirers of Captain William Hobson R.N. down there. Given half a chance, they'd string him up.'

One of the mates, wearing a fearnought and his long hair dripping wet, appears at the doorway.

'We're ready to start unloading the timbers, Cap'n. Opened up the hold.'

'Then, Mr Franks, get this boy a fearnought and woolly Guernsey from the slop chest, would you? He's going to need them.'

The mate looks me up and down. 'Sir?'

'He's signed on to help get those timbers ashore.'

The mate's face is a picture.

I lose count of the number of days the unloading takes. The job seems endless. Maybe fifteen days, or closer to twenty. Nearly all the *Platina* crew and some from the *Anna Watson* are involved, dawn to dusk. Only on Sundays, we get a half-day off.

It is a daunting prospect, as the timbers and boxes and pieces of heavy furniture take up most of the dark, stinking, rat-and-cockroach-infested cave that is the ship's hold. Men posted down there in the depths hoist items upwards through the hatch, for gangs of grunting sailors to grab, and then other gangs to carry to smaller hatches opening onto the upper deck.

From there, as much as is sensible for one load is handed down onto waiting boats. Some timbers are put on lengthwise, others across. In those choppy seas, even just controlling the longboat sitting alongside the ship is tricky, and rowing a heavy load towards the beach, sometimes against the outgoing tide, is always risky. Just one big wave, unheeded, can swamp such a little craft.

The job would have been bad enough in dry weather. But for many days heavy squalls pass through. Men lose their footing on the wet decks, drop slippery boxes, get impatient and angry with each other, are yelled at by the mates supervising. They all swear without restraint, horrible ugly words I'd heard all too often since leaving England. By mid-afternoon, many crew look close to rebellion, their faces grey with fatigue.

I do my best, pairing with a young crew boy to handle the smaller pieces passed up from the hold, getting them up steep, narrow companionways to pile on deck. If I'd found carting bags over the tidal mud to the dry sand bad enough, this is a hundred times worse. By the end of the first day my arms and legs are aching, my back so sore I can hardly sit down.

The fearnought has protected my clothing only somewhat; underneath, all is damp and clammy.

Boys stay silent, I tell myself, they don't whine and whimper and ask for smelling salts, they endure without complaint. The Cascades Female Factory had taught me to endure, and also how to avoid the attention of those with whips and sharp tongues, even though inside I was burning with rage.

Once he's got over his astonishment at my reappearance on the ship, Pigtail Paddy spends our first night's meal in the crew's mess — gummy rice with salt beef, strong-smelling but food nonetheless — telling me what all this effort is for.

A gov'mint house of one storey will rise, he says, 'with a steepish roof, a veranda along the front, chimneys for the marble fireplaces in sixteen — *sixteen!* — rooms. Outside timbers probably to be painted white, quite pretty, if you've got rich masters in London who don't know how much it costs or generally what's going on. Or who do know, and don't care.'

He knows all this from the mate, Mr Franks, who knows everything. And, he adds, under the house there'll also be a big cellar for a deal of wine — *six hundred bottles*! When Governor Hobson R.N. finally deigns to leave his grand house up in the north, he'll no doubt bring down with him a few hundred bottles of the best French claret. The man might be Royal Navy, but ashore he's a pompous fool, a busybody and a hopeless organiser much given to spending gov'mint money on his personal comfort. Or so 'tis said, down in Port Nicholson.

'Well, they would, wouldn't they?' I say, scraping out the last of the rice in my bowl. 'We sailed off with their government house, after all.'

Paddy chuckles. 'Aye, boy, we did. Just followin' London's orders, we were. Crew like a cap'n what knows 'is own mind, does what's right.'

Now I am 'crew', my sleeping place is the crew mess, which is even more cramped and smelly than the passenger deck. One by one, the sailors around us are rinsing out their bowls in a bucket before climbing into their hammocks.

'We've better get yours slung, Harry me lad.'

The hammock wraps around me like I'm a bean in a pod. The canvas is stiff and cold and smells unpleasantly, of what I hate to think. I've been given a rough blanket, but for warmth I've kept on all my clothes, even my woolly Guernsey and fearnought. Turning over requires effort, so I tend not to try.

At least I'm at the end of the row of hammocks, so there's only one body hanging close to mine — but near enough that I can smell his sour breath and be kept from sleep by his snoring, loud and regular, like a cracked trumpet.

The darkness is almost total except for a single lantern near the companionway, I suppose to light the way up in an emergency. I hear squeaking, no doubt rats, more distant snores, then someone with cramp cries out, provoking a chorus of muffled curses which do nothing to reduce either the man's pain or his moans.

Have I dreamed the movement which woke me earlier, or is it real? A rat, sitting on my ear, tail swishing across my cheek? They can climb up or along anything. But one rat can't at the same time also be pushing my knees apart to . . .

I'd heard Cascade girls talk of their fear and shame at the groping hands of men so extreme they are paralysed, can't make a sound. Whatever is going to happen, happens. But I'm not a girl and I vow this will not happen.

My voice echoes shockingly loud around the blackness. 'Keep your grubby hands to yourself!'

The sailor, whichever one it is, gasps. I'm not supposed to speak. His face is inches from mine, his breath foul. His hand is over my mouth, but I twist away.

'You will stop that!' I manage to shout, and am rewarded by irritable voices telling the sailor, by name of Albert, ya miserable poncy bastard, sod off, just leave the friggin' boy alone.

In the morning I'll not be on the lookout for a knowing wink or leer telling me which of the sailors is Albert. Better I don't know. But now they're all aware I won't be silenced.

September 1836

IT MUST HAVE BEEN early afternoon when I accepted Jesse's apple, polished on his sleeve, and took my first bite into the red skin. Being so thirsty only made the juices sweeter. The flesh was as white and crisp as new snow. Jesse smiled warmly when I told him it was the best apple I'd ever tasted.

A stranger's voice close behind me said I should enjoy it while I could, because it would be my last for a long, long time. Someone was grabbing my arms and forcing them behind my back, so roughly that I dropped the apple onto the dusty ground. It took me a few seconds to understand that the voice belonged to the tall constable I'd seen earlier, and the hands restraining me were his.

Also, that the boy standing beside him was Tom the blacksmith's apprentice, his eyes glinting as he told the constable that the apple was stolen. He'd seen me running my fingers longingly over the basket, and then slip an apple into my pocket. That apple was nicked, sir, and that girl is a despicable common thief.

I looked to Jesse, who was calmly telling the constable that there must be some mistake. No mistake, Tom shouted, he knew what he saw. The constable should do his duty.

For a moment, I saw uncertainty in the man's eyes. He could just give me a warning. But by now a small crowd had gathered, and I could hear angry mutterings about rounding up the thieves and pickpockets who'd recently been at work in the market. This girl deserved what was coming to her, a lesson to others.

My struggling to free myself from the constable's grasp only tightened his grip and prompted him to shake out a length of rope to bind my wrists together. Jesse, I cried, tell them that you gave me the apple, you're my brother, I'm no thief, that boy Tom is a lying snitch — but Jesse said nothing further, just kicked idly at stones in the dust, avoiding my eyes.

It was Tom who kept on screaming at the constable and the crowd what he saw with his own eyes, hand on heart the truth, and I was vermin who must be stamped out. Send the little whore to New South Wales, another shouted. A woman in the crowd spat at me, a gob of warm saliva that landed on my neck and I was powerless to wipe away.

I felt myself being forced to stumble through the jeering crowd to arrive at the courthouse. I'd be put in a holding cell overnight, the constable told me. I should calm down and repent me of my sins.

Shivering on a hard bench behind iron bars, I was still too shocked to understand the peril I was in. Or that I would be locked in a damp cell with nothing but the cotton clothes I'd put on that morning. I thought back to the scene outside the tavern. The cooking apples we'd bought were a bright pink. We'd bought no red ones.

Surely my father, hearing of this calamity, would ride over

at daybreak and explain it was all a terrible misunderstanding? Bring me some food and warm clothes and take me back to my family? He would speak to his friends among the gentry, the rich men in the county who stopped by to chat in his shop and bought his saddles. They would help him. I would soon be freed.

Father did arrive early to pound on the doors of the courthouse. I could hear him pleading with the constable for my release. That child is no thief, he cried, she's not yet eleven and as honest as the day. Her accuser is a known scoundrel, a liar and a bully, never to be trusted.

But the constable was doing his duty, and a further plea to his superior fell on deaf ears. The child would be taken in two days' time to the Sussex Assizes, with four other miscreants. A judge would hear the evidence and decide her fate.

My father wasn't allowed to see me. But sometime later in the day a dark blue bundle, which I recognised as my mother's warmest cloak, was wedged between the iron bars.

4. Unmasked

APART FROM SAILORS WITH wandering hands — and there have been no more since that first night — I know I'm safe on the *Platina* so long as there are still materials coming up from the hold.

I have shelter, food, somewhere to sleep, promise of money, even a sort of companionship, with Paddy and Jimmie, the boy I carry with. He's seventeen, and a Scot, not a talkative sort, but we rub along. As the days wear past and the pace of work slows, I fret more and more about what will happen next.

Some revelry, that's what! To celebrate getting a whole government house safely ashore, says the captain, nothing gone missing, nothing dropped in the tide. After the meal, there'll be an extra issue of grog, and perhaps Able Seaman Paddy can be persuaded to produce his fiddle for a jig or two.

On deck, it's raining hard, so the dancing takes place in the fo'c'sle, with the tables and benches pushed to the sides, the hammocks tied back, and the grinning cook serving out rations of grog into our tin mugs.

Curiosity is my undoing. I know I should be cautious, but I drink two mugs, just wanting to see what it tastes like, this tot of rum 'n' water I've heard is served every day to sailors on naval ships. So I take a cautious sip, then a second bigger mouthful, which lights a fire in my throat and burns warmly right down into my belly. Ah, now I understand!

Oh, but I know the risks well enough, too. One being that,

now a little tipsy, I can be prompted by Paddy's jaunty violin to abandon the circle of clapping onlookers and join the dancers. The third mouthful decides it. Up I get.

Through the steamy atmosphere, I hear raucous cries of approval. Who of us doesn't respond to a foot-tapping beat, a good tune? Especially when starved of any laughter and dancing for four years? It isn't only the grog making me reckless.

'Young Harry there! 'E be light as a feather on 'is feet! Dances like a flamin' girl!'

'Never like a *girl*!' I shout, flushed and panting. 'A toff, that's who.'

'Ooooo,' they all chorus, grinning from ear to ear.

'Had me lessons from a French dancing master, don't ya know? Learnt to point me toes *proper*. Comme ci, comme ça!'

I do a few hops, finishing with an elaborate parody of a curtsey, holding out my baggy breeches by the side seams as if they're skirts, which must look ridiculous, before toppling sideways nearly into the lap of a figure seated in the shadows.

'Woops! Sorry, Cap'n, sir! Sorry! Sorry! Pardon me, Cap'n!'

Lowly ships' boys aren't supposed to get anywhere near captains, let alone nearly fall a bit tipsy into their laps.

'Needs be careful, young Harry,' he says, as the sailors, onlookers and dancers alike, burst into applause and laughter. He's smiling, too, but in his eyes I detect a warning.

'Carry on,' he urges Paddy and the dancers. 'You, too, Harry. Pleasure to watch.'

'Nay, sir. Some fresh air . . .'

That dimly lit space throbbing with men who haven't washed their bodies or clothes in weeks, the mingling smells of sweat and grog and cheap tobacco and smoke, the pounding feet, the *noise* . . . it's all too much. I push through the packed jostling bodies towards the companionway, desperate to get up on deck and away from trouble. One of them down there is called Albert.

I'm not so tipsy that I forget the dangers — the steep, narrow companionway up to the deck, and, once there, plenty of obstacles to trip over or protruding edges to get thrown against. The rain has stopped, but a chilly wind bites into my hot cheeks as I stand for a moment by the hatch to get my balance. No stars or moon to be seen this night.

I'm not quite alone on the deck. Two mates are leaning over the rails, smoking and looking across the water to the ghostly, makeshift camp set up on shore. Not all the people there are asleep; inside a few tents, lanterns still burn. Mothers feeding babies, probably, or consoling older children woken by nightmares or shivering with cold.

The mates haven't noticed me.

'They're calling it Mechanics Bay,' one is saying as I creep a little closer. 'Hear tell that some natives have started building huts for the officials in the next bay round. They use some sort of bulrush, tied together in bundles.'

'Suppose one step up from a tent.'

'Tent or native hut, they all leak. Bloody cold and miserable! Dear God, can this place rain!'

I recognise him as the oldest of the mates, a grizzled sea-dog with a bad limp who'd been at sea, he confided one day, since younger than me. Was but ten when he signed on. The limp was from falling off a yard, breaking a hip bone that set badly. But whalers, sealers, all sorts, he knew the Pacific like the back of his hand. So many times around the Horn he'd lost count.

'Canoe races all friendly-like is one thing,' he says; 'savages working on your doorstep, another. Me, I'd be watching out for my women. And my property. All that jolly flag-raising, good way of currying favour, if you ask me.'

He sighs deeply. 'Hard years ahead for those families ashore, though, poor sods. Scrimpin' and goin' hungry, if natives don't get 'em first. No place for young uns.' A match flares briefly, a pipe being lit. With my head clearing, I'm deciding this horrid talk about the natives is not just depressing but wrong. We're all God's children, I was taught, no matter the colour of our skin, rich or dirt poor. And these sailors are reminding me of how the Cascades women talked about the convict settlement over at Botany Bay. The soil was poor, water scarce, the bay too shallow for ships and the aborigines unpredictable, which is why they soon shifted everything over the hill to Port Jackson.

A burst of drunken laughter and singing comes up from below, louder than ever. I'm about to creep towards the stern when I hear my name.

'That skinny boy Harry,' the younger mate is saying. 'Something odd there. Why does Cap'n give him job?'

'Girlish, give 'ee that,' says the sea-dog. 'But Cap'n's no chaser after boys.'

'Family man,' the other agreed. 'The lad's a worker. Not strong, but willin'. Sticks to 'is job.'

'Aye, he does. Well, unloadin's near done. Two, three days more, we'll be headin' for Sydney, then the Horn.'

They're silent for a moment. 'Still strange, though,' says the second. 'Boy that young, travellin' all on 'is own? No money. Joined Port Nicholson? Or was it Hobart?'

'Offloaded by rich uncle, some family scandal. Bedded a maid, p'rhaps?'

'Hardly old enough!'

'You'd be surprised. Mebbe stole a horse? Or showing early appetite for the card table.'

They've turned away from the railing and look to be heading for the hatch. I slip further into the shadows behind the mast as the older mate says, 'Time to rescue the Old Man from that 'orrible racket below. Likes to keep in touch with the lower deck, 'e says. Mad!'

I feel my way along to the deserted foredeck, keeping still while the sailor on watch comes to check the anchor. After a while the noise below subsides: Paddy's fiddle will be back in its case, the captain back in his cabin, the hammocks re-slung.

Numb with cold and the enormity of the decision now facing me, I climb back down into the mess deck, recoiling at the fuggy atmosphere, the lingering smell of liquor. The party is over, the sailors are snoring in their hammocks.

I climb into mine, but I can't sleep, because now I know that this ship is going around the Horn, going home! Yes, Harriet, you can escape from this desolate and hateful place. Speak nicely to the captain, sign on as crew, and get back to England.

The price for this dream will be another terrible sea voyage on a ship that holds so many bad memories. And many more months of playing Harry, an imposter in a man's world. I've grown so tired and impatient of their silly crude banter, their cursing and swearing, their suspicious natures, their mock fights, their bad breath, their scratching and belching and snoring and farting and other dirty habits.

I've noticed the ones who shirk and think they're oh-so-smart, so clever, and those who take pleasure in bullying the weaker, quieter souls. And Lord, how they all complain, loudly and constantly — about the ship, the officers, the food, the weather, about the tasks they're handed out, about their sore backs and aching teeth, about each other.

But put up with all this, Harriet, and one day you'll see Land's End, and then the white cliffs at Dover, and you'll be home.

And then what? Can I count on my parents' forgiveness?

Are they even still alive? Is there a new baby? What about my hated and treacherous brother Jesse? Is he now working in the saddlery as father always hoped, or perhaps even owns it? Or has he taken possession of our comfortable house for himself and a browbeaten wife?

But even as these thoughts go through my mind, reality begins to sink in. Truth is, I won't be able to live in my village, or anywhere in Sussex. I'm not only a convict, but, worse, an escaped one. My father's influential customers and friends will know of my shame so won't employ me, nor any young man in the district see me as his wife. Must I then go to the West Country, work for a pittance in some grand house as a scullery maid scrubbing floors and emptying chamber pots, or become a milkmaid on a farm, or a stable hand? Or go north to spend seven days a week in a cotton factory enslaved to some devilish machine? More agreeable employment is out of my reach. I'm too impatient and restless ever to be a seamstress, endlessly stitching. I'll have no references to find work as a governess, though I can read and write well enough.

I'll dream of a good husband and little ones. But even hiding in a West Country town, or a farm or a factory, I might end up, if not a penniless spinster, then putting up with a bad husband who thinks he's doing me a favour and beats our children and dies of drink and debts, leaving me to scrimp and scrape through life, growing old and lame and lonely.

And if I am to remain here, what does this place offer? Rain, mud, hunger, strangers, fear of native attack, a daily struggle to earn money any way I can just to eat and stay alive.

I can't rely on kindness or pity, that's become clear enough. Those are in short supply here.

October 1836

THE JOURNEY TO THE Assizes took most of the day, to a town called Lewes. Two horses pulled us, the constable with five accused. I'd seen poor and despairing people before in the market, the beggars, cripples and homeless, but the four squashed into the coach with me were not only raggedly dressed and strong-smelling but the most wretched souls I'd ever seen close to, their eyes and spirits dulled by fear.

Two were women about my mother's age, the others younger men, both stinking of liquor. We learned from the constable that we three females were up for stealing food and small items of clothes from market stalls, and the men caught filching silver watches and crockery. We ignored him and each other the whole twenty miles of rutted country roads, rain squalls driving in through the open windows, and several falling asleep on another's shoulder. We stopped only once, at a broken-down inn, for toileting.

Before we finally climbed out, stiff and sore, the constable wished us good luck with this judge, who was known to be a hard man, fond of dispatching people off to faraway Australia. He himself, as a sworn Officer of the Peace, would present his evidence fairly and without prejudice. One of the women spat and swore at him.

With wrists still tied, we spent the night in a big cell, men and women huddled into the corners as far apart from each other as possible. The stench of stale liquor, tobacco and grime was no less than it had been in the coach, the misery even greater. My clothes were still damp. Not even my mother's woollen cloak, which had been eyed jealously by the two women, could still my chattering teeth.

One by one the other four were taken away by two burly,

grim-faced men, never to return. Sometime during that long day I was given bad-tasting water and a hard crust of bread.

Last case of the day, one of the escorts informed me as we walked towards the courtroom. Don't expect no mercy from His Honour, missie. And jurymen just wants to go home. And, no, judge won't let you testify for yourself, don't even try.

My appearance at the door brought forth a muffled cry of anguish. My mother and father, in the public gallery! Lord knows how they'd made the journey, for there were no public coaches on those roads and my mother didn't ride. Perhaps she'd been lifted onto the horse to cling for dear life onto my father's waist, as I had done often enough as a child? But there they were, reminded to keep silent, listening to the constable lying through his teeth, telling the jury how at least three respectable people had seen me slip an apple into my pocket. Stealing from markets, he went on, was rife and must be vigorously stamped out by due process. The court had a duty to impose the harshest of punishments no matter what age the miscreants.

Peering at me, the judge added: this girl pleads she is only ten, but by my reckoning is tall enough for at least thirteen. This provoked my father's one attempt to speak, only to be forced to his seat by a guard and warned any more disturbance, he risked being held in contempt of the court.

As I listened to the evidence that would surely convict me, I knew I couldn't tell the real story. That I'd overheard an argument between my brother and father earlier which now explained everything. But I knew the judge would never hear me out or believe me. The constable's sworn testimony, he was already telling the jury, was proof enough.

Those twelve wrinkled and heavily bearded old men, probably farmers and shopkeepers, no doubt upright citizens, filed out. They were back within minutes, the foreman answering the judge's question without hesitation. 'Guilty, m'lord. Guilty!'

And equally swiftly came the ruling. Harriet Grace was hereby sentenced to seven years in a suitable penal facility in the Australian colony. She would be taken from this court to Newgate Prison to be held in custody to await the next available vessel. Even as the judge's gavel came down on the desk some of the jurors were hoisting themselves upright, keen to get home.

I watched my dear mother jump to her feet as the whack of the gavel echoed through the hushed courtroom. Her face was ashen as she, normally so quiet and gentle, started to howl like a wounded dog. The child is only ten, she never stole anything, she cannot be punished so, even if she did take one apple, one apple, which I won't ever believe, she cannot be sent so far away, she cannot . . . m' lord, have mercy, have mercy on her, I beg you, she is only ten . . . a child . . . we will appeal . . . !

The old magistrate simply stared at her, his face a withered mask, before stating flatly as she drew breath that he hoped she had finished and there was no right of appeal. Tidying up his papers, he nodded to the courtroom guards to remove her. I caught only a glimpse of her stricken face before I, too, was hauled away, more roughly than before because now I was a convicted felon. My father's look of despair, the tears running down his face, I shall never forget. I was numb with shame and fury. It was Jesse, I wanted to scream, and that snivelling, lying Tom — but it was too late.

5. Hard decisions

THE NEXT NIGHT MY resolve — to stay with the *Platina* for her passage back to England — is severely tested, whether by Albert again or some other wretch I can't tell.

No doubt remembering my loud protest that first time, this one comes armed with a foul-smelling kerchief, which I awake from a fitful sleep to find clamped over my nose and mouth. That employs one of his hands, while the other is exploring.

My cries might be muffled, but I have nails that can claw at his unseen face, and legs that can kick. My fingers close around a greasy hank of hair — many of the crew are long-haired, but surely, please God, this is not Pigtail Paddy, not him making my hammock swing violently as I fight for my life. I pull on that hair with both hands as hard as I can, only to smell his foul breath and hear a hoarse whisper: 'A Froggy dancing master taught you, then? And what else did you learn, *pretty boy*?'

Trapped by the enclosing hammock, now in a rage and desperate for breath, I arch my back and kick out as hard as I'm able to where I think his body will be. It's effective enough to provoke a yelp of surprise.

'You little *bastard*!' His exploring hand is tearing at my breeches, the other still clamped over my mouth, and neither my hands nor feet can push him away. He is the stronger, and however much I'm still lashing out, I am being silenced.

Suddenly, the kerchief is gone, the straying hand is gone, and my ears are trying to make sense of the different sounds. Two men now are struggling, grunting, hissing and cursing at each other, while I lie back, gasping for breath, wondering who this rescuer might be. Eventually, a silence suggests one of them at least has slunk back to his hammock. And the other?

'He won't be back,' a voice murmurs. 'Be sure o' that, Harry. Sleep now.'

But how can I sleep or trust anyone? Was that Pigtail Paddy's voice telling me to sleep? Was he the white knight rescuing me from the poncy Albert? Paddy was surely not my attacker?

Breakfast is subdued, the crew not impressed by the mate telling them that, because that damn frame house has taken so long to unload, they need to make sail for Sydney without delay, to load stores and a cargo of whale oil and timber. Then they'll be bound eastwards, to pass through Cook's Straits and set course for the Horn.

The crew might be surly, the unknown sailor Albert always a danger, and the Southern Ocean again a terrifying prospect, but once around the Horn I'll be more than halfway home. Although still badly shaken by the night's episode, I eat my porridge knowing what I must do.

As the sailors clean up breakfast and make ready for a day's unloading, I'm surprised by Paddy, suggesting I come up on deck.

The day is bright, with not much wind. On the shore I can see figures moving between the tents. A Maori canoe is heading towards the harbour entrance, perhaps going fishing. Sailors are lowering the boats for the first load to the beach; boxes sent up from the hold are already piled on deck.

'Goin' ashore today? Leavin' us for life of a colonist?' Paddy asks.

'Not if the captain gives me a job,' I say curtly.

'You want to stay wi' t' ship? Sign on . . . after last night?'

'You mean, drinking and dancing?'

'No, I don't mean the drinkin' and the dancin'. I mean sometin' else.'

I look at him carefully. Surely this is not the face of a cunning attacker biding his time, just letting me know that if I stay on board one more night he'll be back? Or is he the person who saved me from certain harm, not to mention exposure as certainly no boy?

'Fiddlers see things, as they play,' he says gently. 'And what I see is someone with a secret. I keep this to m'self. But come night, in middle watch, what I hear is someone, perhaps a young girl posin' as a boy, in great distress. Confirmin' what I've suspected for some time.'

Oh Lordy! I'm blushing from head to toe. For myself and because I've shamefully maligned and underestimated Able Seaman Paddy. But why would he bother to rescue me? After all, nightly encounters are not unknown. Since leaving England I've learned something about what goes on between sailors below deck. It's common enough.

'God willin', I might've had a daughter like you, similar age,' he is saying, his eyes now averted. 'Me apprentice to a shipwright and married just two years to a dear, sweet girl, but she died havin' our baby, fifteen years since. And God was not willin' — child lived but two days.'

After a long pause, he adds: 'I was nineteen, and it fair broke my heart. So I packed up my fiddle 'n' ran off to sea. 'Tis a good enough life, if you keep your nose clean. From Sydney I'm sailin' as bosun, a step up the ladder.'

'Better pay?'

He nods. 'In all conscience, I can't turn over in my hammock, block my ears to a girl bein' raped. You know that little woofter Albert be not the only one. You'll be safer ashore.'

'I just want to go home.'

'You certain? Four or five months at sea more? I can't always be there to protect you, all the way back to Blighty.'

'I don't expect protection. It's a risk I'm willing to take.'

I've already decided: instead of that vulnerable hammock, I can find a secret space to sleep, perhaps the anchor locker. Curl up among the greasy chains and the rats and the nests of fleas and cockroaches.

I've done a day's carrying work with Jimmie the Scot, and eaten the usual meal at sundown, as much of the stew, tough biscuits and tea as I can humanly put away, given my foul temper. The usual preparation for sleep, but this last night I've hauled my one bag from its stowage, ready for departure. Paddy will wake me when the time comes. There'll be no sleep while I'm so angry.

My talk earlier with Captain Wycherley in his small cabin had been brief and unsatisfactory. Boldly, I thanked him for the unloading work and, before he could say a word, stated I'd become keen on the idea of a sailor's life. Therefore, I had to get back to England where I'd enlist as a loyal AB in one of Her Majesty's ships.

'You don't see opportunities here, in Auckland?' he'd asked me. 'A useful port will soon be established, offering work. Settlers will come, houses and shops built. There'll be plenty of jobs for sailors here.'

'No, sir. My life is not here, in this dismal place. I yearn for my own country, sir.'

And when he remained silent, I added to make sure he understood me: 'I want to sign on, sir, for the passage back to England.'

After a short pause, his answer was brief and final. 'We have a full ship's company. I'm sorry, m' boy, I cannot carry extras; I'm bound by Board of Trade rules and regulations.'

He reached over to his desk and gave me a small pouch, heavy enough that it might contain coins. 'The money you're owed. Remember, when you leave, take your Guernsey and fearnought.'

I was paid off and dismissed, and any pleading was useless. And I'd thought him kind and caring. Trustworthy. A friend.

'Thank you for a job well done, Harry. Talk to the mate, he'll arrange to get you ashore.'

I find Paddy straight away and vent my anger and frustration, to be told that the captain is only doing what's best for me. That's for me to decide, I rage. *My* risk to take.

'Not yours alone,' says Paddy, his fingers busy tidying up the frayed ends of some ropes. 'Captains don't knowingly put to sea—'

'Knowingly? Knowing what? Did you *tell* him?'

'Sooner or later, you'll be exposed. Probably sooner.'

'I've kept it up for weeks, all the way from Hobart—'

'The Tasman's a nasty stretch of water, but only a thousand mile. Believe me, it's nuttin' compared wi' high latitudes to the Horn. Months o' gales, followin' seas the size o' mountains. Sheer hell.'

'I know about hell,' I growl softly, conscious of crew nearby. 'Three years ago this same *Platina* was a convict ship, London to Hobart, and I was on it. A hundred and thirteen women chained and cooped up like animals. Fed muck. Kept in the dark. Beaten and abused by the sailors.'

'You a convict girl! *You?* Jesus and Mary! Why?'

'They *said* I stole an apple.'

'English bastards!' He doesn't look at me, but I can feel his anger. 'Feckin' *bastards*. They're not human.'

'I was ten, the youngest on the ship. Non-stop to Hobart. Five months of purgatory! You can't tell me anything about the high latitudes. So, did you betray me to the captain?'

'Beg pardon, missie, but he told me! And why me? Because he'd seen me takin' a friendly interest. He could trust me to explain his decision.'

'I'm not convinced. They'll not find out—'

'Listen to me, girl. They *will* find out, and once the sailors know the truth, there'll be trouble, sure to God. You'll not be safe, the ship neither. No female would be safe, they're not particular — young, old, strumpets, poxy, they don't care. And sailors are superstitious creatures—'

'You mean women bring bad luck.'

'Any incident, bad weather, bad food, gear failure, man overboard or dropped off yards — you and you alone will be blamed. Chances are, you'd meet wi' accident. I'm sorry, but it's God's truth . . .'

He inspects the twine he's been binding up, avoiding my eyes. His sailor's fingers are gnarled and cracked from years of handling coarse, salt-laden ropes.

'I'm instructed to take you ashore tomorrow.'

'Making sure I don't stow away!' I say bitterly. 'I want to go early, then. Before dawn.'

He doesn't flinch. 'There'll be no moon.'

'*How* did Cap'n know? No one else did — apart from you.'

'Intuition, he says. He's got four daughters, three granddaughters. He says if they grow up with half your spirit, he'll be a proud man.'

Flattery does little to calm my mood. For all its known and future dangers, I've come to think of the *Platina* as home, the Captain and Paddy as my friends. Cruelly, I'm now to be cast adrift from the only world I know.

My best hope now is to earn enough money, somehow, until I can pay for a passage back to England. However long it takes.

Paddy doesn't need to wake me, since I haven't slept a wink. 'Gone four,' he whispers. 'It's calm outside but chilly, so wrap up.'

Silently, lugging my bag, I climb the companionway for the last time and take a deep breath of the clean night air. Paddy has rigged a rope ladder down to the boat, and warns me to make no noise that will alert the sailor on anchor watch, huddled on the foredeck.

He's careful, I notice, to row steadily without splashing the oars on the still water. Where the blades dip, a trail of tiny lights flare briefly, like shooting stars. ''Tis thought, some tiny sea creature,' he breathes. My fingers leave smaller twinkling trails, so pretty.

And up there, as well as the Milky Way, a sight never seen in England: the four bright stars that the *Platina* mates told me are called the Southern Cross. My dear father, so alive to beauty, would be astounded by the brightness of all those heavenly bodies looking down on our little boat.

'Please, take me to the other side of the headland,' I whisper suddenly. To change my clothes I must be well away from any wakeful eyes. When I get back to Mechanics Bay I'll be wearing my skirts and bonnet, just one of the young girls. The *Anna*

Watson people will think I'm from the *Platina*, and vice versa. They won't notice Harry's absence.

'You mean what they're calling Store Bay?'

'Yes.'

'Half-tide, some mud to walk through,' he warns.

'No matter.'

As the boat grounds, I take off my boots and roll up my trouser legs. Stepping into the cold, slimy water, I take the bag held out to me. The captain's money pouch is tucked into my jerkin pocket, next to my heart. Without that, I'm nothing.

'You're a good man, bosun Paddy,' I murmur. I feel his warm hand grasp mine in a squeeze of farewell. 'Just remember natives are not savages, they're people.'

He chuckles. 'I'll be prayin' for you, Harr— Wait, I don't know your proper name.'

'Harriet,' I say, adding because I won't see him again: 'Unjustly sentenced for seven years to the Cascades Female Factory in Hobart, Tin Ticket 103.'

October 1836

THE GUARD ESCORTING US to Newgate Prison turned out to be a genial old fellow, who treated the six of us females not as dangerous criminals but with a rare measure of kindness. From Lewes to the City, he said, was a full day's travel, leaving before dawn, some eighty miles, so no high jinks, ladies. Make the most of clean air and sunshine, nowt of those where you're going.

In the coach were myself, the two older women also convicted in Lewes, and three others, equally ragged and dejected, smelling strongly of liquor. All cast envious looks at my blue cloak. But our guard made up for their hostility. Fortified by swigs from a hip flask, he barely stopped talking the whole journey. Though occasionally dozing off, I still learned much.

We should, he said, thank Betsy Fry that we were going by public stagecoach with four horses, not in an open wagon for the jeerin' folks at the prison gate to pelt with rotten eggs as they once did. She'd put a stop to the open carts many years ago. Like she read aloud the Good Book to the inmates, and set up a school for the children to read and write. She even visited the docks to comfort the female prisoners boarding ships for the other side of the world. That'd be all of you ladies, I'll wager. You might get to meet 'er, good Betsy Fry! Sorry, ladies: Mrs Elizabeth Fry!

His last act of kindness was at the entrance, helping us down from the coach, which was difficult with heavy chains around our ankles and our wrists still tied. After sitting for so long, we all stumbled about like broken puppets while a small crowd threw insults and wedges of rotten cabbage. In the guard's brown eyes, as he steadied me for the walk through the gates, I saw pity.

It wasn't the foul air that overwhelmed me first, nor the particular stench I was to grow used to, but the unholy noise. From one area we passed came groans, growls, screams and tuneless singing that were male. Down a long corridor of grey stone, as our party approached huge locked doors, the sounds changed to screams, moans, wails, sobbing, tuneless singing but higher in pitch.

Behind those doors stood a matron dressed in black. We were patted down for weapons, given a tin bowl, a wooden spoon, and two pieces of sackcloth, one to lie on, one to cover. The other women willingly surrendered their ragged clothes for a clean cotton shift, but I fought to the end when two attendants appeared, to hold my arms while the matron stripped me of my skirts and jacket. As she carefully folded up my mother's precious cloak, I heard a whisper, that'll fetch 'er a nice little penny at the pawn shop.

It was a cruel introduction to the greater horrors that awaited us. There was the noise, all day and most of the night, too, and the vile smells of nigh on three hundred women and children cooped up in two adjoining spaces. The only windows were high up in the stone walls.

I saw half-naked women in frenzies, clawing the walls, thrashing around on the floor; women, even young girls, who wasted away just staring into space, oblivious to everything. I learned who had been convicted of murder and were awaiting their hanging day, or those guilty of fraud, or poisoning, or assault, or prostitution, or just petty thieving.

I learned where I should toilet, and to tread carefully wherever I went. I heard women sobbing in pain or weeping over dead children, or laughing wildly, so drunk they couldn't stand up, or brawling over a game of cards. I learned to close my ears to foul swearing, insults and lewd songs, and which of the guards, male and female, I should avoid at all costs.

I learned that many of us were awaiting our transportation to Australia, and that most had been waiting for many months. There were only two or three ships a year for female convicts, and they chose only the most fit, because the colony badly needed women who could provide healthy children. The rest would die in this purgatory, probably before serving out their sentences.

I would have wasted away and died, too, I'm sure, of dysentery or one of the plagues that swept through, or from hunger or just from despair, had it not been for the visits of the woman we'd heard about from the guard in the stagecoach.

Mrs Elizabeth Fry taught us that even here, and therefore *anywhere* in this cruel world, there can — and always should be — human kindness.

6. Return

I'D NOT EXPECTED TO feel regret stepping out of my boys' breeches. But tying the long, dark brown skirt around my waist I realise how much less free I now am. Harriet can't walk in the shallows or run over grass without gathering up all this heavy material from around her ankles, vainly trying to keep the hems clean and dry. For a brief moment before he disappears forever, I'm quite envious of Harry.

Paddy's boat has slipped silently into the darkness, leaving me standing barefoot and clutching my bag on one end of a broad beach. At the other end are the dark shapes of pitched tents. Poor Paddy — landing here has meant a longer row for him back to the tiny gleam of the *Platina*'s riding light.

Behind those two lumpy volcanoes on the other side of the harbour, a pink glow in the sky promises sunrise. I've never felt more abandoned, not even after my escape in Hobart. So dirty and parched.

Where now? I recall that tinkling stream running into Mechanics Bay. With all the rain, there are probably other riverlets running from these hills into the harbour, places for a drink and a wash. The weather feels settled: I should strike out inland.

Impatiently, I watch the glow deepen to orange, and chew at the several pieces of ship's biscuit that I've found tucked into the top of my bag. Paddy must have sneaked it from the galley, or given me his ration, bless him. My fingers have also felt something hard and smooth: oh my — a piece of scrimshaw. There's just enough light to see the billowing sails of a tiny ship carved onto a snowy whale's tooth.

I wonder if it's Paddy's work. Perhaps I've been, for a brief time, the daughter he never saw grow up. This melancholy thought is all that's needed, for at last I give way to tears, for myself and all the world's lost daughters.

As I climb up and away from the beach, I'm proved right about the possibility of other freshwater streams, but wrong about expecting that a path through the bracken would be tolerably easy.

From the ship, these slopes had looked quite gentle, but the bracken is shoulder-high, dense and prickly, and the uneven, stony ground will be wearing down my one precious pair of boots. I must hold my skirts close, to avoid rips in the cloth which I have no way of mending.

And in this dense undergrowth are there really no snakes or venomous spiders or leeches or caterpillars with a hundred legs? What about foxes, or jackals, or monkeys, wild pigs or even bears? Large cats with long claws?

But in the trees I see and hear only birds: a plump, handsome pigeon with a green and white breast that just stares lazily down as I stumble close by, and a smaller bird, about the size of a house sparrow but with tail feathers in the shape of a fan, which flies twittering behind me.

The first stream, prettily fringed by ferns, tumbles over some rocks and flows on down, I imagine, to the big bay I've just left. I hobble — with all this climbing my boots are beginning to rub painfully on my heels — to the bank where I can scoop up some water, clean and cold. But looking down into the harbour,

I know the stream I seek is still some way distant. There I'll wash away weeks of sweat and grubbiness and unpleasant memories. Meantime, some thick leaves, folded and stuffed into the heel of my boots, might help lessen the rubbing.

The sun is high in the sky before I realise with great relief that the undergrowth has given way, and I can now look along the ridge to where some tents are pitched and, beyond them, the flagpole and the *Platina* still lying at anchor. It doesn't take me long to find what is probably another native track alongside a considerable stream running from the ridge towards the harbour.

A little way down, I strip off skirt, jacket and boots, put my jerkin with the captain's money pouch and Paddy's scrimshaw safely into my bag, ready to step under a small waterfall. Above, several handsome black birds with white tufts at their throats sing and chuckle, like no bird I've heard before. The cool breeze deliciously caresses my whole body. In all my adventures far from England this is a new and most wonderful experience, so free and close to nature I can raise my arms to the sky and feel . . . well, almost reborn.

Splashing into the clear water, I come up from ducking my head to see a figure standing just a few feet above my bag and clothes. A very old and frail-looking native woman, barefoot, thin and much wrinkled, stands there, bent over a stick. Her cheeks are sunken, and long, grey hair straggles down to her waist. Her sparse clothing is just a short skirt, some sort of flax, so that her droopy little breasts dangle uncovered. The expression on her face is hard to read.

Is she shocked at my whiteness or my nakedness, or both? My short hair? We stare at each other for a long moment. I'm wondering how I can protect my only worldly possessions. Am I already too late?

But I needn't have worried, for when I reach the pile of clothes I find nothing has been taken, and look up to see the stooped figure limping into the undergrowth, as silently as she has arrived. Not a thief, I think sadly, hoping I haven't given her offence, just an old, pitiful woman, probably taking a lonely walk to pass the time. Standing under the waterfall, I had likely appeared to her as some sort of pale apparition arising from the mist.

I am wondering why she looks so downcast, even furtive, when I remember the young priest from Port Nicholson telling us that Maoris had slaves, usually taken captive after battles. Men, women and children, too, doomed to a life of drudgery, constant danger and of course complete obedience to their masters' every whim. The fate of some, he added, was even worse. Their freshly tattooed heads were shipped back to England and America, where collectors paid high prices for such curiosities.

Pushing aside this disgusting and hideous thought, I listen to the birdsong while the sun and breeze dry my skin. I sternly remind myself that, despite my present situation, I'm young and healthy and my wits have served me well enough, so far.

If she is a slave, that old woman has had none of these advantages, or if she was captured as a child, never had. There are worse lives than mine.

Not finding any continuation of the track, and weary of fighting my way through the bracken, I follow the stream down its narrow valley, with the flagpole sometimes visible on the headland above. Before long the water runs through a beautiful wooded area, and opens out . . . This must be Official Bay, the middle of the three bays.

Before me is quite a little settlement, the beginnings of what

Paddy has told me is going to be 'the better part of town', just for the *Anna Watson* officials. It's the smallest and certainly the prettiest. Six tents, one bigger than the others, are pitched on the flat grassy area above the sands. A couple of grazing brown and white cows complete the rustic scene.

Behind the tents, Maori men, perhaps ten, are putting up bulrush huts. They're wearing only a sort of short flax skirt, the bronze skin of their broad backs glistening in the sun. A canoe is pulled up high on the shore, and on the sands lie some of the neatly bound flax bundles that I see they're using for the walls of the huts. I wonder if that beautiful paddler from the founding day race might be among the builders, but no, these men are all older.

For many minutes, I sit unobserved on a rock under the shade of a large tree hanging over the stream, watching the activity. The walk has left me very hungry, but I know I must keep what's left of Paddy's biscuit for later.

Two Englishmen can be seen outside one of the tents; one I recognise as the short, round fellow who'd talked loudly at breakfast all those weeks ago about the urgent need for a wharf.

But their appearance isn't the only reason for my sudden anxiety. Since Hobart, I've been in breeches, to all appearances a shy, gawky boy, not yet old enough to shave or for a man's voice. But now here I am, back in long skirts. I'll be treated differently, and not to my liking.

Reluctant to step out into this new world, I slowly tie on my girl's bonnet.

I'm about to leave the shelter of the tree when I see two figures in skirts emerge from the bigger tent. Two women! This is unexpected, but then I remember that there'd been a woman among those rowed ashore for the flag-raising ceremony. Perhaps she is Mrs Mathew, the owner of the horses and the piano. Her dark burgundy dress with modest lace trim and black shawl is certainly a cut above those of the wives around in Mechanics Bay. The other is a girl, perhaps twelve, more plainly dressed in a dark green skirt and blouse. She looks cold and resentful.

I watch their activity at the back of the tent, sheltered from the wind. The cooking fire and the aroma wafting my way tell me they're baking bread. The older woman is instructing the younger, but more like she is a servant than a daughter. I have a vague memory of seeing that girl on our first day ashore, looking after two other children. They were probably from the *Anna Watson*.

Hunger and the possibility of a kindly reception emboldens me to start walking towards their tent, but my timing is terrible. Before I've taken more than a few steps, the chubby official stands up from the chair where he's been reading, stretches with a loud, unrestrained yawn, and makes for the stream where it runs into the harbour. He has a quick glance around to check that the women are busy, and, not spying me, begins unbuttoning his breeches. Unable to move, I avert my gaze, thankful I'm seeing only his back.

Judging it safe as he walks back towards his tent, I take a few uncertain steps onto the grass. The two women are still preoccupied, but, before I can approach them and say anything, the short man has headed me off.

'How long have you been standing there?' He means, have I seen him pissing in the creek?

'I just . . .' How I so want to laugh. Looking demurely down, I note that not all his fly buttons are yet done up.

'This is not your place!' he shouts before I can collect my wits. 'This bay is exclusively for the government officials, so we're not disturbed by nosey children and crying infants.' Taking a threatening step towards me, he calls out: 'Mrs Mathew, please come and tell this child she is not welcome here.'

I catch her glance quickly summing up the situation. 'I'm sure you can convey the message suitably well, sir, without any help from me,' she replies, while the girl stares at me impassively. The voice is that of a genteel English lady, quite high and clipped. 'I'm about to take bread from the oven.'

The man grunts. 'Understand this, girl: your place is in the next bay. *Mechanics* Bay. Fortunately, a convenient physical barrier prevents us from seeing and hearing what happens around there. So be gone!'

I go, but cheekily not with any great haste, lingering enough to exchange smiles with the Maori workers. Although they would not have understood exactly what has been said, I'm aware they've watched with interest. I swear one gives me a broad wink.

At the foot of the low, rocky promontory which is the rude man's 'convenient physical barrier' between the two bays, I'm stopped by water too deep to paddle through. The choices are to clamber over the rocks, which are thickly covered with some kind of small black mussel that will ruin my boots, or wait for the retreating tide. As I wait for the water to recede, I try prising off some of the mussels, and use a smaller rock to break them open, but the edible part is tiny and very salty, and five or six leave me still hungry and thirstier than ever.

Harriet, I remind myself, you have until sundown to find a family who will feed and shelter you, or face another cold and hungry night.

Forsaken and desperate though I feel, I cannot deny a certain beauty to the scene. The sun, at somewhat past noon, is warm on my face. The light is brighter here than on the Sussex coast, the colours stronger and the air clearer.

Across the water, those prominent green hills, rounded like kitchen spoons, shimmer with their covering of vegetation. Between them, more distant, lies that strange twin-peaked island noticed on our arrival in the harbour. *Platina* is now the only ship at anchor, with sailors in two boats still doing the back and forth run into the beach, on what must surely be the last deliveries. I can't yet see around to the Mechanics Bay encampment, but I can glimpse the stern of a Maori canoe pulled up on the sands. Perhaps a second one in the harbour is out fishing; I've heard tell that the natives are great fishermen.

The very thought of a piece of fried fish, or my mother's rich stew of mussels, cockles, potatoes and onions, is enough for my sight to blur with tears. At home it must be autumn, and in the kitchens mothers are stirring their Christmas batters, for cakes heavy with sultanas and hazelnuts and almonds. They're boiling up sweet jellies from summer apples and berries picked on Sunday walks along narrow lanes . . . fattening up their turkeys and pigs . . . roasting a joint of beef with crunchy golden Yorkshire puddings . . .

November 1836

I WAS IMPRISONED INSIDE the stone walls of Newgate the whole of that long winter, late October to April. Small fires lit in broken grates did nothing to blunt the chill. Some mornings a woman or a child, supposedly asleep under her piece of sackcloth, was found to be dead. I remember days when the pails of water froze over, and we breathed out small clouds of mist into the freezing air.

I made no friends in that place. I expected no pity; each of us was just trying to stay alive and keep our wits. There were other children, but they were mostly suckling babes or younger than me. Girls my age whose mothers had been sent here would have been taken in by relatives, or put into a parish poorhouse, or left to fend for themselves on the streets. I tried to make friends with a crippled girl of maybe fourteen, but she was unresponsive, and I found out later that she was a deaf-mute and had been raped. Soon after I arrived, she took ill with convulsions and died. Sometimes I sat with the little children, playing finger games and singing the nursery rhymes my mother taught me.

I survived only because some hope arrived almost daily in the person of Mrs Fry or one of her lady friends. They swept into the wards in their bright, clean gowns, pretty bonnets and warm shawls, smelling of lavender water, ready for a Bible reading, or a lesson in needlework or writing. Afterwards, they would stay longer to comfort those who were sick or in the depths of despair.

Mrs Fry was a big woman, more plainly dressed than her friends, and the best Bible reader, her voice low but strong. She read quite slowly, giving us time to think about the parable story, or the verses about faith, hope and charity — 'these three; but the greatest of these is charity'.

When I found the courage, one day I asked one of her ladies to tell me about her.

Dear wonderful Mrs Fry, she said, her whole face aglow. For twenty years or more she has been visiting Newgate. She is a Quaker — and when I looked puzzled added: a special sort of Christian. They believe in a simple life and that in every one of us, no matter how wretched or impoverished, there is God.

She knows many important people, even the Queen herself and Sir Robert Peel. Rich people give her money for her charitable work. They call her 'the Angel of Newgate', but truly she is more than an angel, she is a veritable saint! And doing all this even with eleven children of her own!

This conversation led to another. It was probably January by then, as snow could be seen battering against the high windows. I was in a side room where the light was better, with ten or so others. We were seated on the straw, stitching patches together for a quilt. My mother had taught me to use a needle and thimble, but the cold made my hands clumsy and I kept pricking my fingers. I glanced up to see Mrs Fry in the doorway, inspecting us, but then she drew up a chair and sat down near me.

She asked my name, and the village where my parents lived. I added my father was the best saddler in all Sussex, and she smiled. And how did I come to be here? They said I stole an apple, I replied, but I didn't; my brother stole it and had me blamed.

She looked pensive, then asked my age. Soon to be eleven, ma'am, though the judge decided I was tall enough for thirteen and I was lying. He gave me seven years in Australia. I saw a look of horror flash across her face. Can you read and write, child? A little, I said, my father was teaching me and we read books together, but I want to be better. Then you shall be, she said; I'll see to it.

She was true to her word. Either she or one of her ladies took classes for the older children most days, providing us with the books, the slates and chalks. Sometimes she made a point of watching my attempts at neat writing, or listened to my halting voice trying to spell out a hard word. She was always smiling, always encouraging. In Australia, she said, I must be brave and endure, and when my sentence was done, find ways to make the most of myself.

One morning, perhaps it was April, some of us were summoned to the matron's office and told to collect whatever belongings we had. Today we were boarding a ship bound for Van Diemen's Land.

But first, even though we could hardly walk, let alone run anywhere, the matron made sure that each one of us was weighted down with iron chains, around both wrists and ankles. The guards who fitted us with these manacles lost no chance to breathe beery fumes into our faces and call us vile names.

But despite the chains we were soon going to breathe fresh air and raise our eyes to an open sky, even if it were grey. Might there even be the sun that we had not seen for nearly seven months?

7. Finding a family

ON MY PERCH ON the rocks, waiting for the tide to go out, I must have briefly fallen asleep, as what seems only moments later I feel a sharp prod and hear a rustle of skirts close by. 'You were about to topple over. What happened to your hair?'

I'm suddenly wide awake, with the girl in the green skirt perched beside me. She puts up her hand to feel the bristles at the nape of my neck, under my bonnet. 'I thought so, no plait. What happened to it?'

I have to think quickly. 'When we got to Hobart, my mother ran out of money. Her breast milk dried up. She sold my plaits to pay a wet nurse. Else the baby would have died.'

Oh, what a storyteller I've become! I add: 'They use it to make wigs. They like fair hair best.'

'Is it fair, your hair, when it grows?'

'Yes. Very. Thick and fair.'

'Lucky you,' she says, reaching for the single gingery plait which hangs down her back and twirling it at me. 'Nobody would want mine, it's so fine and thin. Suppose yours will grow back.'

'Suppose. A year, maybe two.'

'Where's your mother now?'

'She died. And the baby, a boy, died too, the day before. I didn't like Hobart, so I got on the *Platina* to go to Port Nicholson, but I didn't like that place either. So I came here. You were on the *Anna Watson*?'

She nods, but doesn't elaborate. I ask, 'Is that woman back there your mother?'

'No. She's Mrs Mathew. She says it "*May*-thew". Her husband came from Sydney with the governor, to be a surveyor or something. She hasn't got any children. I'm her servant girl. I come here every day.'

'Is she kind, this Mrs May-thew?'

The girl hesitates. 'Strict, but kind enough. She was on the *Anna Watson*, too, and the *Westminster* before that, from Sydney. She gets horrible seasick. She thought the *Anna Watson* a very badly run ship, plain dirty, the captain lazy. I think she picked me because she thought I was quiet and biddable.'

'And are you?'

'When I have to be.' For the first time, she looks at me directly, with a curious, even sly smile. Her face is freckled, plain and rather bony, as are her wrists and long fingers, sure signs of there never being enough food, long term. People probably notice the same of me.

She asks: 'How did you come to be walking down onto the beach from the stream?'

'I went for a walk up behind all the tents and got a bit lost. It's all thick bracken.'

She looks pointedly down at my bag.

'In case it rained,' I say. Adding hastily, to change the topic: 'My name's Harriet.'

'I'm Tillie.'

We sit in companionable silence for a while, watching the little waves slowly recede from the rocks. Soon we'll be able to paddle through the shallows back to our own beach. In the meantime I need more information.

'What will your father do here?'

'He's a sawyer. He says he'll earn more money here than in

the Bay of Islands. That hasn't happened yet.'

'Mrs Mathew pays you, I hope?'

'A little. She gives me dinner. But my mother is so anxious, all the time crying, that I'm glad to be away. When the officials get organised, there'll be work for father, and better wages. I've heard them talking about putting up a government storehouse around in the big bay.'

I say: 'On my ship there was a whole mansion for the new governor, in bits and pieces in the hold. With marble fireplaces and a wine cellar for six hundred bottles. Can you believe that!'

She's taking off her boots. 'Oh yes, I can, very well. Father worked on the governor's grand house up at Okiato. He got angry about the waste of money, trying to make it look like Buckingham Palace. We can go now, if you don't mind getting your feet wet.'

As we walk around the little headland, the Maori canoe and the tents of Mechanics Bay come into view. It feels like a homecoming, of sorts, both reassuring and depressing.

There's the little stream by which I'd spent that first miserable night ashore, those many days ago. Above the high-tide mark now sit heaps of cut logs and stacks of firewood. The tents look more established, with clothes hanging on lines. Three Maori bulrush huts have already been built, with two more nearly finished.

A quick glance tells me that the beautiful young paddler of my foolish dreams is not among the natives now preparing to launch the canoe.

The sun has sunk behind the hills, and the first fires for the evening cooking have been lit, so that a delicious smell soon reminds me that since the last meal on the ship I've only nibbled at the edges of Paddy's rock-hard ship's biscuit.

'Mmm, that smells good!' says Tillie. 'Which is your tent?'

Oh Lordy. Yet another lie. 'I . . . the wife took against me; she says I'd been rough with the children, which I hadn't. More likely she didn't like her husband always touching me. That was why I went for a walk.'

'She asked you to leave?'

I nod.

'That was very unkind,' she says indignantly, 'to someone who's lost their mother and baby brother and is all alone. Well, you must come and eat with us. Don't mind my mother if she's crying. She cries a lot.'

By now faint with hunger and gratitude, I follow my new friend to a tent where two very young children are playing with cockle shells, and Mrs Roberton — for that is her name, I discover — is sitting on a box, dully stirring something in a pot.

'This is Harriet,' says Tillie. 'She's from the other ship, but she's got no family here. She can help you look after the twins while I'm with Mrs Mathew.'

Mrs Roberton has indeed been crying. Behind her the open flap of the tent allows a glimpse of disorder. And I know what she will say. That there's barely enough food for the family. Our stores are getting low. An extra mouth — the Lord only knows how we will survive . . .

I squat down in front of her. 'Your daughter is very kind, but I'm not asking for charity. I've got money. I can pay for my food. And I can mind the children so you can get some sleep.'

She overflows with tears. 'Our food is very plain, miss . . .'

'It's food.'

'I've hardly had a wink of sleep since . . . We couldn't afford proper mattresses . . .'

Tillie says, 'One or other of the twins is awake most of the night. I don't think she's got enough milk for them both.'

I know nothing about feeding little people, but I ask, 'Aren't they old enough for milky porridge?'

Tillie says, 'Yes, but breast milk too. There's only two cows here. The milk goes to those who can pay the most.'

'That is *shameful!*' I say, leaping to my feet. 'Don't the babies get preference? Where are these cows? Who owns them?'

Tillie points to a tent set back from the rest. Beside it two animals are munching the meagre grass, while a young woman draws a thin stream of milk from their teats into a wooden bucket. 'That's Abigail. She milks morning and evening. She was a dairymaid back in Devon, so she's good at it. But the men, the owners, don't give her any money.'

'That's even more shameful!' From a combination of hunger and outrage, the world suddenly spins and goes black. When I come to, Tillie's eyes are wide with concern.

'Just got up too fast,' I mumble. 'Sorry . . . I'm . . .'

'Needing food,' says Tillie, helping me to sit up. 'Here.' And glory be, she's holding out a steaming bowl of meaty soup, which I fall upon like an animal, forsaking any remaining dignity. She gently brushes aside my attempts to reassure them that I can pay for my food, at least while my money lasts and I've found myself paid work.

And meantime — I fumble to get my pouch from inside my vest — here are some coins to get milk for the twins.

Although reluctant, Tillie comes with me to approach the owner of the cows. He's quite young, but red of face and already losing his hair. At first he treats us with disdain, and names an outrageous price for a billy of milk, but starts to listen when I suggest it would not be hard to persuade the women of the camp to refuse to buy his milk until he charges a fixed and fair price. The milk will quickly go sour in the heat. Does he not know that he is already regarded by the women as a scoundrel, callously taking advantage of poor people in a terrible situation?

The owner counters that his purchase of the cows from the missionaries up in Paihia has taken all his savings. He bought four, two for the mechanics and the two I saw around in Official Bay. He's entitled to recoup his costs.

I say, we don't care what you paid for them, that's not our concern. We just know that, because of you, babies are going hungry, and their mothers made miserable. Do you want starving or dead babies on your conscience?

He begins to bluster, but Abigail the milkmaid has been listening to what is being said with her mouth open and, now emboldened, states that she'll not milk another single cow unless he agrees to our terms. And as an experienced milkmaid, probably the only one among all the women here, from tomorrow morning she wants a wage. He will agree, here and now, and these girls are her witnesses!

We come away with our billy of milk, costing what Abigail says is a fair price. Mrs Roberton's gratitude is almost embarrassing.

At sundown Tillie's father appears, to kick off his boots and silently eat the food kept for him. He announces that he started work today helping carry the materials for the new government house up the hill. It will be erected on a vantage point over the harbour. He doesn't need to tell us he's completely done in, and is fast asleep even before we women have tidied up after supper and bedded down the twins. Soon after it starts to rain, heavy and loud, so there is nothing left to do but turn in and pray the canvas keeps us dry. Lordy, how this place can rain!

I'm sleeping next to Tillie. The mattress laid on the ground is thin, but at some point Tillie snuggles closer, and we share some blessed warmth, cuddled like two spoons in a drawer.

She can have no idea how much her caring and offer of food and shelter from the pelting rain means to an escaped and homeless convict girl.

April 1837

DURING THAT WINTER BEHIND prison walls, I'd dreamed of sunshine on my face, air fit to breathe. But when we stumbled out of Newgate it was into drizzling rain and air that smelled of dirty smoke. Guards herded us roughly into coaches, jeering at those so weak they couldn't manage the steps, or laughing at the younger women who, because of the chains, couldn't avoid their groping hands.

We were lucky, someone said, that the *Platina* was tied up at the London docks, not anchored in the river, thus sparing us a very wet trip in an open boat. The sailors who pushed us up the gangplank were no gentler than the earlier guards, and just as given to insults. Some of the women swore back at them, or spat, but most looked bewildered, cold and lifeless. A few were carrying babies, or had little ones clinging to their skirts, or were obviously with child.

I don't know how many of us joined the *Platina* that day, or how many others were already aboard brought from prisons in Ireland or the north. Maybe thirty; we were the last. Altogether, I heard later, we numbered a hundred and thirteen, along with twelve children.

Once, I thought tall ships seen in the distance were so noble, their billowing white sails so beautiful. The *Platina* was just another prison, a floating version of hell. From the slippery main deck, we looked up to a forest of ropes and wooden spars. Steep, narrow stairways led down to pits of creaking darkness, to the orlop deck where we would sleep and cook food and pass the days. Everything was damp, the air already foul — and would get far worse.

To most of the crew we were just a cargo of untamed animals, though our chains were removed that first day by a huge bare-chested sailor wielding a large hammer, watched by his jeering shipmates.

Then the surgeon in his fine naval uniform took over. His manner was kindly, even sympathetic, as one by one we were recorded, our heights measured (he wrote me down as five foot two inches), our mouths checked for disease and our scalps for lice. We were told to sponge our hair and feet with soapy water, then to sign the register with our name or an X. Next, we were given a clean cotton shift, a bowl and a spoon, a blanket, a thin mattress filled with straw. And last, they showed us the water closets below, only two for us all. The sailors, we'd learn, would simply piss into the scuppers or hang their bare buttocks over the side, uncaring of who might be watching.

Somehow all of us passed the surgeon's inspection, swallowed the cook's thin cabbage soup, and found the narrow berths where we would sleep. Before locking us in for the night, a crewman announced that we'd sail in two days, but tomorrow there would be visitors. A Mrs Fry and party, come to wave us thieves and whores goodbye — and feckin' good riddance, he couldn't help adding.

Next morning, we were ordered up on deck for the arrival of a fine closed carriage pulled by two horses. Mrs Fry stepped down first, followed by three other ladies, and two footmen each carrying a large box. When a sailor muttered from the rigging 'Lookee 'ere, shipmates, famous Betsy Fry is come to send ya scum o' the earth off to—', he was shamed into silence by a brief but withering stare.

We are here, Mrs Fry announced, to bring some cheer to these poor creatures about to undertake a long and hazardous journey. We pray for their safety, and that the good captain will see they are treated with kindness. The women around me sniffed and snorted at that, a faint hope.

It wasn't a short visit. Luckily, instead of the previous day's rain, a pale sun shone through a dirty yellow haze. Mrs Fry read from the Bible and prayed at some length for us to mend our ways and become useful members of society. But then she sat herself down on an upturned cask and asked for the boxes to be placed nearby, and for each of us to come forward, one by one.

'Ah, Harriet, I believe,' she smiled as my turn came. She remembered! 'Aged nearly eleven — perhaps now turned eleven?' I nodded. 'A saddler's daughter who will serve out her unjust sentence but make something of herself in Australia.' She held out the small Bible handed to her by one of her ladies. 'Keep it safe, my dear. Read some verses daily. Remember who you are: a girl from a good family. I shall pray for you.'

The Bible was not her only gift. I also received a small bag with quilting patches, needles and a thimble, 'for idle fingers on the long voyage'. Also an apron, a cotton cap, and finally my tin ticket, a small metal circle on a red cord, inscribed *103*. As she put it over my head, I caught her scent, not lavender water, something sweeter, perhaps roses. 'I have grandchildren your age,' she murmured, and I thought her voice faltered.

By the time she had spoken with all hundred or more of us, and blessed the babies and the little children, the sun was low in the sky. The four ladies drew their pretty fringed silk shawls around them, bade farewell to the captain and climbed into their carriage. I wasn't the only one watching them go with tears in my eyes.

8. Settling in

THE *PLATINA* HAS GONE. Before dawn the sound of men singing wakes me, rough music that I recognise as a shanty song. From the lights and movement on deck, I guess they're trudging around the capstan to haul the heavy chain aboard and house the huge anchor against the side of the bow.

Mr Franks, as the first mate, will be on the foredeck directing the operation, the captain beside the wheel, sniffing the air. The sun has risen by the time I hear a shout — 'Anchor's a-weigh!' — carried by a light breeze across the gold-streaked water.

I stand outside the tent and watch the sails fill as the *Platina* silently slips out of the harbour, finding myself unexpectedly tearful. I'd had both terrible and good times on that ship. Now my last link with home is held only by the thinnest of threads: the letter that Paddy had the day before promised to get one of the young officers on the ship to write, telling my parents that I am in New Zealand, in the new capital Auckland, alive and well. He has assured me he will see it properly addressed and delivered.

I knew they were going: the previous day a familiar lanky figure had walked up the Mechanics Bay beach to where I was feeding breakfast to the twins. It was the first time Paddy had seen me in my girl's clothes, and was clearly amused — 'amazin' how a bonnet makes you a girl' — and by my domestic duties, so different from a cabin boy's menial tasks.

If favoured by a fair wind, he said, they were leaving at first light, on the outgoing tide. He had a small package from the cap'n, being final pay due to me, along with his best wishes for my good fortune in the colony. Final pay? I was not due any.

'I still wish with every bone in my body I was coming with you,' I said, only to be told that halfway to the Horn I'd surely be wishing I was dead. The southern Pacific to the Horn was wild and terrifying and relentless, no place for young bones, male or female.

And it would be dead of winter when, God willing, they arrived back in England. Snow, sleet, winds straight from the North Pole, long hours of darkness. Here was warmth and summer sun, rain on green and fertile land, birdsong echoing around the valleys.

Then why did he not jump ship and remain here himself? I asked.

'I'm a sailor,' he shrugged. I caught the sadness in his eyes as he looked out at his ship. He was just as much trapped by his circumstances as I was by mine. 'One day I'll be comin' ashore, swallowin' the anchor. Not yet.'

'Then God speed ye, bosun Paddy,' I said, conscious of the weight of the package in my hand. This 'final pay' was more than just a few coins.

'Thank the captain,' I called out, but he didn't look back. Sailors were always saying goodbye to loved ones and learned not to linger.

So, here I am, marooned on the shores of the Waitemata.

For many days, the harbour is empty of ships, none yet arriving with either new immigrants or supplies. Facing north, our tents get sun all day long — but also a tiresome wind when it blows in from that direction, as it does often.

We settlers are living in three quite separate bays, according to our station. At Mechanics Bay the poor families in tents draw water from the little creek, sufficient for cooking, washing ourselves and, occasionally, our under-clothes. The communal privy is steadily filling up, and in certain winds the nearer tents complain of the stench.

All the fine talk about establishing a new capital for a brand-new colony in the great British Empire has been replaced by an air of sullen acceptance. At sunrise, the wives wake to the daily routine of tending the children, preparing food, laundering their babies' soiled clothing and their men's sweaty shirts in the creek. The older children look after the younger ones, or are sent to find driftwood for the cooking fires.

The men leave early, to walk up onto the point where the governor's house is to be built. Tillie's father, now kept busy sawing timber from dawn to dusk, tells us that the men are still carrying five or six loads of materials a day, from Store Bay up the steep track to the building site.

It's well known that the governor, true to form, wants to choose the *exact* spot *himself*, and only then, when his mansion is finished and ready, will he bring his family down from Okiato.

What justice is there, I wonder, in requiring these men to break their backs on erecting his abode of sixteen rooms with marble fireplaces and a wine cellar before being allowed to build humble one-room shelters for their own children?

Around in Official Bay, Tillie tells me, there are now nine officials' tents as well as that large marquee I saw earlier. There, Mrs Mathew, as the only wife, cooks the food served to the officials and occasional visitors. My friend Tillie is dish washer, potato peeler, sweeper and general maid-of-all-work. Walking there daily as the tides allow, Tillie may seem quiet and biddable, but she has sharp ears, too, and brings back many a piece of gossip.

An example: the very proper husband Mr Felton Mathew, charged with drawing up a town plan, is off daily on his horse to ride up the volcanoes to take measurements and draw sketches of the harbour and countryside. When it's fine and not too windy, the surgeon Dr Johnson can be seen at an easel, painting watercolours.

Captain Rough, a dapper little fellow who often wears white gloves, is busily building himself a boat. The stout gentleman who is to be the police magistrate spends much time at his writing desk, Mrs Mathew says, occupied in drawing up laws and regulations. These are necessary for the township, to ensure public order and bring scoundrels to book.

Also, there's a much younger man named Edward Williams. Tillie blushes behind her many freckles as she tells me that he's the official interpreter. According to Mrs Mathew, this handsome Edward, aged twenty-two, is the son of the mission family up in the Bay of Islands, just five when they arrived in the country. Having grown up among the natives, he speaks their tongue fluently. He is almost one of them, Mrs Mathew had sniffed, much given to singing — not good English songs, either! — and the wearing of native ornaments made of feathers and whales' bones and green jade.

Still, adds Tillie, he has at least acknowledged her presence in Mrs Mathew's marquee and spoken kindly to her, which is more than some of the older men have done.

I'm beginning to dislike the sound of them and Mrs *May*-thew.

What no one has expected is the almost daily arrival of the canoes, three or four at a time. Only when there are white caps in the harbour do they fail to appear — but even then some brown figures might suddenly emerge from the bush behind our bay, having come from who-knows-where using tracks as yet unknown to we English.

They don't seem to feel the cold at all, as their clothing is scanty: only a sort of short flax kilt, and sometimes over their shoulders a cape made of flax and other leaves. Whether arriving by canoe or on foot, they come armed with bundles of reeds and large flat stones with sharpened edges. We're quickly reassured by Mr Williams that the stones are tools for gardening and wood-cutting and they have only good intentions — to help us build these bulrush huts. Their chiefs have welcomed us as settlers likely to be a presence for peace in an area where there have been many tribal wars. Their helping us become established is in everyone's interests.

But my beautiful paddler, of him there is no sign. Every day I eagerly scan each canoe as it approaches the beach and the paddlers jump out, and every day I'm disappointed.

Not that all aren't handsome in their own way, well muscled, strong-looking. I find myself often staring at these groups of men in wonder. Before Cascades, back in England I'd known only puny village lads — and even the pudgy ones like Jesse — all needing warm clothing even in summer, and on the *Platina* underfed sailors, also well clad against the weather. That is, except when crossing the tropical doldrums when their pale and skinny frames were revealed and soon turned a bright pink by the sun. But among these brown visitors, barefoot, bare-chested, going cheerfully about their building work, I don't find the one I seek.

Sometimes the canoes continue on past our beach to disappear behind the headland and land at Store Bay, where I'd come ashore from *Platina*. As the days pass, I'm beginning to fret at the confines of Mechanics Bay and my child-minding responsibilities.

From the wives' chatter, it seems that I'm most likely to find work in Store Bay, where shops and businesses are soon to be established and then ships arrive with goods to sell.

So one fine morning, I walk with Tillie around the rocks to Official Bay, where five or six of the shelters we now call 'raupo' huts have been completed. Mindful of my first encounter with Official Bay, Tillie explains to Mrs Mathew that her dear friend Harriet is only passing through, heading for Store Bay.

'You'd best take the inland path, alongside the stream,' she says, civilly enough. She is red-faced, engaged in vigorously kneading a large mound of bread dough. 'Up on the ridge, you'll see the wide track running down to Store Bay. Mr Mathew tells me there's much activity there. The Government Store is built and being used. I've a large chest waiting to be delivered, all my precious ironmongery for the kitchen. My oh my,' she sighs, stopping briefly to stretch her back, 'the men here are hearty eaters! Would you believe — this is only two days' worth!'

With Tillie sent to fetch wood and build up the fire under the camp oven, I set off up the stream path, stopping at the waterfall where earlier I'd come across the old native woman, and wondering why I can faintly smell smoke.

The ridge soon opens out, allowing a view of the flat area being cleared of fern to accommodate the site and all the materials for the governor's house. At the very end of the point stands the lone flagpole. The smoke is coming from below the ridgeline behind Store Bay. I note a nor-east wind is blowing the smoke inland and away from the stacks of timber.

Panting from the climb, I sit myself on a grassy mound and watch the activity for some time, appreciating the quiet — just distant voices and the cries of a few seagulls — and the rare chance of solitude. I grow drowsy, the noon sun warm on my back as the breeze drops right away.

What arouses me, I don't know, but one glance tells me that

the smoke is now being carried by a westerly, and will soon be drifting directly down into Store Bay. Flames will follow!

Evidently the men over there are immersed in their work and haven't yet noticed. Should I hasten down the track to warn the people in Store Bay? In my cumbersome skirts, damn them? No, I've seen a big fire before, in a nearby village, when a spark from the smithy set alight a whole hillside. I know it's bodies to carry water that are most urgently needed.

I start running towards the workers.

'Fire! Fire!' I scream, pointing wildly at the smoke. The men turn, puzzled by this crazed girl running across the tussock towards them.

'Only clearing scrub, miss,' shouts one; but another yells, 'She's right, you blockhead! All those tents — the storehouse! Come on!'

No more urging is needed. Twenty, maybe thirty, men have dropped their tools and are now sprinting across the ridge towards the track. They soon leave me behind, except for two older men who are taking their time, not convinced of any danger.

'Didn't you hear the man, dearie? Clearing scrub, that's all,' one calls to my departing back. 'Remember the boy wot cried wolf?'

Some men are so blind and so *stupid*!

The track is well trodden but steep. I stumble down helter-skelter, thinking of the men who've carried up on their backs every last length of timber for the governor's grand house. And window panes, slates for the roof, those heavy marble fireplaces.

On the grass above the beach there certainly are tents pitched, below them the newly completed storehouse and some unfinished raupo huts. By the time I arrive someone has organised two chains: one handing along buckets of water from the small stream which flows onto the beach, and a longer chain stretching from the shoreline up to the first trees. Luckily, the tide is fairly well in.

If the idea is to douse the area above the tents with water, to stop the red fingers of fire in their tracks, they're doing it none too soon. Flames are now to be seen below the ridge and rapidly working their way down the slope.

Natives stand side-by-side with settlers to pass heavy buckets, which are then tossed back down for refilling. There's much shouting, a sense of great urgency and, now, much coughing as thick smoke engulfs the men.

What can I do, in my cumbersome skirts? Besides the storehouse itself and the tents, there are other piles heaped around. Some are covered with canvas, some are collections of shrubs and trees, their roots tied up in sacking.

In the confusion, no one notices me going into the tents and searching for anything — buckets or basins or jugs — that will hold water. I find five or six suitable containers and take them to the men scooping water from the stream.

No one notices me carrying the shrubs and small trees brought from Australia down onto the sands, two or three at a time. Some, quite big and heavy, I grab by their trunks. If that is all I can do, it is at least something. As it turns out, if not for me they would have been destroyed, along with the two tents that can't be saved.

The sun is below the western hills before someone decides that the flames are contained, and the government storehouse safe. Where the fire has been stopped, smoke still rises from a broad band of blackened vegetation. The two lost tents are just smouldering piles, the contents unrecognisable.

The chain quickly breaks up. Scanning the crowd of men now busy shaking hands and congratulating themselves, I'm yet again disappointed. The one I'd hoped to find is not among the natives standing in a group apart, watching.

'Thank you, men,' a black-coated man is shouting, I think Mr Mason the government engineer. 'Your timely arrival saved the day. Whoever noted the wind change and so quickly raised the alarm should be commended.'

Hearing this from where I'm resting behind a shrub, I don't expect that even one man there might speak up about a mad girl running across the tussock — and none does.

No one thanks the natives who've so willingly helped, either.

I'm so tired from running up and down the expanse of beach to save those plants — and take them all back again when the fire is doused — that I fall asleep right under that bush.

I'm holding a spluttering candle, and walking up a steep, narrow staircase. My small bedroom holds only a bed, a chest of drawers and a single chair, but my mother has lit a fire in the grate, and shadows flicker across the ceiling. Once in bed, at my feet is a warmed stoneware bottle, and I'm snug under two blankets and an eiderdown.

My mother is tucking me up, stroking the hair back from my forehead. She smells of lavender, of the scented water she makes from her garden bushes. The song is the same every night.

> Lavender's green, dilly dilly, lavender's blue,
> You must love me, dilly dilly, 'cause I love you . . .

Or sometimes it's the other way round:

> Lavender's blue, dilly dilly, lavender's green,
> When I am King, dilly dilly, you shall be Queen.
> Who told you so, dilly dilly . . .

I snuggle further down into the bed, pulling the blankets up to my chin. The stone bottle at my feet is almost too hot. 'My darling wee sparrow — sleep now, snug as a bug in a rug,' my mother murmurs as my eyes grow heavy . . .

A man's voice awakes me, with words that make no sense. I'm suspended in time and space, trying to catch a dream of a song, a lullaby, my mother's voice. Why am I crying?

Gradually I understand where I am, and that this grey-haired native man with a tattooed face and a bone pendant hanging from his neck is gesturing at the headland. He has realised that if I am to get around the rocks to Mechanics Bay before nightfall, I need to go now.

The words must mean wake up, see, the sun has set and soon it will be dark. His face is fearsomely tattooed, but his smile is tender, grandfatherly.

I start off, stumbling across the sand towards the rocks. Tears blur my sight. That fragment of dream was my bedtime ritual, warm in my own nest, the sweet smell of lavender, in a village on the other side of the world.

April–October 1837

AUSTRALIA? WHAT OR WHERE that was, I had very little idea — until the day one of Mrs Fry's ladies arrived at Newgate bearing an enormous book. An atlas, she announced, opening it up, and this is a map of the world. Our world is a big round ball, so try to imagine the surface lifted off and laid out flat, like so.

A group of us had leaned over the table as she pointed. Here is England, here Ireland. Here London, the River Thames, the English Channel. The glorious white cliffs of Dover you will see as you leave. The continent of Africa. The Cape Colony. And here, this very large island — Australia!

As a group we gasped in horror, for the first time getting a sense of how far away we were going. We might as well, I thought, have been going to the moon. Yes, she said, you are shocked, and rightly afraid, but Mrs Fry believes it better you know, rather than be kept ignorant.

So, she resumed pointing, you will sail down the river into the Channel and out into the Atlantic. At first it will be cold and grey, but gradually it will get hotter. Here, on the Equator, you will likely be becalmed under blazing hot skies. Then good winds south, to round the Cape of Good Hope. Through the Southern Ocean to this smaller island, Van Diemen's Land, right here.

You'll be at sea maybe four or five months. The distance is some ten thousand miles. By the time you arrive in Hobart it will be early summer; the seasons are topsy-turvy, the opposite from England.

As the last thick ropes tying our ship to the wharf dropped into the water, I remembered those words and shivered. Had I known what lay ahead, I would have jumped into the Thames right there and then, and let my boots and skirts drag me to the bottom.

Mrs Fry's lady friend hadn't mentioned the sickness that the ship's motion would bring on, from the minute we left the calm of the river. Nearly all the women were struck down, unable to move from their bunks or eat or even stand upright. The surgeon gave us nasty syrups which seemed only to make it worse. Several had to be tied down to stop them jumping over the side.

Nor had she warned us of the huge seas that rolled and pitched and tossed the ship about like a toy, the wind shrieking and the sails torn, while we huddled in the foul-smelling darkness of the orlop deck for days on end. Or the doldrums, when for many days there was no wind at all, the seas oily, the sails useless, the heat unbearable. We were permitted on deck during daylight to prick idly at our quilting patches, but the only women allowed to sleep on deck were those chosen by crewmen for certain favours. For the rest, the heat below made sleep impossible.

I lost count of the days, of day and night, of right and wrong, good and bad.

Though good, I suppose, was the kindly surgeon tending the women coughing up blood, or in agony with dysentery or its opposite malady. He could do no more than he did.

Good, certainly, was the captain who knew how to steer his ship safely through storms and calms in the right direction. Also the barefoot crewmen who went aloft in terrible winds to reduce sail and save us from capsizing.

Bad were the babies born but who soon died despite the surgeon's efforts. The mothers who died, their bodies put on planks and tipped over the side, while the captain mumbled a few prayers. Bad were the sailors who got out short lengths of rope to flog women with insolent tongues or who refused to give favours. Bad were the sailors who violently forced women into these favours.

And especially bad was the food: cabbage soup, salt pork, a disgusting slimy meaty gruel, oatmeal porridge, hard ship's biscuit from which you shook weevils, boiled rice, hunks of tasteless bread — all horrible, but you ate it, otherwise you starved. A treat was a few sweet currants, which you first checked for wriggling white grubs.

I learned which crewmen to avoid, and which convicts, too, those poor creatures who lost their reason, wailing and screaming and lashing out, beyond help. I became indifferent to the fights which sometimes broke out, the squabbles over food, the accusations of stealing, as if most of us had anything to steal.

Only the children kept me from throwing myself overboard. Early in the voyage, when I had stopped vomiting and had got my 'sea legs', I took to sitting with the little ones as I had in Newgate, singing, playing finger games, making up stories.

One mother, older than the rest, repaid me with rare kind words, and several times pushed away sailors who came snooping around our deck for girls to take into some dark corner. Though slight, she was surprisingly strong as well as sharp of tongue, and the sailors grew wary of her. She told me she was being transported for the murder of her husband. He had beaten and abused her in every possible way. Even Australia, she said, could not be worse than those seven years of torment. One day, she had simply sunk a kitchen knife deep into his back. Because of the children, a lenient judge sent her to Australia for life rather than to the hangman's noose.

Rounding the Cape of Good Hope, the Southern Ocean still to come, I was grateful to have one friend, a good woman, whatever she'd done.

9. Fire, again!

MY MOOD, AS I take off my boots, lift skirts and wade through knee-deep water in the twilight, is melancholy.

I know now that over at Store Bay there's no chance of the likes of me earning money for many weeks, not until the shopkeepers have something to sell and are needing help. Apart from the money occasionally going to Tillie's mother, I must save the rest for my passage home.

News of the fire in Store Bay spreads quickly around our camp as the builders return to their families for the evening meal. Loud voices proclaim their fear and reported acts of heroism. But Tillie bursting into our tent provides a sharp reminder that my grumbles are trifling.

Breathlessly, she informs us that Mr Mathew had arrived back in Official Bay much upset, having to inform his wife that her large trunk and everything in it was utterly destroyed — the crockery, china, glassware, cutlery and utensils shipped from their former home in Sydney for the proper house soon to be built in Official Bay — all utterly ruined. The tent had gone up like a bonfire on Guy Fawkes night.

Until ships arrive with goods, Mrs Mathew must make do with the few essential pieces being used in the marquee. Her oak dining tables, stored under a tarpaulin, had been spared, scorched only lightly.

How people relish being the bearer of bad tidings, even mousy little Tillie!

'Mr Mathew says the wind changed and only the carpenters raising the alarm and rushing down in time from the governor's house saved the store and most of the tents,' she continues, her words tumbling over each other. 'They had to throw water on the flames for hours and *hours*. You saw everything, Harriet? It must have been so frightening.'

'I saved a few plants,' I reply sourly.

'Poor Mrs Mathew. She must be most distressed,' says Mrs Roberton, who would never know what nice china and quality cooking pans look like. Her own kitchenware comprises cheap tin billy-cans and clay bowls handed down in her family or bought at some county market. 'Perhaps a visit from the twins would cheer her up?'

And so it happens that two days later, the tides being right, Tillie and I are shepherding two stumbling young-uns through the shallows around to Official Bay. Wearing what passes for their best clothes, they delight in being barefoot, kicking at the water and splashing each other. Both fall over at least once. Lucy is a sweet child, but it's Thomas who steals my heart.

I'm prepared for gentlemen to emerge from the tents and demand that we return to our proper station. Sure enough, we're confronted by two officials stating that mechanics' families are not welcome in this bay. They decline to accept our explanation, until Mrs Mathew hears the raised voices and walks down from her marquee to tell them that the previous day Mr Mathew himself had given permission for a visit. It is easy to see that as the only official wife, and the person who cooks their food, she commands a grudging respect.

Much progress, I notice, has been made on the raupo huts here. Some of the natives working there recognise me with friendly waves, and smile broadly at the twins. But I have just about given up hope of ever seeing that beautiful paddler again.

'See how we have borrowed a little local knowledge?' says Mrs Mathew, ushering us to the sheltered area behind the marquee. Reed bundles tied to poles now form a makeshift cooking area. A small fire under the three-legged camp oven is heating something in an iron pot.

'The natives bring us wood,' she says, gesturing at a large pile nearby. 'Please keep the children away from the fire. It's inclined to send out sparks.'

She had greeted the twins rather coolly, I thought, like a maiden aunt unused to children, but now she sits herself down at a low bench beside the rough-hewn dining table and calls them over. They're not quite two years old, Tillie informs her, and named Thomas and Lucy. 'Such bonny little people,' says Mrs Mathew, pinching their pink cheeks. 'Were they born in England?'

'On the ship, during a storm, the very end of the passage,' says Tillie. 'We were two days out from Sydney. My mother hoped we'd reach Sydney in time, but she had a fall and her waters broke and the pains started.'

'Your mother must be so brave and strong,' murmurs Mrs Mathew, looking down at the twins, who are playing with the little charms dangling from the silver bracelet on her wrist.

'Not really,' says Tillie. 'A midwife on board helped her. I watched and it was bloody and horrible and went on for hours. She screamed a lot, and the second baby was a shock.'

'I'm sure it was,' says Mrs Mathew.

'And since we left Sydney she cries all the time. She wanted to stay there.'

'I sympathise,' says Mrs Mathew. 'I lived in New Town, just outside of Sydney Town, for three good years. My husband was town surveyor, until unjustly relieved of his position.'

'Why?' I ask.

Mrs Mathew looks a little surprised by my directness, but replies: 'He was caught between the dictates of the Colonial Office in London and the dullards in Sydney who grandly call themselves officials of the state. It was grossly unfair and wrong. Mr Mathew's work was known to be very satisfactory.'

She sighs deeply. 'I had such a nice garden at Penselwood Cottage in New Town. I do miss it terribly. I grew roses and hollyhocks and planted thick hedges of lavender. This time of the year we had golden daffodils and cherry blossoms, and roses coming into full bloom. The apple trees were smothered in white. All grown from seeds and cuttings, shared between the wives. Saplings, too. Oaks, chestnuts, sycamore, elms . . . A change from the ever-present eucalypts.'

She's a thousand miles away, in a springtime elsewhere. She brings herself back with a start.

'Have you girls noticed, there are no flowers in this landscape? Practically none at all. We go for long walks, Mr Mathew and I, and I've seen only one little white flower, a creeper, something like a clematis. All around us is endless dull green. A sea of bracken as far as the eye can see.'

Her face registers a happier thought. 'Oh, but there's Mrs Fairburn. She grows a few flowers around at Maraetai. Hollyhocks, daisies, that sort of thing. No roses. The soil there is not very good.'

'Where's Maraetai?' I ask.

'Follow this coast around to the east, about half a day's sail, you come to the mission station. She and Mr Fairburn and their daughter Elizabeth run a school for native children to learn English, and of course recite their catechism. They sang the alphabet for us, would you believe, to the tune of "God Save the Queen"!'

'So you've been there?'

'Twice, with Mr Mathew. Last May, on our voyage from the Bay of Islands aboard the *Ranger*. Mrs Fairburn and another daughter Sarah were very hospitable. They employ a few native workers, housemaids and gardeners.'

Breaking the long silence that follows, I say, 'That bracelet is so pretty. Do those silver letters mean something?'

Tillie's frown tells me that this is impertinent. But Mrs Mathew replies that on the *Anna Watson* the cabin passengers had much admired her unusual bracelet, a fashion begun by Queen Victoria herself. Each charm has its significance, marking a special memory, maybe happy, maybe sad.

Mrs Mathew takes off the bracelet for the twins to dangle between them, enjoying the tinkling sounds. We watch them for a while before she speaks again.

'Mr Mathew gave me the chain in Sydney, when I first arrived, hence the letter F and the little heart. We married two weeks after my ship docked.' Another long moment, before she continues. 'The E is for Eliza. The J is for James.'

Tillie swiftly gestures to me to remain silent.

'They were both stillborn,' says Mrs Mathew calmly. 'Such pretty little things. Mr Mathew buried them in our garden at Penselwood, beneath a beautiful willow tree.'

'That's so sad—' I begin, but Tillie cuts me off.

'I know about stillborns,' she says. 'My mother had two before the twins. That's why I'm much older than them.'

'Then, my dear, you'll know something about heartache,' says Mrs Mathew. 'Your mother should be very proud of Thomas and Lucy, who are very much alive!'

Reaching down for Lucy to drop the bracelet into her cupped hand, she adds: 'It's true, though I don't often admit to this, but yes, I should like to have had children. Mr Mathew doesn't mind so much, so he says, but I—'

Our conversation is interrupted by shouts from the shore, where the native builders are now preparing to push their canoe out to sea. Evidently they've finished work for the day.

'Harriet, take the twins down to watch the launching,' Mrs Mathew says, her tone resuming its normal briskness. 'It's quite a ritual. Tillie and I have some work to do.'

I've noted before how there's a special way of readying the canoe for sea. First, it's dragged into water deep enough to float. Some men hold it steady while one by one the paddlers climb aboard, to clamber over the seats to their places, until only two or three men are left in the water. They push the canoe off and jump in at the last moment, as the paddlers take up the rhythmic stroking. Two men usually stand, to steer and call the speed of stroking.

My two little charges watch this with great interest, and wave them goodbye. There is still time before we'll be cut off by the tide, so we wander over to the stream, to sit under the trees and dangle our bare feet in the running water.

Soon that isn't enough: they want to splash about, to step unsteadily from stone to stone, and scoop up water in their chubby hands to throw at each other. They gleefully chase seagulls with black bills, and then a pair of peculiar black and white birds with long red legs and long red bills that came to wade where the fresh water meets the tide.

For me, the twins' carefree games bring more pain than pleasure. I'm reminded of a stream not far from our home where I spent many an hour making tiny square-rigged boats out of leaves and sticks to be launched into the slow current and finally tumble over the weir to certain doom. We had competitions, the village boys and I, and gave our ships famous names like *Golden Hind* and *Victory* and *Redoubtable*.

But it's more than that. My last night at home before that

terrible day in the market, my mother had told me she was carrying another child. Unexpected, she said, so long after you, my darling Sparrow; but I could tell she was pleased.

If she has lived, and the child has lived, how old will this brother or sister now be? Around three or four, and bonny like Thomas and Lucy? Will I ever know?

'Are they twins?' says a voice.

Turning, I see it belongs to a young Englishman who I suppose — from his youth, his good clothes and the large pendant of a shiny green stone on his chest — must be the interpreter Edward Williams. Tillie has told he is handsome, and so he is: tall and erect with crinkly eyes, a wide smile, dark hair worn quite long.

But he also knows how to entertain very young children, because he quickly takes off his boots, hoists up his trouser legs and paddles into the water to use rocks to create a small dam. The twins quickly respond, dancing about in the pool of rising water.

'I'm Edward Williams,' he says. 'And you?'

'Harriet. I mind the twins for Mrs Roberton. That's Thomas and that's Lucy. They're nearly two.'

Oh Lordy, how conscious I am of my stained brown skirt and the absence of a plait of hair hanging down my back. 'And that's their big sister Tillie, over there with Mrs Mathew. You've met her. Tillie, I mean.'

'Indeed I have. We were on the *Anna Watson*. You're from around in Mechanics Bay?'

The little lake has filled up rapidly, so he shows the twins how to place more stones to raise the height of the dam and contain the water. 'You know they call this "Exclusion Bay"?'

'That's no great surprise,' I say. 'I've already been asked to leave, twice.'

'The Maori hut-builders have told me they find this amusing. They consider our English ways very strange, especially how these three bays have been so strictly apportioned. You know, officials *here*, mechanics *there*, and all the merchants around *there*. Actually, I find this odd, too. I grew up in a missionary household. We were all kept too busy to worry much about such matters.'

His voice is unusually deep for a young man, and the accent interesting. English but with an unusual rise and fall, I suppose because he's grown up also speaking the native tongue.

'These two look healthy enough,' he says, watching Thomas remove a rock from the dam and shout with glee as the water breaks through and rushes down towards the shoreline. 'My youngest brother — Joseph — is about the same age. We're eleven all told, six boys and five girls. Three eldest born in England, the rest up in the Bay of Islands. I miss them, oddly. And you?'

Conveniently, I've noticed that a ship with a fair spread of sail has appeared in the harbour. 'Oh look!' I cry. 'The first big ship since ours!'

'That's the *Britomart*, doing a survey of the harbour. She's Royal Navy, a brig. They need the survey done quickly before the settlers start to arrive, so the ships know where it's safe to drop anchor.' He turns back to me. 'You came on the *Platina*?'

'Yes.'

'From Port Nicholson — but before that? Are you with family?'

Again I'm rescued, but less pleasantly, as we both turn to look at the source of shrill women's voices, raised in obvious alarm. From behind the marquee a thin column of black smoke is rising. Not a second fire! *Another* one? Mr Williams utters something in Maori and sprints away to help, leaving me frustrated and annoyed.

Oh, why can't Mrs Mathew have had her fire on another day, not interrupting a rare opportunity to talk to the one good-looking, unmarried young gentleman in this whole place? The only one who can tell me about the Maoris hereabouts, where they live, how they make those canoes, if I can perhaps visit their village. Even go for a ride in a canoe, learn to use a paddle.

Besides, is not a girl of nearly fifteen allowed to dream, just a little, that such an interesting man might find her attractive? Enough to want to know her better? He *had* asked after me!

Given time, he would learn I'm not the ordinary plainly dressed girl I might appear. I can read well enough, and my writing is improving. My father has read me poems by Mr Keats and the legends of Camelot, and we'd just started reading the first episode of Mr Dickens's *The Pickwick Papers* when . . .

I stare up at the marquee, where there is still much activity and noise but the smoke is diminishing. There's nothing I can do to help and I can't abandon the twins. The tide will soon be coming in. Tillie can get herself back.

Ignoring their protests, I hoist one twin onto each hip and set off across the sand to walk back to our proper lowly station.

July 1837

WE WERE TOO FAR south of the Cape of Good Hope to see any land. The surgeon warned us that even in the southern hemisphere where it was officially spring, we could still expect gales, snow, crusts and pendants of ice on the rigging, seas like the Himalayas coming up behind. The westerlies would blow us due east towards Van Diemen's Land. We were now a little over halfway.

Shivering with cold, sullen and exhausted, we needed no reminding that the safest place was our bunks. Only two lanterns lit the orlop deck, so there was no day, just endless night. Our needles and patches lay untouched, Mrs Fry's Bibles unread. We covered our ears to muffle the noise — the pounding, banging, creaking — expecting at any time the one mighty crash telling us the masts had fallen and the hull was breaking into a thousand pieces.

Most of the children had become mute ghosts of themselves. Some women were still able to walk, bring down the food from the galley. We got used to living with fleas, rats and cockroaches. We pissed without shame into buckets, and knew from the smells when bowels were emptied, too. Some were still vomiting, whether from sea sickness or something worse, only the surgeon knew.

From him we heard that some on board, crew and convicts, were complaining of sore and bleeding gums. He feared that this was the beginning of scurvy, the mariners' disease which struck on long voyages, but with no limes left on board there was nothing he could do.

We saw less of the sailors, up above us keeping disaster at bay. The surgeon told us of torn sails being mended day and night, and one immense wave that had crashed over the stern and brought down the mizzen mast. Three men were needed to hold the ship's wheel steady, and whole teams to man the pumps day and night. But never fear, the captain — and he himself — had been through worse than this!

One morning the surgeon announced that the wind was dropping, and gulls were being seen around the ship. Sixty days since rounding the Cape, land had just been sighted. Some of us were able to climb the ladders up to the deck to gulp in the clean, cold air. The land was just a tiny smudge on the horizon, but the younger sailors were dancing about, as pleased as we were.

With lighter winds, we were now allowed a few hours on deck as each day the land drew nearer. Most stayed on their bunks, their spirits crushed. I knew I must look as sickly as any: gaunt, thin and listless, face and hair greasy and grimy, clothes filthy.

But a few like me were still able to line the rails and see us sail past high cliffs and rocky shores. Large sea birds soared overhead, and for a while huge silvery-grey creatures swam alongside the ship. Dolphins, said the surgeon.

For the last few days we were locked down below. Coming into port, explained the surgeon, the captain needed no distractions while finding the river entrance and a spot to anchor.

At first we barely noticed that the ship's familiar noises had quieted, the rocking now as gentle as a baby's cradle. Then above us footfalls and shouting, a jumble of rattling noises, followed by some much louder clanking sounds towards the front of the ship. These lasted some time, then suddenly all was quiet. Shockingly, impossibly, *quiet*. Someone was heard to whisper: was that the anchor?

Into the silence came a new sound: a hundred or so women sobbing, slowly coming to understand that the ordeal was over. My murdering friend next to me was giving thanks to God, hugging her bewildered children, and then me, wet kisses that mingled with my own tears. She declared nothing would persuade her to go on a boat ever again: never, *never*!

Perhaps the surgeon tactfully waited for the sobbing to subside before he came down the ladder. He had exchanged his usual stained aprons for his smart navy uniform. You can tell your grandchildren, he announced, one hundred and seventy-two days at sea.

We were told the five in the infirmary, alas very sick, would be taken ashore first, today, on stretchers. Those with signs of scurvy would also go first. Then those remaining, in groups of eight on the longboats. We'd not be put in chains; on this small island anyone who tried to escape wouldn't get far. We'd not go ashore today, though, the surgeon warned us. There were processes to observe first. Even so, we could begin by packing our bags and then going up on deck.

I was a mouse emerging from its winter nest. First, the joy of breathing fresh air, then, with eyes still unused to such strong sunlight, peering around a bend in the wide river, a number of ships also at anchor. Sea birds squawked above the masts, some swans cruised by, but — glory be — these were not white but as black as night. A bare mountain loomed over the wharves and buildings of the township.

As we women assembled on the deck, some officials climbed aboard. They looked English, stiffly dressed in black, pleased with their importance. We were lined up, examined, deemed fit for work, or not.

Two days later, the first of us supposedly fit ones were directed into the longboats. Some could climb by themselves down the rope ladders, most could not. The sailors handled them roughly, like rag dolls. Those who looked to be pregnant fared no better than the rest. I hung back, carrying one of the little children down into the last boat.

We weren't officially told, but the word had got around: at the foot of that tall mountain was our destination, the Cascades Female Factory.

10. Changes afoot

THAT NIGHT TILLIE DOESN'T come back home. I delay telling her anxious mother about the fire until after supper. Surely she's just been detained helping with cleaning up and has missed the tides? We wake to our normal breakfast, the twins more fractious than usual and Mrs Roberton tearful, convinced that something terrible has happened to Tillie. The morning passes slowly, buying milk from the cow man and taking the twins to build dams and paddle in the stream.

The men, of course, have all gone to their work, since the rules about keeping to our 'proper station' don't apply to those who labour, those who do the actual work.

I'm watching the twins, all three of us out of sorts. The sun is high in the sky before Tillie appears around the rocks, looking drawn and weary. Like most of the other women and children squatting at the open flaps of their tents, we're having a meagre lunch of tough bread, a few ends of salted beef and some old cheese.

'Why did you just leave?' Tillie demands as she approaches the tent. Her hands are filthy and she has black smuts on her cheeks. 'Didn't you want to know what happened?'

'There was nothing I could do to help,' I reply testily. 'Should I have left the twins? Anyway, what did happen?'

She slumps down onto the grass. 'A spark from the cooking fire jumped onto the raupo reeds. The whole hut went up, but two men and Mr Williams came running and helped put out the flames. Mrs Mathew keeps two big pails of water nearby. The camp oven was ruined, and the pot with some soup bubbling was burnt to a cinder.'

'How frightening for you,' says her mother, wide-eyed.

Taking off her bonnet and running blackened fingers through her limp hair, Tillie gives way to tears.

'When it started, and we were screaming, Mrs Mathew first asked if I'd done anything foolish, been careless with my skirt or used the fire poker in a stupid way. It wasn't fair, I did nothing — the spark just jumped. She did apologise later, said she was sorry, in the heat of the moment . . . I was not to blame . . . just for a spark jumping.'

Yes, I'm thinking, true to form. Cascades proved to me over and over again how the lowly people always get the blame. Female and young especially. But usually we don't get an apology.

Tillie sniffs. 'She was most upset about her new boots. She'd put them out to dry, but they got burnt up, too.'

'Oh the poor soul, what a calamity!' cries Mrs Roberton. 'But I suppose such a fine lady has others?' Most of us in Mechanics Bay would have only the one precious pair, irreplaceable.

'Only some older ones, which she said might just last until a ship comes. Or a bootmaker arrives and begins business.'

'Dearie, look: your skirt is all soiled from the fire,' fusses her mother. 'It will need a good scrub.'

Tillie brightens, and reaches out for the crusty remains of bread.

'I do have better news,' she says. 'Mrs Mathew wants you to see if there's a seamstress here, to take an older skirt of hers and make two skirts. One for me and one for Harriet. She says the amount of material in some of her skirts is just ridiculous, even up to twenty-five yards!'

A new skirt — even if sewn from material already used. It

might even be a prettier colour than depressing Cascades grey, or the nasty brown one I stole in Hobart. I'll twirl around and around like the daughter of the manor! Mrs Mathew must like me, despite my impertinent questions.

But I'm sure there's another reason, when we hear Tillie say that today she is packing a bag to go and stay with the Mathews in their tent in Official Bay.

Tillie explains, as the only official wife Mrs Mathew must offer hospitality to important visitors — missionaries passing through and captains of naval ships. The governor himself is expected any day now to inspect his new capital. Mrs Mathew would be needing more help, what with the earlier loss of her chest of kitchenware and now this smaller fire.

And, I'm thinking a little sourly, with the governor himself visiting, Tillie the servant girl must be properly dressed.

Tillie departs that afternoon, carrying her burlap bag, a pillow and a blanket, promising to return as often as she can. She will bring around the cast-off skirt from Mrs Mathew, in the hope that among the wives at Mechanics Bay there's a former seamstress. Most would be carrying a sewing kit for mending, but a seamstress would have a bigger kit of really sharp scissors, plenty of pins, needles, thimbles and different-coloured threads. Mrs Mathew would pay her, of course, for her work.

The farewell becomes strangely drawn-out and complicated. She's only going around to the next bay, for goodness' sake! But her mother fusses over the packing, and asks me to mind the twins while she has some private time with her daughter. When they return from their walk along the beach, both are tearful and the final goodbyes more emotional and suited to Tillie leaving on a journey halfway around the world. I can't imagine what confidences or secrets have been exchanged.

'Shall I walk with you over to the rocks?' I ask.

Tillie nods in reply, gives her mother and the twins final hugs amid a fresh torrent of tears.

Not far from where we will part ways, she stops. 'Will you promise me to stay with Mother and the twins? She needs you now.'

I think my silence gives her the answer. Despite all their kindness over these past days, I just can't promise to remain. How can I, when I must earn money to pay for my passage home? And I can't do that staying forever in Mechanics Bay.

We're both staring out at the harbour, when she suddenly blurts out: 'Do you . . . Harriet, do you know about the bleeding? Is it true?'

How can I not know, from being cooped up with women for all those months in Newgate, many more at sea and then those three years in Cascades, where they constantly complained of their stomach cramps, their sore breasts and headaches, thinking no one notices them secretly washing blood from their clothing or the two small and useless squares of cotton we were given for our bleeds when we first arrived. Some hung these kerchiefs to dry under their hammocks. We all knew those who just bled into their skirts, or walked around dripping blood onto the floor. The unfortunates on any sort of punishment duty were required to mop up these sticky trails.

I ask: 'Is that what your mother . . . ?'

'I've never been away from her. She says, now I'm nearly a woman, leaving home, she can't bear it. I'm growing up too fast, she says.'

'It may not start for ages yet. Perhaps when you're fourteen, even fifteen.'

'I'm nearly thirteen. How often . . . ?'

I didn't trust her mother to have told her all she needed to know. 'About every twenty-eight days, like the cycle of the moon. To begin with, only bleeding for two or three days, but then usually about four days. Until you're too old to have children.'

'You mean, my whole *life*?' she asks, horrified.

'Nearly. Perhaps until forty-five or fifty.' As we near the rocks, I push aside the unwelcome memory of some of the meaner Cascades wardens making those they decided were bleeding sit apart at meals or even stay away from the chapel services, so everyone was aware they were 'unclean'.

'How do you know all this?' she asks.

'My mother,' I swiftly lie, although maybe not so much of a lie, as Martha, the old warden at Cascades who'd told me about the bleeding, was nearly a mother to me for those years.

'Have you started?'

'No.'

We resume walking, but reaching the rocks Tillie stops again.

'Just one more thing?' she asks, looking sheepish. 'It's only when you piss, right?'

'No,' I say. 'Anytime. It just drips. Now you must go. You can talk to Mrs Mathew, you know.'

'She's very—'

'She's had two babies!' I say, firmly. 'She knows about these things. She's not a dragon. Well, not quite.'

As Tillie turns to go, I know there's something I need to say.

'Tillie, wait! Look, I'm really sorry, but I can't promise to stay with your family. I'll sleep here for a little while yet—'

'Then you—'

'—but I won't be minding the twins during the day. I need to earn money to pay for going back home, to England.'

'Going *back*? To all that cold and misery? Factory work or no work. Children sick and dying. People drunk, homeless people living in the filthy streets. Endless winters. Always hungry. Are you mad?'

She's so stricken that I can only guess what sort of life she and her family have left behind in England. 'For pity's sake, Harriet, why?'

'It's home.' Perhaps that's still true. I must have faith it is true. Blinking back tears, I point at the desolate, lumpy landscape all around us. 'There's no place for single girls here. You have your family. I don't and . . .'

'But another terrible journey? A few years here, you'll marry . . .'

'Maybe, maybe not. But when I'm an old lady back in England, I'll remember you! We'll exchange letters.'

Perched on a sunny rock, staring across at the encampment, I'm asking myself: is this really so bad, this collection of scruffy tents before me on a muddy beach far from anywhere? Still better than the England that Tillie remembers?

The children playing in the late afternoon sun seem happy enough; the women are preparing food, some gossiping in small groups. There's a smell of cooking, a sense of settling in: clothes are hung on lines strung between tents and the few trees, or draped over bushes.

Beside the children's cries and a few yowling babies, there are the farmyard sounds of chickens, the cows and the goat. Not horses — those brought by the officials are kept around in Official Bay. And according to Tillie, already stabled in their very own raupo hut.

On the sand above the high-tide mark are heaped-up piles of logs and sawn wood for the proper house-building that they say is soon beginning. Small gangs of Maoris are working on the raupo huts, which are nearly ready for the first lucky families. We've got used to them coming, almost daily.

Down on the tidal mud sits a native canoe, also several small sailing vessels now starting to arrive with food and firewood, perhaps from the mission station at Maraetai around the coast. On these days, when it's sunny and the harbour twinkles, even at low tide it's actually quite pretty.

But I'm trying to make sense of Tillie's sudden departure for Official Bay. Harriet, are you a little jealous? I would be the better maidservant; kitchen and laundry work, how to use a needle are useful things I learned at Newgate and Cascades, though Mrs Mathew would prefer Tillie's meekness.

I must sleep alone now, always cold, missing my friend's warm back on these chilly spring nights. Yes, I like Mrs Roberton well enough, despite her constant weeping. I'm truly grateful for the family food and the shelter of the tent, and the twins are sweet, no trouble.

But I'll never get back to England if I stay in Mechanics Bay just minding children.

As I wander to our tent I stumble over a rope and earn myself an ill-tempered outburst from a woman feeding a baby. Bad enough, she shouts, to be stuck on this godawful beach without having yer bloody tent collapse around yer ears. Watch where yer going, why can't ya!

Mumbling an apology, I decide it's time to explore what is happening and the possibilities of work around in Store Bay.

October 1837

WE WERE ASSEMBLED ON the Hobart wharf, clutching our pathetic bags and the children too sick to walk. It was the first time since Mrs Fry's visit in London that we'd all been as one group in the open air, and a wretched, bedraggled sight we made, reeling as if drunk, our legs weak from lack of use. The very boards of the wharf seemed to tilt and rise up as if we were still at sea.

Our arrival was quite an event for the men of this town. The black-clothed officials were joined by a squad of armed soldiers in red jackets, here to escort us to our new home two miles away. But many more men, young and older, ordinarily dressed, had gathered at the wharf to remind us that we were criminals, strumpets, whores, bitches, *convicts*. To whistle and hoot as they pointed out which ones of us might provide a bit of easy fun, which ones were just petty thieves or which actual murderers.

I told myself, don't look at them. Look at the wooden shops, the wooden cottages behind white picket fences, the English spring flowers. Keep walking, past a white mansion — the governor's, probably — with the strangest of creatures strutting in its gardens. Birds six feet high, an animal with long ears, short front legs and an impossibly long tail.

Keep walking, even though the child on your back grows heavier, the muddy track steeper. Walk past makeshift workers' huts and alongside a narrow river, longing for water, but knowing the soldiers would not allow stopping for a drink. Keep walking.

At sundown we staggered towards the high walls surrounding Cascades. The mountain loomed above us, blocking the lowering sun. The air was cooler here, and damp. We were marched in twos into an inner courtyard, and then one by one to a small set of rooms. I was told to strip off the shift I'd been wearing ever since leaving London — fit only for burning, said the warden in charge, holding her nose.

Next, a bath in a tin tub, the water very cold but at least washing away months of salt and dirt; next, given two shifts made of scratchy dark grey wool, two pairs of stockings, two aprons, two caps and two cloths — 'for when you start to bleed'.

That night, we first tasted the food that would be served to us three times a day, every day of every week: a hunk of brown bread with a bowl of oxhead soup. Sometimes bits of gristle or a few grains of barley floated in the thin liquid.

Afterwards, we learned from the superintendent the reason for the eerie silence. This was a house of correction, so there would be, as we went about our daily tasks, no talking, no laughing, no singing of any kind. There would be no smoking or foul language. Any transgressions would be severely punished. We would attend a short chapel service twice a day, morning and night.

And now, at last, we could sleep. On the ship we had lain down on our narrow wooden berth, but here we were shown low-slung hammocks. My conviction being 'minor', I was put into a dormitory of twelve for Second Class, Yard One. I think my murdering friend and her children must have gone into the Crime Class, Yard Two, for I never saw them again.

Later I found out that because she was a skilled baker, despite her crime, she had quickly found a position in the town, and that children aged over three went to the orphanage. Some others of 'good behaviour' from the *Platina* also went to settler families wanting servants they could work to the bone and didn't have to pay.

That first night I drifted off to sleep in my hammock still feeling the ship rocking, quite beyond tears.

11. Trapped!

STORE BAY HAS BEGUN to feel like another country, as events conspire to delay my visit and finding work. During the next night there is a great commotion, the noisiest since we came ashore over a month ago.

Usually, night noises are babies crying, or men snoring, or a man and wife arguing. But this is from the tent right next door, mostly a woman screaming and sobbing, a man's voice brusquely telling her to be quiet, Mrs Roberton dashing over to help, and other women aroused from their sleep all trying to understand the reason for the uproar.

Candlelight from the neighbouring tent casts ghostly shadows, and from the raised voices it's soon clear to me that something is terribly wrong, a child is missing. There's a lot of shouting — a boy's name, Joshua, over and over. But before too long I hear a different sort of screaming and even laughter. All, apparently, is well.

Gradually, peace is restored, except for Mrs Roberton, on her return to our tent, whispering insistently to her husband and getting only grunts in response. Sawing timber all day long, he's always asleep the minute his head touches the pillow, and sleeps like the dead. Six in a tent, you're aware of these things, even if you pretend not to notice.

In the morning, the talk is all of Joshua, just four, who'd gone sleepwalking. His mother, woken by a hungry baby, discovered the empty mattress and convinced herself that he'd walked into the sea and gone out with the tide. Or been kidnapped by the natives, taken into the interior, never to be seen again, perhaps killed and roasted. But in the end he'd been found quite quickly, not far away from his tent.

We've had several incidents of children wandering, but this one seems to unsettle all the mothers, perhaps because it's the first at night. I hear men saying that we're getting a bit too friendly with the natives who come every day; we need to be more cautious.

Others want to post night-watchmen, armed with muskets and orders to shoot on sight. The boy's mother is especially disturbed, lavishly hugging and kissing the child, who, of course, has no idea why he's getting all this attention. Listening to her talking with Mrs Roberton, I think she is slightly mad.

'Of course Harriet can help you,' I hear Mrs Roberton saying. 'She's very dependable. The twins adore her, and now that Tillie's gone, she's . . . Oh, oh, forgive me . . .'

One sets off the other into torrents of tears. For both, it probably isn't only the sleepwalking, but everything — the making-do, the rationed food, the constant worrying about the children, the rain and the mud. I hadn't yet seen Mrs Roberton take comfort in another woman's arms. But neither, I think unkindly, has actually lost a child. Not to actual death.

I need to be party to this conversation. 'Pardon me, ma'am,' I begin, squatting at the door of the next-door tent. 'How am I to help?'

'Joshua here is a good little boy,' says Mrs Roberton. 'He'll be no trouble.'

'Am I to mind him as well as the twins?'

'Oh, just for a few days,' she trills. She knows, and I know, that it will be longer than that. This is what young single girls, 'dependable' but dependent on the charity of others, are expected to do, and not to question or complain. 'Until Mrs Harris gets over her shock. She is quite worn out, the poor darling.'

In a whisper she adds, 'She's got it into her head some constant fear of snakes, no matter what the missionaries say.'

Mrs Harris, who can't be more than five years older than me, looks up, pitiful gratitude written all over her swollen face. The restless baby on the ground beside her starts to wail. She picks it up roughly and opens her thin blouse. It sucks at her greedily. I may be no great expert in these matters, but her breast doesn't look to have much milk.

'I *told* Mr Harris we should'na sleep with the tent flap wide open,' she says peevishly. Her accent is Scottish. 'But he gets so hot at night, and needs his rest and — ach, how this bairn hurts me.'

'There, there,' soothed Mrs Roberton. 'You need your rest, too. Tomorrow you needn't worry about Joshua. Harriet will take care of him.'

So, here I am again, a third time trapped, held captive. Not in a stinking rolling ship, nor a convict prison, not with chains or locks, but on a beach, bound to three little people for all the long daylight hours.

One day slips into another. We fetch water from the stream and build dams. On warmer days I scrub down the children's white little bodies, amidst much splashing and squealing. They help me wash the family's clothes, slapping them down onto the wet rocks. We buy milk from the cow man. By the shoreline we paddle or throw stones into the sea, build sandcastles below the high-tide mark to watch the sea inch closer and then wash them away.

Sometimes one or other of my charges becomes irritable, so we return to the tent, and I sing them off to an afternoon nap. Or tell stories of a poor kitchen servant who went to a ball and lost her glass slipper and ended up marrying the prince.

My frustration grows by the day, as the men come back from their work at nightfall and rumours fly around the camp.

Around in Official Bay, the government offices are being built first, so the officials can have somewhere to sit and push their pens. Several raupo huts have been completed, and more started. The governor is expected daily!

And Store Bay is apparently also a hive of activity. The small vessels we saw sailing past our bay to anchor off Store Bay are bringing new arrivals, early birds hoping to buy land when the first sales are held.

As well as the hut builders, Maori traders are now arriving with canoes loaded up with food — fresh pork, potatoes, pumpkins, melons — and huge bundles of firewood to exchange for blankets, cloth, tobacco and nails.

Even in our bay, there are some small excitements.

One day, after breakfast we go down to watch a Maori canoe being pulled up on our shore. Instead of heading straight over to begin work, one of the paddlers hesitantly approaches us, carrying something that looks like a mat of leaves, plaited together. He's a handsome man, probably about the same age as Tillie's father.

Through miming and a good deal of laughter, I learn that this mat is actually a kite. That he also has children, three in number, and this is a gift. The only word I catch, as he lays the kite carefully down on the sand, sounds like 'koha'. I guess that this might be a native custom, so I pick it up solemnly.

He shows us how to run along the sand and let the wind take it aloft, not very successfully, as there isn't much of a breeze that morning. But later in the day, when the afternoon winds have got up, Thomas is able, with a little help from me, to get the kite up into the air, high enough to have him laughing with delight.

This incident is noticed, of course, and whispered about. I'm warned by Tillie's father — and two or three busybody wives — not to talk to the natives, nor accept gifts. But Mrs Roberton persuades her husband there is no harm in it, and it surely makes the little ones happy.

And a few days later, look what the incoming tide brings us! Mid-morning, around the headland comes a small boat with two people in it: perched in the stern is my friend Tillie no less, waving energetically, being rowed by the affable interpreter, Mr Williams. I don't mind admitting to a stab of envy as he runs the boat up into the shallows, leaps out and gallantly lifts Tillie onto dry sand.

Mrs Roberton leads the way down to the waterline for a smother of hugs and kisses. Tillie is clutching a bulky packet, the famous skirt no doubt, for making into two. I peek inside; the material is a lovely blue, the blue of deep oceans.

'You've found a seamstress?' asks Tillie. The sea passage has given her a healthy glow, or perhaps it is Mrs Mathew's pork and potato dinners. Or perhaps the excitement of being rowed by Mr Williams. 'Well have you, Mother?' she presses.

'Oh dearie, no,' says Mrs Roberton. 'I clean forgot. Oh, silly me. I promise I will ask about. There will be someone. Can you stay awhile?'

Tillie rolls her eyes at me. 'I'm just here to deliver this, I can't stop. Mrs Mathew is expecting the governor, and we're so busy. He'll be staying on his ship, but dining with us. And having meetings and inspections, you know.'

Her mother is more interested in the young man rowing her daughter. 'And you are . . . may I ask, sir?'

'Oh yes, sorry,' says Tillie, proceeding to introduce her mother to the official interpreter, who is attractively flushed and panting slightly from all his rowing. He listens patiently to Tillie's breathless summary of his life story.

As soon as is polite, he begs leave to row Miss Roberton back to Official Bay, as he has promised Mrs Mathew. He's expected to be on hand for the governor's arrival, probably tomorrow. They will no doubt be meeting with the local rangatira. The local chiefs, he adds.

As he turns the boat around and helps Tillie back into the stern, I take off my boots, hitch up my skirts, and wade out a little way to help push the boat into deeper water.

This gesture isn't actually necessary, but I need to show them and reassure myself that I'm not completely without my uses.

It's a still moonless night, so no one notices me as I creep from the tent and go for a walk along the wet sand. My bare feet enjoy the cold mud, although occasionally I stumble on a rock, a piece of driftwood or a sharp cockle shell. The tide is a long way out. A fair-sized ship, thought to be carrying the governor, arrived today with the last of the light. We heard the usual shouts, and the clanking of the anchor chain going down. Now a faint riding light pricks the darkness.

My thoughts as I walk are so confused. I'm not a jealous person. I learned many harsh lessons in Cascades, and one of them is that being jealous of others only makes you bitter and gets you nowhere.

But Tillie's mousy little face beaming at Mr Williams has roused unkind thoughts. She has her family here; her position, therefore some wages; a kind enough mistress providing decent food and a bed. And around her interesting people coming and going, even a young man who for whatever reason took the trouble to row her around the headland to deliver a package. Perhaps he just likes rowing.

Whereas here I am . . . No, no, no, Harriet, you'll *not* succumb to self-pity. Tomorrow after breakfast you will talk to Tillie's mother and tell her that she must find another girl to help look after the twins and Joshua. The time has come for you to look for work over in Store Bay.

She'll probably warn you of the dangers for young girls in such situations. Nothing is more certain, men will take advantage. You'll assure her, you can look after yourself. She will reluctantly agree to ask among the families for a suitable girl to mind the children. *Urgently*, you say. You feel a little heartless, but resolute.

You thank her for her understanding and kindness, and yes, you'll be walking over to Store Bay every day but returning to sleep in the tent, and partake of her family's food — if this arrangement is acceptable? She doesn't need to know about your need to earn money and your grand plan.

October 1837

MY TWO PRISONS SO far had been such noisy places: the never-ending wailings and babble of Newgate, and the bangs and creaks and clatter of a ship at sea. I'd become alert to what particular sounds might mean, what calamities — a fight, an injury, a death, some failure of gear — might be unfolding.

Cascades was different. Barred from talking, laughing or singing, the women here moved around like phantoms. The silence was eerie and strictly enforced by the wardens.

Woken before dawn by the dreadful clangs of the brass hand bell, we shuffled from dormitory to food hall to chapel to whatever task we were assigned. It was called a factory because we all worked at something — laundry, sewing, sorting firewood, picking oakum and other tasks — until we sank into our hammocks and the last candle was doused.

There were other reasons why Cascades changed me. For all those months in Newgate, I knew there would be a daily visit by Mrs Fry or one of her ladies, and I knew my stay there should end, sometime. For all those months at sea, I knew we should arrive at our destination, sometime.

But at Cascades there was no end. Only seven years of days and months merging into each other, the silent shuffling routine, the food not fit even for animals, the punishments for the slightest of sins. Because of that mountain looming above, we hardly ever saw the sun. And though the governor's wife, Lady Jane Franklin, was said to take an interest in our welfare, even corresponded with Mrs Fry in London, she never once visited the prison, at least in my years there.

And I realised there would be no end to the whispered teasing and insults that soon started. I was picked out as different, not a poor orphan, or a wronged homeless mother, or a victim of abuse as most inmates were. I'd never given thought to how I spoke, but in Cascades it became a reason for mockery and envy. They decided I must have come from a good family, but must have done something especially bad to be transported so young.

As the months went by, and the tedium became unbearable, I grew cunning and impudent. I found myself objecting to inmates' teasing or the wardens' scolding, muttering curses or insults of my own just loud enough to be heard. Several times I was rewarded with three days' solitary on bread and water. I dragged my feet going to chapel, and was purposely last out of my hammock, which infuriated the others, who were made to stand shivering while the bell clanged on and on and on until I was upright.

That stumpy hook-nosed warden with the bell was especially hateful. Most were stern and impatient, determined to keep us to the rules. They seemed to be women from the town, widows or wives abandoned by their husbands. Miserable themselves, they enjoyed wielding their power.

But the one called Martha showed me some kindness. She was older, her voice gentle, and I learned she'd come from England three years before, had two sons but had buried five other children. Her late husband had been a fisherman, lost at sea.

It was she who warned me one day about the reverend who rode up from the town to conduct the daily chapel services. You may be young, she whispered, but Holy Willie is not particular, for all that he is a priest and a married man with children. Never find yourself in a room alone with him. He preaches Christian values, but he preys on women and a greater hypocrite never lived.

This underground knowledge was only the beginning. I gradually learned that Cascades was not always a place of obedience, silence and penitence. Some nights we heard singing from Yard Two, the Crime Class, where the most criminal and rebellious females were put. A group there was known as the Flash Mob, famous for rude songs and dancing, and the bribing of wardens and constables for things like tobacco and tea, sugar and liquor. Some even occasionally bribed their way out of captivity to run down to the township and spend a night in the brothels.

I could understand their desperation for breaking the monotony — so when hearing from the matron one day that

I was being sent as a servant to a family in Hobart, I was almost excited. I'd done two years in this loathsome place. But I had forebodings, too. I'd heard mostly bad things about how convicts sent from Cascades were treated — but surely, it couldn't be worse?

Just walking out from behind those walls would be something.

12. Store Bay

MY TALK WITH MRS ROBERTON goes exactly as predicted. She is not pleased with me and my plans. What I do not expect are the full twelve days that it takes for her to bestir herself and find another girl to mind the children and a proper seamstress for our skirts. She keeps pleading headaches and other indispositions.

I'm minding the children, counting the days, frustrated beyond belief, but trying to be understanding. Is it just shyness that makes her reluctant to leave the tent? She sleeps a lot, so has few visitors and seems to have few friends among the wives. Yet in the camp she has some status: her daughter works for the only 'official wife', in the bay where the toffs live.

I know it's twelve days because on the thirteenth, two things happen. Around noon, I notice an imposing, official-looking flag on a small square-rigger leaving the harbour, and in the early afternoon Tillie returns to us for a visit.

The twins are the first to spot her walking around the rocks, and rush squealing across the wet mud to greet her. Joshua and I follow. Her surly greeting tells me she's out of sorts.

'Is that the governor leaving?' I ask.

'On the *Ranger*,' she replies. 'Mrs Mathew whispered to me as he left: "not a moment too soon".'

There's little wind this day, so the *Ranger* is still to be seen out near that strange island the Maoris call Rangi-toto, her sails flapping listlessly.

'He set up his office in the big tent and dined with us most days,' she goes on, kicking at the wet seaweed brought in by the tide. 'Such a fussy man, always interfering, demanding this or that. Not just to me. To his secretary Mr Shortland: "find these papers!" "Mr Mathew, tell me of your progress with the survey." "After supper, Mrs Mathew, play me something on your little piano!"'

'Well, you'd enjoy that, surely?'

'Briefly, yes. Though it was odd, hearing nice tinkly music in a shabby tent. She said it was Mozart — written when he was only twelve, would you believe!' Tillie isn't finished with her list of grumbles, though. 'To me, the maid: "you may take my plate" . . . "clean my boots" . . . "it feels like rain, bring in my shirt" . . . "a glass of water".'

'I suppose being a captain used to—?'

'Oh, it wasn't just ordering us all about. He's such a busybody. "Mrs Mathew, the cooking fire needs wood placed *across* the embers, like so" or "A little salt makes porridge taste so much better, don't you know." And at supper, he drones on about his time staying in India being a *burra sahib*, or his capture by pirates in the West Indies. Then getting a horrid tropical disease called yellow fever. His eyeballs going bright yellow. Perhaps once he was handsome, but now . . . Well, he's just sad, so thin and ill. And nearly bald, but Mrs Mathew says he's not so very old. She worries about him, with all that's expected.'

'I missed him when he came here,' I say. 'I was taking the children around the rocks.'

'He never stops,' she continues. 'Up to the flagpole to meet the native chiefs, or to check progress on the house building. The next day over to the other harbour — I'm not sure why.'

'Probably to meet the chiefs. There's a big Maori village over there. But it's miles away.'

'They went on horseback. But everything wears him out.

He gets terrible headaches. I heard someone say that when he's in pain he howls like a young rhinoceros! Mrs Mathew says it's all the criticism and the nasty letters, especially from the south — those people with the New Zealand Company. They absolutely *hate* him, everything he does, everything he stands for.'

'Then how can he be governor,' I ask, baffled, 'when he's sick and can't walk far and people hate him?' I remember Captain Wycherley's comments on the *Platina*.

Tillie looks a little guilty. 'I overheard Mr Mathew whispering to Mrs Mathew that up in Okiato, when he got para . . . pal . . .'

'Paralysed?'

'They thought it was a stroke.'

I'd heard that word at Cascades. An older warden, with a crooked back and a vile temper, hated by the convicts, had suddenly been struck down, unable to speak or move her limbs. Not long afterwards, she died.

'Mr Mathew and some others wanted him to resign,' says Tillie, 'or write to London asking to be recalled.'

'Better if he had?'

'Probably. But, to me, sometimes he was kind. He asked where did I grow up and what my father was doing here. His daughter is my age, he said, presently up in the Bay of Islands. I felt sorry for him.'

We stand a moment by the shore, thinking about poor fussy Governor Hobson, while Joshua and the twins amuse themselves tossing tendrils of seaweed at each other. The *Ranger* is making slow progress past Rangi-toto.

'Has Mother found a seamstress for our skirts?' she asks.

'Yesterday, yes.'

Tillie sighed. 'Why did she take so long! And has she found someone for the children? I've only got two free days — more visitors are coming.'

Ah, so she has not forgotten that I am serious about seeking paid work, and why.

'Her name's Verity,' I replied. 'I think she was on the *Platina*.'

So, with Verity arriving this morning to take charge of the twins and Joshua, I'm finally able to go over to Store Bay in search of work. I set off up the path to the ridge. Rain is threatening, but that won't stop me, in my new-found freedom. I've got my fearnought with me in a bag, anyway, just in case.

From Tillie, the quiet spy, I've learned that Mr Mathew has been greatly frustrated and irritable. Principally because the governor wouldn't allow work to begin on government house until He Himself had come back and *personally* chosen the actual site. Well, that is hardly surprising, Him being such a meddling fusspot, wanting to control everything.

So now that He Himself has decided on the exact site overlooking the harbour, when I reach the top of the track I can see that the carpenters are at last hard at work. The first timbers are in place, indicating the foundations and the eventual size of the building. The harbour's waters today are a dull green, and a chilly wind is whipping across the ridge.

As I start down the track leading to Store Bay, I note that it is now wider, the bracken cut back further. I take care not to slip or trip on the broken surface, but caution is abandoned when I feel the first drops of rain on my face. I should have been warned by those heavy dark grey clouds from the north.

Dashing recklessly down the track, I decide the only shelter from what's now a downpour is a single large tree standing above a stream flowing on down to a small flax swamp. Viewed from here, all of Store Bay lies before me, and it's nothing at all as I expected. It has certainly transformed in the few weeks since last I was here.

Just below, stretching away around the curve of the bay stands an uneven line of raupo huts, some finished, many not. Below them is an assortment of tents, some large and some meant only for a single person. Down by the shoreline stands the Government Store, with stacks of materials piled up alongside it. Several canoes and small sailing vessels are drawn up on the sand or anchored just offshore.

Most astonishing are all the people — maybe a hundred or more. Bare-chested natives working on the hut-building, untroubled by the rain. Pale-skinned Englishmen, also bare-chested and drowned-looking, working those long two-handed saws in pairs. Men in thick jackets scurrying with loads between tents. More men down by the boats, doing what men do around boats. If there are any women, they're not to be seen.

Where have all these men come from? Not one big immigrant ship has yet arrived, only those many smaller vessels constantly passing our bay. If it's true and they're land-sharks coming from Australia, intending to make big profits at the land sales, they're in for a long wait. According to Tillie, Mr Mathew is taking far longer than expected to do his survey and produce a town plan, and until he does the governor can't hold any land sales.

But as I stand under that dripping tree, tugging on my fearnought, it's the general air of disorder that really makes my heart sink. Everywhere are untidy stacks of logs and sawn timber; also heaps of shells, clay and sand, probably also destined to be used in the building construction. The other stuff strewn around is just rubbish, left to rot and for busy seagulls to feast on.

Has anyone organised a communal latrine for all those men? Or do they just piss and squat in the creek, or wade a few feet out into the shallows for the tide to take away their waste?

And what is that being unloaded from a canoe that's just arrived?

I blink the rain from my eyes and — and, yes, it's a pig being unloaded. Several pigs, in fact. A small crowd immediately gathers, and it looks like an auction is underway. People pushing and shoving and shouting, pigs shrieking. Are they killing the animals on the beach, right there?

Suddenly, I feel my heart racing. That tall figure among the natives around the canoe is surely the paddler? My first sighting of him since the flag-raising day! They have finished unloading, and are standing knee-deep in the water, watching impassively as the settlers yell their bids and pump their arms high in the air. I can hear them even from up here.

But is it him?

There is only one way to find out.

I leave the shelter of the tree and plunge down the track onto the sand, all the while thinking: Harriet, my girl, you are so *foolish* — what will you do when you reach the canoe? Just stand there in the rain, hoping to be noticed, feeling stupid? Why would he, or any of them, take any notice of a white girl with nothing better to do?

But halfway down the sand I make myself stop. The paddlers have turned the canoe around and are climbing back in. He — if it *is* he — is already climbing aboard.

I am drenched, and for nothing. My heart thuds dully in my chest. The auction finishes, the pigs are being led off. The canoe pulls away from the shore, the paddles flashing in perfect time.

I stand amongst the muddle, watching the canoe disappear into a squall, and ignored by all the men going about their business. It's even more obvious that there'll be no work here for the likes of me for many weeks. I turn and trudge back up the beach.

In desperation, I ask Tillie to see if there's any chance of work in Official Bay. If Mrs Mathew has so many visitors, could I be useful as a second scullery maid? But Tillie reports back that there's no call for extra help at the moment. All the official gentlemen dine with the Mathews, but, as they spend most of their time over in Store Bay, there's no call for more servants.

So with Tillie gone, and hearing that the new child-minder Verity has lasted just six days, I'm again summoned. Verity is abed in her tent with a high fever and a terrible cough, her return anytime soon very unlikely.

I'm finding it hard to be gracious or even enjoy the children's company. Cooped up inside the tent while rain squalls pass over, they're irritable and demanding. And little Thomas is not well, sleeping a good deal, and his hot forehead a cause for concern.

'We'll find another girl,' I tell Mrs Roberton. 'Tomorrow.'

'Maybe,' she replies listlessly. These days, aside from sleeping, she isn't doing much more than the absolutely essential cooking. I'm helping her knead the bread dough when I can. 'I'd prefer you to stay, Harriet dear. I can rely on you. Oh, I so miss my darling Tillie!'

Rather than respond, and seeing that the rain has cleared, I wander with the children around the tents I know to house suitable girls. Two are possible, though younger than ideal and their mothers reluctant, even when I mention a small purse of money. They have their own little ones to keep safe.

Mrs Roberton is horrified when I ask why a boy can't be employed to mind the children. 'It's not boy's work,' she replies.

'Why not?' I ask.

'Boys are not trustworthy.'

'Why so?'

'They just aren't.'

How convenient, I think — and also most unfair. Girls mind children; boys have fun. So again I'm trapped at Mechanics Bay, amongst a camp of people getting more miserable by the day.

That the natives — as well as building us huts — are also now bringing potatoes and occasionally pig meat and bundles of firewood might sound an excellent thing. And of course it is; we would otherwise be nearly starving, as happened to those folk over in Botany Bay. But with only two or three canoes coming at a time, the natives can't bring enough for everyone and progress on the building is slow.

So how to decide who shall get the firewood or the food? Or who shall move into the next raupo hut to be finished? Who chooses which family will have the hut? Is drawing lots the fairest way? Or priority given to those who have sick children? Or just to those who can offer more money?

With no one in charge, it's hardly surprising that when canoes arrive and their loads are lifted onto the sands there's immediately a crowd, and squabbles, even scuffles, break out. Usually the woman with the loudest voice and most hectoring manner prevails. And the language can be pretty ripe! The more timid wives don't stand a chance. Tillie's downcast mother doesn't even stir herself from her mattress to attend.

The husbands, of course, are mostly away dawn to dusk, so play little part in these scenes. But the men around in the two other bays — the officials and the new arrivals, particularly — are soon exerting another sort of influence. Come December, we realise that the laden canoes are generally heading past us, straight to the officials in their bay and the workers further around in Store Bay. The natives aren't to blame. And they're canny, driving a hard bargain for the things they're now wanting: the blankets, bolts of calico, figs of tobacco and, of course, iron nails.

We poor Mechanics Bay folk have little of worth to barter with, and to survive *we* don't need much in the way of fresh food like potatoes and kumara and pig meat; *we* can get by with what we brought from the ships, our horrible oaty gruel and hard biscuits and old rice, what's left of them.

But, oh, how the very thought of a ripe peach or a sweet juicy pear makes my mouth water.

It's the arrival close together of the first three ships bringing proper immigrants that convinces me that it's again time to look seriously for work.

Tillie's taciturn father, returning nightly, is persuaded to tell me that the newcomers, mostly mechanics with families, are pitching their tents at Store Bay or on the beach further up the harbour, known as Waipiro. They've set up a sawpit there. The first wooden houses are going up in Store Bay, he says, and some buildings that look like they'll be premises for shops.

And there was the arrival of the first soldiers, who'd been marched straight up to the flagstaff area to pitch their tents. Apparently, there are plans to build a barracks there, not far from the flagstaff.

So with Verity still unwell, and 'untrustworthy' boys ruled out, I renew my efforts to find another girl to mind the children. Eventually Maisie, whose father is a stonemason, agrees to help. She's only ten, but her mother says she's reliable and honest, and, being the youngest, is fond of playing with little children.

Mrs Roberton raises no objection, other than to remind me — several times over — that she would much prefer that I stayed. The twins have grown to love me so. Can't I just delay my quest for work a little longer? Just until Thomas is better? For their sake, if not for hers?

I'll be back each sundown, I reply in my firmest voice, for supper and to tell them their bedtime stories.

The morning dawns fine, the sun rising behind Rangi-toto wearing a misty veil. I leave the tent early, as soon as Maisie arrives.

I'm wearing my new indigo skirt, courtesy of Mrs Mathew and finished by the seamstress a few days earlier. A shawl lent by Mrs Roberton hides my shabby jacket, and covering my short hair is a white bonnet borrowed from Joshua's mother. You look almost quite respectable, Mrs Roberton declares, meaning to be kind. But I still have no plait hanging down my back.

Up on the ridge the governor's house now has its four exterior walls, though not yet a roof or a veranda. The governor has ordered haste, so the men are already hard at work, their number now also including some burly natives. That's new.

Leaving behind the sound of hammering, I start down the steep track to Store Bay, strangely nervous. Will this visit be more successful? All I need is one person who thinks I can be useful and is prepared to pay me adequately.

With skirt hems held high, I'm stepping so cautiously between exposed roots and clumps of cracked earth that I don't see the tree until I'm nearly underneath it. Before, I'd only appreciated its spreading branches for the shelter they gave me, when I'd leaned back against the several gnarled trunks. I'd not looked upwards.

For some unknown reason, this day I did, and now I can't look anywhere else. Those leafy branches I've earlier barely glanced at are now coloured a deep red provided by clusters of thousands of crimson needles. A red brighter than fresh blood, or any red I can remember: Christmas holly berries, summer strawberries, even the royal guards marching past Buckingham Palace those times my father took me up to London, innocent and happy.

Apart from blue skies and the occasional pink or golden sunrise, my earthly world has been so entirely composed of the duller shades of green, grey, brown and black that I stand dumbstruck at such scarlet beauty, tears starting to my eyes. I've not seen a living thing so brazenly, magnificently *red* my whole life. Close up, I discover that each little red needle is topped by a tiny ball of pure gold. How my father would love this tree.

I survey the scene below me with renewed purpose. That dismal rain-swept vista of my last visit is now bathed in bright sunlight. Such bustling activity! Three ships in the harbour, many smaller ones under sail, and now some bigger Maori canoes also carrying sails. Those, too, are new.

It's nearly high tide, so the smaller vessels, maybe twenty, have been drawn up above the tide mark. How many dozens of men going about their business amongst the raupo huts, the tents, the piles of materials, I can't tell. Maybe now two or three hundred, a good many of them natives.

And at the far end of the beach, some sort of a marketplace. A small jetty of stones now juts out into the bay to enable goods to be unloaded. At its base is a wooden platform on which wares can be displayed, also a pig-pen. Even this early in the day, a small crowd has gathered for trading.

Where to start? I decide to wander through the area of raupo huts towards the marketplace. I'm hailed by some of the native workers with cheerful waves and shouts. The man who gifted me the flax kite I certainly recognise, and wish I had the words to tell him how much the children have enjoyed flying it, these days past. And not just Joshua and the twins, either.

I stop by one hut to stare, perhaps rudely, at a younger native man, but realise that the memory of the beautiful paddler on that day of the canoe races has faded. This one smiles in greeting, but his eyes lack the paddler's intense curiosity.

I see some familiar faces as I wander down through the tents towards the beach: the Mechanics Bay men coming here daily, bent to their various labours. Besides the newly arrived soldiers, something else is new: I pass several women, clearly recent arrivals from their bemused expressions and clinging children.

I divert to inspect the framework of a small building that will probably be a shop, but this brings me into the path, fatefully, of someone I'd once prayed I would never ever *ever* set eyes on again.

November 1839

SO, TWO YEARS AFTER arriving at Cascades, a gruff constable escorted me on the two-mile walk to my new home on the outskirts of Hobart Town. I felt giddy with the freedom. It was late springtime, judging from the flowers and the bright green new leaves on the fruit trees.

In the house, rather bigger than a cottage, lived a carpenter, his wife and several children, one a girl my age. At first I was kept busy trying to remember the routine, the tasks, the rules, where everything was kept. They were civil enough, and my cot in the little laundry was comfortable compared to a hammock.

But I quickly became more than just a house servant to help out the often bad-tempered and demanding wife. My days began even earlier than at Cascades — clearing grates, lighting fires, preparing breakfast. Then followed sweeping and scrubbing floors, bed-making, doing the laundry, cooking chores, scouring pans, cleaning up after the smaller children. Outside: chopping firewood, pulling out weeds, feeding chickens, and every day walking a mile to Macquarie Street with two large pails to fill with water. Occasionally, I was sent down to the wharves to fetch food stores landed by a ship from Melbourne or Adelaide.

Inside the house and out, I often found myself looking at a snake and fearing for my life. Copperheads, the man said, nasty vicious biters, but if the governor's wife — that Lady Jane Franklin — thought he was going to risk life and limb to catch any sort of 'orrible snake for a measly shilling a head, she had another think coming. They'd not ever rid this damnable island of snakes.

I was never allowed to rest, even to sit down for a brief moment. I had few thanks from the wife, none at all from the man or the children. The girl my age ignored me. On my two free hours on Sunday afternoons, I just went for a short walk to find a nook in a tree or a dry, grassy bank where I could sleep.

I began to understand why they had chosen a younger girl. I would be more biddable, less likely to complain or cause trouble. And, walking daily to Macquarie Street, I was less likely to be molested by sailors or peddlers. For the husband, less likely to object when he began to touch me.

One day, staggering into the yard with my two laden pails of water, I heard a voice in my head saying 'Leave, girl! Just leave!' My shoulders ached. There were callouses on my knees, and blisters on my feet and on my swollen red hands. That morning there'd been a large snake on a pantry shelf, and that was not the only peril: the man had stumbled against me in the kitchen and cupped his dirty hands around my breasts. It wasn't an accident.

So I dropped the pails, packed my meagre belongings and walked out the gate. No one shouted after me, or ran to restrain me. My thoughts were wild: could I hide in the backstreets of the town, stow away on a ship? But I was wearing Cascades grey, and any passing constable or worthy citizen would be suspicious.

My unease must have been plain to see, because before too long a constable stopped me. I was just running an errand, I stammered, but he was not convinced. I was soon being escorted in handcuffs up the muddy path, two miles back to the Female Factory.

In my time at Cascades, I'd heard many whispered secrets, but not the one about how they punished inmates who ran away from their oh-so-privileged positions as servants for the townspeople. I was met at the locked gates by the superintendent and the matron, his wife, ravens in black. Their eyes glittered with pleasure.

I would not be going back to Second Class, Yard One. I was a wicked, ungrateful, sly and insolent girl, and would pay for my sins by confinement in the Crime Class, Yard Two. With hard labour, and, if my insubordination continued, indefinitely.

Being the most criminal and difficult inmates, of course we were given the worst jobs. Cascades took in the town's laundry, sheets, clothing, tablecloths, anything washable. We stood sweating at the washtubs ten or more hours a day, up to our ankles in dirty water, up to our elbows in suds. The ever-burning fires heating the water made the rooms as hot as the doldrums. We tottered out to the lines with huge baskets, and heated the little pressing irons over the fires.

From the first day, it was clear that the skin of my hands and arms was soon going to be as reddened and swollen, my feet as puffy and wrinkled and sore, as all the others around me.

But even that wasn't the worst. Because I had sworn at the constable, and been insolent with the matron, first I was to receive the very worst punishment they could hand out.

13. Violet

STANDING BEFORE ME: VIOLET. Not only today, but tomorrow, the day after, and the day after that . . . my tormentor will be here, large as life in Store Bay.

I take a deep breath and step out from behind the half-finished shop. We look each other up and down, like the prize-fighters who once came to our village and glared at each other before sparring until one was knocked down senseless. She takes in my respectable dress; I her attire, plain and of good quality, but the green overly bright. Her boots look new. She has tucked her left hand inside her right, just not enough to hide a ring.

'You escaped,' she says finally, with that smile baring those ugly yellow teeth.

'As did you, it would seem,' I say. 'But I'll wager it took a man foolish enough to make a proposal.'

She has the grace to colour slightly, then flaunts her wedding ring. 'I got my Ticket-of-Leave. My husband belonged to the military in Hobart Town, but he had the wanderlust and I'd had my fill of Van Diemen's Land — so here we are, all set for a fresh start.'

'What was your crime again? Stealing a handkerchief or a fancy ribbon? Selling yourself? Cruelty to animals?'

Even as I say this, I remember the gossip. She'd arrived in Cascades heavy with child, convicted of assault but also marked as a fallen woman. The baby had died in the nursery, which was set up so the mothers were free to work ten, twelve hours a day. Before I began to get into trouble, I'd worked in that awful place, cleaning up after children sick with fevers or just screaming with hunger.

'Let me guess,' I go on. 'Being so willing, such a good and helpful inmate, you were promoted to a better class in Yard One. And then sent to a comfortable position in Hobart.'

'A military household,' she says. 'Respectable.'

'Where you smiled sweetly at a defenceless solider.'

'An officer, please.'

'Oh, pardon me. Congratulations!'

I make to push past her. I've had enough of this reunion, but she holds out a bony hand to stop me. I recoil from the touch. 'And *your* escape?' she asks.

'Don't tell me you're curious.'

'Oh, but I am. You were the only one who succeeded in all my years there. Now how did you manage it?'

'My secret to keep, yours never to know. Except . . .'

I hesitate, deciding that a morsel of information might just prick her conscience. 'Except that there was one who took pity on this young girl, just fourteen. She took a great risk. So, you did me a favour, really.'

'Convict or staff?' she asks sharply.

I smile and turn away. I've sworn on my mother's grave never to tell a living soul.

'Harriet,' she calls. 'That skirt is made of good cloth and such a pretty colour. And such a handsome bonnet! It looks as though you're earning good money. Now, tell me, your employer wouldn't know your . . . interesting history, would he? I don't suppose he's ever seen you without your bonnet.'

Violet, I decide, must be stupid as well as wicked. Sure, her husband might know about her troubled history and have nobly forgiven her, and she's arrived here as a soldier's wife. But she was still once a prostitute, and the traces linger, for all that she tries to speak like a lady.

I decide that I, too, can play this game. 'My employer is a woman' — this is more or less true — 'and I've been living around in Mechanics Bay for three months nearly, since the founding day. I don't suppose you've lowered yourself to visit there yet?'

'I've not had that pleasure,' she says, smirking.

'You have to climb up the track and over the hill with the flagpole, up there on the point, see? It's quite steep. But, even so, it's truly amazing how rumours and gossip spread so quickly from one bay to the other.'

The flash of fear in her eyes tells me she understands.

Now there's a further compelling reason to put the shores of the Waitemata harbour behind me. Here, Violet will haunt me on my daily visit to Store Bay, a smiling apparition, tall and thin as a twig, brandishing the truth of my past like she once did a cut-throat razor.

I'm shaking with anger and dread that this woman can ruin any immediate prospects I have here, although I'll make sure, if needs be, that I keep my side of the deal to remain silent.

Oh, why could she and her sadly duped husband not have chosen another settlement? Port Nicholson, say, or those way down in the southern parts? Better still: have stayed in Australia!

Any excitement I'd been feeling from my new-found freedom to look for work — now gone.

As I walk down towards the shoreline, I look out at the three big ships in the harbour, sitting there, mocking me. One by one they will leave, for Sydney probably, but maybe one is bound for the Horn.

But there's no point asking the sailors down by the shore; I don't have enough money for the passage.

My mind elsewhere, I don't at first notice what's different. Since fleeing from Cascades, I've become used to being invisible: just a plain, underfed, shabbily dressed immigrant boy, and later a girl too young and poor to be of any interest. It has suited me to go unnoticed.

But today something has changed. I've washed my face, and I'm dressed in a clean skirt and sporting a ruffled bonnet, and now men are glancing up from their work or pausing their conversations to watch me as I pass by. I can feel my cheeks colouring.

My path takes me between sawyers at work, groups of gossiping men, some holding jugs of the ale being brought ashore in large barrels from the ships. Though it's not yet noon, they're already tipsy. I'm aware of low whistles, muttered comments, as I pass.

I can't go back, the only way is onwards, head held high.

I've been in plenty of markets back at home, but this is something quite different: rougher, noisier, with seagulls overhead adding to the clamour. Natives are briskly trading their flax baskets of potatoes, pumpkins and other vegetables for woollen blankets and pouches of tobacco. Other native men hold up bloody hunks of pig meat.

All is good-humoured, with much shouting, laughter and gesticulating, yet in all their faces I sense desperation, on both sides. Probably some of those red-faced Englishmen bartering for pork haven't tasted fresh meat for a very long time. And, having no sheep, the natives are very keen to get their hands on one or more of those warm woollen blankets. Those who have theirs already wear them draped like Roman togas.

'Miss Harriet?' Standing beside me is Edward Williams.

'Mr Williams!'

'Kia ora, Miss Harriet. I hope you are well.'

'I am, thank you, sir.' Oh Lord, how handsome and clever he is! Like me, he seems quite captivated by the busy scene before us. 'Are you not required for translating today?'

'I should be at my desk round in Official Bay. But this is such a diverting spectacle. And, as you can see, the traders are managing very well without me.'

'Indeed. "Kia ora"— what does it mean?'

'Hello . . . greetings . . . sometimes, more like good luck.'

'Well then, kia ora.' My eye is caught by a tall, slender man, unusually well dressed, engaged in purchasing some pigs. He seems to have some knowledge of the native language. 'Who is that gentleman over there?'

'A Dr John Logan Campbell. From Edinburgh. He's been camping over on the Coromandel with local tribes. He and another canny Scot have bought the island of Motu-korea. They're calling it Brown's Island.'

'Where's that?'

He points down the harbour. 'It's that small volcano, see? But the good doctor will be here for the land sales, mark my words.'

'Do you know him?'

'We've met briefly. He's said to be setting up here as a trader.'

My heart leaps. 'So work might be available?'

'For . . . ?'

'Myself. Clerical assistant? Messenger?' He looks surprised but doesn't question me. 'Might you introduce me?' I suggest.

'Very well, but now may not be the best time.'

And nor is it. But as Edward Williams strikes up a conversation with the Scot, I note that the dapper Dr Campbell, for all his commanding manner, is not much older than the young interpreter. Closer to twenty than thirty, I'd hazard a guess. Their conversation is short. The doctor is far more interested in unlacing his boots, prior to corralling his five piglets over the tidal mudflats, with the help of the native sellers. For we onlookers, it's a messy, noisy and amusing spectacle.

I don't have to ask Edward the outcome of his approach as he returns to my side.

'Why is he buying pigs?' I ask.

'To add to his stock of breeding pigs, so he can keep selling new piglets for good prices. I asked about work, and he says he has no money to be taking on assistants at present. Perhaps in a month or so.'

The doctor has not even glanced my way. I suddenly feel very foolish, dressed in my best, and of no interest to anyone other than a passing smirk or two.

'If I hear of anything . . .' Edward gets out a timepiece and regards it intently. 'Alas, duty calls. Miss Harriet, kia ora.'

I suppose, here, that means good luck. But it's becoming clear I'm going to need more than luck.

Nursing my disappointment and sense of failure, I sit for a while under the canopy of the lone tree and drink in its splendour. I suppose the sprinkle of red needles on the ground is a sign that all those clusters will soon drop, and only a memory remain. I hope that Mrs Mathew, missing any colour and flowers in this landscape, has seen this beauty on one of her walks.

My beloved father sees beauty everywhere, and used to take great pleasure in sharing it with me. Never with my brother Jesse, whom he thinks a lost cause.

Come, daughter, he would say, please admire this saddle of the finest Italian leather, ready for its buyer — I'll wager no saddle better made in all of England. Walking through the village, he'd note a newly thatched cottage; look up there, Harriet, even for something so commonplace, such precision and craftsmanship.

Standing beneath the old copper beech, he'd be spellbound by the play of sunlight on the bronze leaves.

Or on a clear night, look up, little Sparrow, to the magnificence of the Milky Way. There's Orion the Hunter, sometimes lovely Venus, the beautiful North Star. Or, all of us dressed to attend Matins on a Sunday morning: your mother's new gown, see how that shade of blue so perfectly matches her eyes!

To those rough men on the beach below me, is this all it takes? A colourful skirt, a well-fitting top and a frilly bonnet? Have I recently got a mite taller, my breasts a touch fuller without my noticing? Certainly it's not been so easy of late to fasten buttons and ties.

Oh, Harriet, don't deny you are a little flattered. You've just forgotten how well-dressed women attract attention: those haughty women in their top hats riding side-saddle along Rotten Row. The shoppers in the Kensington High Street with their monstrous skirts — twenty-five yards at least — the huge leg-o-mutton sleeves and enormous hats, all flowers and feathers, ribbons and bows.

You've grown used to a convict's dowdy attire: grey shifts already worn by several poor souls before you. Skimpily cut from perhaps five yards of cloth, now patched, stained, ill-fitting. And always that ingrained smell you can't escape, the smell of despair.

I gaze long and hard at the scarlet magnificence of this single tree, trying to summon up my father's voice. See, my little Sparrow, how each slender stamen finishes in a tiny ball of bright gold? . . . So delicate, yet the effect overall . . . so . . . so . . . Sometimes even he couldn't find the words.

February 1840

THE VERY WORST MEMORY of Cascades, the one I've tried my utmost to forget, involves hair and Violet. But in a heartbeat I can be back there, sitting on a low stool and holding a fancy mirror with a tortoiseshell back.

There were two faces in the mirror. The lower one was me, Harriet, surly and now as bald as an egg. The upper smiling one belonged to Violet, who had eagerly volunteered to carry out the order that, before joining the Crime Class inmates, I should be punished by being shorn of my hair.

Earlier, I'd been made to stitch three large letters — yellow *Cs* — onto the back and the right sleeve of my jacket, and another to the hem of my shift. Thrice over, I was branded a criminal.

And then there'd been Violet, with her ice-blue eyes, and wielding a long leather strop on which she was sharpening a cut-throat razor. As she went about her grim task, she breezily told me that the razor and strop had been generously provided by the matron's husband, a true God-fearing gentleman, not merely superintendent of this hellhole, but a Methodist minister no less. Some months had passed, she added, since the last female convict had received this punishment, that time for continued insolence and disobedience.

But before she could get to work with the razor, she had to send for a large pair of shears from the seamstresses working in Yard One. They were needed to chop away my long tresses to within an inch of my scalp. At first I struggled, but she summoned three — three! — constables to hold down my legs and arms while she did her worst.

As she put aside the shears and picked up the razor, I howled. I wailed like a banshee while she scraped the blade back and forth over my scalp with more enthusiasm than skill. I flinched as some strokes nicked and broke the skin, and I bled. One constable held my jaws and neck cupped rigid in his smelly hands; for my own safety, Violet said. Another stood behind me and pinned my arms to my body, the third held down my legs and feet.

My shrieks must have been heard by other convicts, not that I expected them to do anything dramatic, like rise up in protest. I was expendable, only one of hundreds. If Violet's blade had slipped to cut a red gash across my throat, no one would have cared. One less mouth to feed.

Her task completed, she handed me the mirror, which she must thoughtfully have procured from one of the wardens, or perhaps from the matron herself, because I'd certainly never seen one within these walls.

I stared at the bald person in the mirror. That was *me*?

I was determined not to cry, but I couldn't stop the tears welling in my eyes. The person staring back at me was gaunt for lack of food, cheeks hollow, neck scrawny. The lips were blistered. Blood was dripping down the forehead and onto the nose and ears. The face was a mask of death.

I vowed to that image: *I will escape from this place if it's the last thing I do.*

Above me, admiring her handiwork, Violet was still smiling. I'd never noticed her front teeth before, quite yellow and crossed over. She murmured, as she wiped down the razor: well, madam, no worries now about lice for a while.

Then she asked if I'd like a drink of water, dear? With all that hullabaloo your poor throat must be quite raw.

I told her to go rot in Hell.

14. A death

RELUCTANT TO RETURN TO Mechanics Bay, I go for a long walk, avoiding the men at work on the governor's house site and the fire-blackened area that would ruin my boots and tear my skirt hems.

My mind is in turmoil, trying to push aside that shocking image of myself in the mirror. Accept, instead, that Violet is here, large as life, flesh and blood, and a real and terrible threat to any plans to get work and return home.

On an impulse, with the sun now high in the sky, I turn down the track to Official Bay. Why should I not visit my friend if I choose? Where are the fences or laws to stop me?

As I step out from the copse of trees onto the sand, I register how much progress has been made here, too. Natives working on several nearly finished raupo huts hail me. My cry of 'Kia ora' in return amuses them greatly.

There's no other sign of life, but a small fire is burning under the cooking pot near the Mathews' larger tent. Inside, Tillie stands at a long table, wearing a floury apron and kneading a large ball of bread dough. She looks tired, and shows no surprise at my unexpected appearance. After a quick glance and a wan smile, she returns to her kneading.

'You look pretty,' she says. 'The bonnet suits you.'

When I don't reply, she adds, 'I've not worn my new skirt yet. We've got missionaries coming to stay. The governor, too. Maybe I will then.'

'Is Mrs Mathew here? I wanted to thank her.'

'She's away on her horse with Mr Mathew, riding up the volcanoes. Taking measurements for his surveys. She helps carry his chains and instruments.'

She pauses her kneading briefly. 'I should like to ride. But Mrs Mathew would say I'm a servant girl getting ideas above my station. She's kind, but particular.'

'I can teach you, if she'd let me.'

'You can ride?'

'My father is a saddle-maker. The best in the county.' I'm not going to tell her that of course he owns a horse and has taken me riding, sitting behind him astride like a boy, not like the women who have to ride side-saddle with the local hunt.

'So you know about horses?'

'A little.' But I know more about saddles, how a woman's side-saddle differs from a man's, how to work dubbin wax into the stiff leather and buff it to a smooth shine.

She's gone back to her kneading, now panting slightly with the sustained effort.

'That looks like hard work,' I say. 'How often do you have to do this?'

'Every two days. I'm the primary bread-maker now,' she says wearily. 'This dough makes five loaves. All the officials still eat here, with us. They like their food. And their drink.'

I watch how she presses the heel of her hand down to stretch out the dough, then folds and twists and reshapes it into a ball to do all over again. Her forehead is moist with the effort.

With no great enthusiasm, she asks: 'How are my parents? The twins?'

'Your father I never see. He leaves early. Your mother sleeps a lot. She misses you. A girl called Maisie is helping her look after the twins and Joshua.'

'Why not you?'

'I told you,' I say brusquely, aware of how ungrateful I must sound, 'I need paid work for my passage home.'

'Still homesick? I don't understand: you're much better off here. For poor people like us, England is a cruel, nasty, horrible place.'

I'm in no mood to remind her that not everyone in England is poor and miserable, living in foul-smelling cities. And not for the first time, I wonder why her parents chose to leave, to risk everything for a supposedly better life. Did she grow up in an over-crowded hovel, always shivering with cold, always hungry, often sick with fever? She has never told me, and I sense she's not about to tell me now.

Gathering up the dough into a ball once more, she says, 'Let me see your hair. How's it growing? Enough now to make a plait?'

Reluctantly, I untie the bonnet ribbons. I'm months away from a plait.

'Goodness, is that all!' she says, as I shake my head, enjoying the sudden freedom, the feel of the wind coming through the tent flap ruffling my hair. 'You know, with those tight curls, in boys' attire you could be mistaken for a street urchin.'

Not *mis*-taken, Tillie. Oh, how little you know about me.

I'm keen to change the topic, but I decide not to mention Thomas, how poorly he is. There is no reason to worry her, as there is nothing she or anyone can do, except keep him comfortable and wait for the fever to break.

I gaze out at the small vessels making their way down the harbour. In one of them is the barefoot Dr Campbell and his five muddy piglets, he being apparently more enthusiastic about breeding pigs than being available to tend sick children.

'So why are you all dressed up?' She gives the ball of dough a final slap, places it inside a large basin and covers it with a cloth. 'Just to go to Store Bay?'

She has no need to add 'oh, and the young men now to be found around there'; her arch smile says enough.

Annoyed and embarrassed, I fight back pangs of resentment, envious for her position, her wages, her interesting and secure life with the Mathews, even if she does have to make five huge loaves of bread every other day.

'Has Mr Williams the interpreter been here at Official Bay lately?' I ask pointedly. 'I thought he rather enjoyed taking you out rowing.'

'Don't be silly,' she replies sharply, turning her back on me. 'I haven't seen him, and anyway . . . he's too busy with the natives, I suppose.'

'I should go,' I say. 'I'm sorry you seem to be out of sorts.' I don't want to quarrel, nor to justify myself.

With the tide too high to get around the rocks, I start off towards the hill track.

'You might meet the riders on the path,' she calls out. 'They have to walk the horses down, as it's too steep and rocky for them.'

And halfway up, meet them I nearly do. Hearing the clatter of hooves, I dive into the bracken, lacerating my hands on the stiff prickly foliage, and wait until the riders have passed. I suck at the blood spurting on my palms, knowing that if discovered and scolded for intruding on their precious Official Bay I doubt I'd remain polite — no matter that I just came to thank Mrs Mathew for the pretty skirt.

The group of women gathered around our tent warns me that something is amiss. Joshua is clinging for dear life to his mother's skirts. Seeing my approach, the women silently make way for me to look down upon Mrs Roberton slumped on her mattress, holding a child close.

I've seen dead children before. On the ship four babies were born to convict mothers and somehow survived. But six others were stillborn, or died within hours, their tiny stiff corpses taken away by the surgeon, probably later to be tossed by a sailor into the sea. At least five of the women arriving in Australia were made pregnant on the voyage.

And in the Cascades nursery I grew numb to seeing babies dosed with laudanum to silence them, and sickly children breathing their last, their grey bodies then wrapped in rags by a grim-faced warden and flung, it was said, over the wall for the dogs and rats and large birds to find. Maybe the dignity of an unmarked mass grave; no one knew. The mother would arrive at the end of a fourteen-hour day to find her child simply gone, the dirty clothes and soiled sheets already sent to the laundry. Few if any words of explanation or comfort were offered.

But this is different. I *knew* this child. I'd built sandcastles and dams with him, helped him fly a kite, washed his gingery curls in the stream. I'd wiped blood from his knees and food from his chin. We'd splashed through mudflats and clambered over rocks and thrown stranded starfish back into the tide. I'd once saved him from being swept away by a rogue wave. I'd sung him to sleep.

Lavender's green, dilly dilly, lavender's blue . . .
You must love me, dilly dilly, 'cause I love you . . .

I'm still capable of feeling horror, pity and a nagging guilt. No one needs to tell me that Mrs Roberton is keening over the body of her dead little boy.

There have been some injuries and sickness in Mechanics Bay since our arrival, but this is the first death.

'We thought he was just sleeping,' wails Mrs Roberton. 'Maisie couldn't wake him up.'

'Where's she now?' I ask.

'Taken Lucy for a walk, to get milk.' She looks up at me helplessly. 'What do you say to a child of not even two? That their twin, their brother, is . . . has just . . . won't ever . . . won't wake up? Not today, not tomorrow, not ever.'

Unable to hold back my own tears, I fall down beside her on the mattress. Some warmth lingers in the child's wee hand and forehead. His face is slack, with deep shadows under the eyes, but peaceful.

'Why did we not stay in Sydney?' Mrs Roberton sobs. 'There are doctors . . . medicines . . . And him not yet baptised . . . we should . . .'

The women crowding around the tent opening now find their voices. You mustn't blame yourself. It is God's will. He will be merciful. Put your faith in the Lord. You must not ever blame yourself. There is nothing you can have done.

And because word has obviously got around the camp, they are joined by the young priest from our ship. He kneels down beside the mattress. *'Suffer little children, and forbid them not, to come unto me: for of such is the kingdom of heaven.'*

'Kingdom of 'eaven? Save your breath, reverend! No gold thrones, no fucking cherubs 'ereabouts.'

The sarcasm belongs to the bad-tempered older woman who'd once sworn at me for tripping over her tent rope. 'Ain't no kingdom of 'eaven in this dammed 'ole. Trapped like animals, we are. Doomed, I tell 'ee . . . if it's not snakes or the friggin' pox, it'll be them odious black savages . . .'

I feel Mrs Roberton tense with anger, see the pain in her

eyes. I can't bear it. Before the priest can say anything, I'm on my feet.

'Take your miserable self away from here! You're not wanted.'

The woman laughs at me. 'Away, she says! And where to, missie? And how? Walk on water?'

'This wee mite didn't have the pox, no rash either, just a wasting disease no doctor can cure. Have you no respect for the dead? For the living?'

The women behind her are staring at me, wide-eyed. Girls my age do not scold married women. Before she can find her voice, I go on: 'And if the Maoris around here really are . . . what you say . . . why are they bringing us food and building us shelters—'

I remember that she and her husband and two children had been one of the first families to move into a raupo hut.

'—that *you* are not too proud to occupy, oh no, ahead of families with twice as many children.'

There are immediate murmurs of agreement — 'Aye, that's true enough.' 'Yes, why did *she* get priority?' — and some anger — 'Did you pay them?' 'Think you be so special?' 'I've got *two* sick children!'

The priest, who I'm sure is more used to the sedate parishioners of a Kentish village, has momentarily lost his voice as the clamour increases.

'Please, Harriet, send them all away,' sobs Mrs Roberton. 'Leave me alone with my poor wee babe.'

I find Maisie and Lucy buying milk from the cow's dim-witted owner. Ignoring him, I tell Maisie the reason why she must keep little Lucy away from the tent for as long as she can. I need time to get around to Official Bay to fetch Tillie.

Tillie's father is not due back from Store Bay until dusk.

The tide is still too high to go around the rocks, so I take the inland route, up onto the ridge and down to the Mathews' tent to deliver the terrible news.

Tillie turns as white as the linen sheets she's helping Mrs Mathew to fold. I'm bitterly — and yes, rightly — rebuked for keeping news of her little brother's sickness from her. Then we are both scrambling up the track at speed, running along the ridge and stumbling down the other side.

From the moment Tillie pulls up short outside the tent, gasping that seeing dead bodies always gives her palpitations and nightmares, it becomes a long afternoon of tears, awkward silences, arguments and refusals of all well-intentioned offers of food and help.

Except for Mrs Mathew, who knows all about losing a child. For her first visit to our bay, she carries her boots, and daringly pulls up her skirts and splashes up to her knees through the dropping tide. She also carries a large billy of boiled pork and potatoes. Mr Mathew, she says grimly, can make do with bread and cheese tonight. And the rest of them, too.

There are some unbearable moments, including Lucy's untimely return, before Mrs Roberton is ready to surrender her son. So that Lucy, running unrestrained by Maisie into the tent, is at first puzzled, then annoyed and angry at her brother's refusal to wake up. And it's to me — not her sobbing mother, nor her big sister Tillie, nor mute Maisie — that the bewildered child turns for comfort, and then to cry.

By sunset, Mrs Roberton has agreed that the priest should take the body for keeping overnight, for burial in the morning, rain or shine. Mrs Harris, Joshua's mother, has also delivered food, a thin over-salted gruel, but with the special treat of a few thin slices of potato.

Tillie's father arrives with the last of the light, and is told the news. He says nothing to either his wife or his daughter; just takes a candle, and for the next few hours we hear the sound of sawing and hammering: a small coffin being made from discarded timber lying about on the beach.

I'm still awake when he collapses onto the mattress beside his wife.

'My son will be given a proper burial' is all he says.

Sleep eludes me. I'm pinned between two bodies: Tillie clasping my back so tightly that I can barely breathe, while little Lucy has chosen to cuddle up to me rather than her mother. I can't decide whether the sounds coming from Tillie's father are a stifled weeping, nightmare noises or just normal snoring.

In the morning there'll be a burial. I think of funerals at home: darkened church, a hard pew, mournful hymns, the vicar's reedy voice droning on and on, endless collects and lessons and prayers. Family all in black by a churchyard grave; the coffin being lowered, handfuls of dirt thrown down onto the lid. Earth to earth, ashes to ashes, dust to dust . . . Something like that.

I remember coffins containing my Grandfather Harrington, his terrible hacking cough finally stilled. The village simpleton who stumbled into the duck pond one moonless night and wasn't found until two days later when he floated to the surface. The squire's hunting-mad son whose horse failed to take a jump, and his mother so crazed with grief she tried to throw herself into the grave.

Here are no church, no graveyard, no people in black. Tillie's stricken parents have persuaded the priest that before the coffin is finally closed, he'll mark the forehead with the sign of the cross, a simple affirmation of his infant baptism, stating his name, Thomas Richard — after his grandfather. I heard someone whisper that this is most unorthodox, but the priest hadn't taken much persuading.

Then they'll take the coffin for burial on a flat area somewhere on the hill behind the beach. A brief service will be said. A small cross inscribed with name and date can be placed. May the child's soul rest in peace.

Sometime before dawn it starts to rain heavily, a waterfall of tears.

March 1840

THE CRIME CLASS WOMEN mostly ignored me. I was just some chit of a girl wot spoke a bit proper, Lord knows wot she done back in Old Blighty. Now she runs away from a good position, silly thing, and gets shorn like a sheep for her trouble. She's learning the hard way, she is!

I stood at the washtubs day after day, scrubbing and wringing and rinsing and pegging up on the lines until my shoulders and arms ached. A lot of the laundry came from the town hospital, so there was blood and worse.

But I listened to the chatter in the dormitory — the 'no talking' rule didn't seem to apply there — and soon identified the Flash Mob members, those who had killed a husband or were guilty of a second offence. I knew who were the heavy drinkers, and who were considered the best at taunting and bribing the constables for treats or trips into town.

They talked freely about their escapades. That time one of the Flash Mob actually attacked the superintendent, gave the old fart a real fright. Or the riot not long before I arrived. Or the time they set upon Holy Willie after a chapel service and stripped his trousers right off, and would probably have done some real lasting damage to his manhood had the constables not arrived promptly.

One day they were all agog with news of an attempted escape. Two women had ripped up bed sheets for a rope to fling over the lowest part of the walls. They got as far as the top, but then, spotted by the night watchman, one had fallen back inside. The doctor set her broken leg in splints before she was put in solitary on bread and water.

Some remembered an earlier incident, a famous rebel who got some way digging a tunnel with a spoon under the walls of her solitary cell before she was caught. And of course, after her hair was shorn off, she was put straight back into solitary for double the time.

From the chatter, I learned which of the wardens were best avoided, which were likely to spot and quickly punish any small wrong-doing. We were depraved, wicked and irredeemable sinners, and deserved everything we got. In the laundry, on our single file to chapel or at meals, the guards circled us like dark shadows, ready to pounce.

Standing mute at the washtubs day after day, I could feel myself fading away, getting thinner, always hungry, bone-weary. I had no energy to be defiant or annoying, which is of course just what they wanted.

But the stories about escaping had set me thinking. Without some help, it was impossible. But who would so put themselves at risk, just for one miserable inmate, only one among hundreds?

So I could escape only in my daydreams, picturing myself back in my village, riding across the fields with my father, walking along the clifftops, picking blackberries. I recalled conversations between Father and local gentry come to pick up their expensive new saddles, or the times when we visited those smart shops in Oxford Street and stood at the gates of Buckingham Palace, listening to the chatter around us about the young Princess Victoria set to become Queen when the old King William finally dies . . .

15. And a funeral

AT FIRST LIGHT I hear Tillie's father rise and leave the tent. He comes back with the priest, between them carrying the child-sized coffin. Because of the heavy rain, it has to be put inside the tent.

The lid is raised briefly for the naming ritual. I can see only the upper part of the face, a small white nose.

Name this child. Tillie's father replies *Thomas Richard.* The priest says *Thomas Richard, I affirm that with your baptism you entered the fellowship of the Holy Catholic Church and the hope of everlasting life safe in the arms of Our Lord, in the name of the Father, and of the Son, and of the Holy Ghost.*

We all mumble *Amen.*

I'm glad the lid is then closed and that Lucy has earlier been taken over to the Harris tent, to be minded by Joshua and his mother. I can do nothing to comfort Tillie or her mother, both alone with their grief.

When the rain eases to a drizzle, our procession sets off, followed by many of the Mechanics Bay families wearing whatever waterproof clothes they possess. The coffin is carried by Tillie's father and another man. We look like a parade of beggars.

We proceed up a narrow track beside the streambed, to stop at a small, flat area, already cleared of bracken. In the silence, the ever-present seagulls and that bird that sings like a chiming bell can be distantly heard. We fifty or more huddle together to watch Tillie's father and two others take their shovels and begin digging a grave.

They are strong, the deep hole is speedily dug. The priest has the good sense to keep his prayers short, getting quickly to the burial prayer:

> *Forasmuch as it hath pleased Almighty God of His great mercy to take unto Himself the soul of this child here departed, we therefore commit his body to the ground . . . earth to earth, ashes to ashes, dust to dust . . . in sure and certain hope of the Resurrection to eternal life, through our Lord Jesus Christ, Amen*

before indicating that the small coffin should now be lowered by its two ropes.

Unlike all the others' heads bowed at that solemn moment, I raise my eyes, to blink through the drizzle at the leaden sky. I want answers: tell me, cruel God up there, how would it have *pleased you* to take the soul of this little boy? To what possible purpose? By what '*great mercy*'? Tell me!

The handfuls of earth are thrown onto the coffin lid. Shovel-loads of soil are thudding down, and the usual mournful hymn is about to be sung, when something happens that abruptly lifts the head of every man, woman and child.

A woman's voice: a high-pitched, full-throated, continuous wail. It comes from somewhere up the slope above us. As one, we stand wide-eyed, transfixed; the chant is on one note, occasionally dying away. The language must be native, the singer native. The song sounds like a lament for a dead child.

I've never heard a human voice like it. I know what boy choristers sound like, and actors of the travelling mystery plays and the Punch and Judy shows that came to the village. I've heard loose women carousing with bawdy ballads in the local tavern. Even a famous singer of opera on her way to London, exercising her voice when forced by a storm to sleep at the village inn. At Cascades the Flash Mob could often be heard through the thick walls, their singing loud and defiant.

But this? The power of it — so confident, strong and eerie — thrills me. All the pent-up emotion of the day is suddenly released, our grief translated into this unearthly music. No native singer can be seen, yet the voice seems close by and can surely be heard down on the beach, several hundred yards below.

Although most of us are too astonished to move, I hear stirrings behind me. The chant is lengthy and soon ugly voices are muttering damn natives, confounded cheek, utter disgrace, what a racket, no respect. Two or three men are pushing through the crowd and heading in the direction of the voice.

As they do so, another astonishing thing happens. A group of maybe eight natives steps forward from the undergrowth, led by an older woman whose chin and lips are tattooed and who is probably the singer. I recognise several of them: the tattooed man who'd given us the flax kite, and others who'd been building huts in our bay. Two or three men are wearing blankets Roman-style, but most are bare-armed. The other women I've never seen. One younger girl, about my age, wears a flax skirt, but is bare-chested, her nipples upright with the cold.

The kite man has left the group, and singled me out. He grips my upper arms and leans forward to put his nose close to mine. The message in his eyes is perfectly clear to me: we're here to share your sorrow. On the beach that day he'd told me he has three children. He'd shown little Thomas how to run along the sand to get the flax kite airborne.

But any understanding I have is not shared. As the native

steps back, I hear cries of 'Get him away from the girl!' 'Watch out now!' And mutterings that are louder now and less polite.

I can see Tillie's father is about to explode, but I explode first.

'How can we be so rude and ungrateful?' I exclaim to no one in particular. 'These people have come to show their respect. They waited until we'd finished—'

'Mark 'ee, so's to dig up the body and—'

'Shame on you, what a vile and wicked thought!' I cry to the woman behind me. 'How dare you! They've built huts for us, brought us food—'

My voice is lost in the general outburst. I hear cries of 'The girl's right', ''Tis true enough' mixed in with 'Leave us alone!' and 'Get back to your grass huts!', and from Mrs Roberton and those around her much renewed sobbing and wailing.

This commotion is not what should be happening at a child's burial. I see the priest try to make himself heard, but what silences the crowd is the native, who has correctly decided which of the men is the father of the child just buried. He walks over to where Tillie's father is looking down at the filled-in grave, and turns him by the shoulders to stand close, face-to-face.

For a terrible moment I wait for Tillie's father to push him away or use his fists, with who-knows-what consequences, but he submits to the gesture of pressing noses. The two big men stand embraced for some time, perfectly still. Perhaps the native has also known the anguish of losing a child.

Mercifully, as they disengage the priest's voice breaks the silence with the familiar blessing. *In the name of the Father, and of the Son, and of the Holy Ghost, Amen. Let us depart in peace.*

We do depart in an uneasy peace, but this day, not even that is simple. With the native group silently watching, the crowd stands back to let Tillie's parents, Tillie and myself follow the priest, but we are surprised by two more native women, both grey-haired, who stand either side of the narrow track. Each holds a roughly hewn wooden bowl full of water and makes it clear that before passing we should wash our hands.

When Tillie and her parents hesitate, some instinct urges me that we should comply, as do all our party before stumbling silently down the hill back to our camp.

I think it might be a gesture to send us back to our lives cleansed of the dark spirits around that place of death.

Little Thomas's passing has some unexpected effects on the folks of Mechanics Bay.

Mrs Roberton rises from her bed the day after the burial, declaring that she doesn't need Maisie or any other girl to take care of Lucy. Now, day and night, the child will never leave her sight.

Tillie's father, having buried his only son, becomes more taciturn than before, leaving ever earlier for his work in Store Bay and returning for his supper well after dark, haggard and worn out. Tillie, unable to offer any comfort to either parent, returns the very next day to Official Bay.

And Thomas's death has left me despondent and listless, putting off a return to Store Bay and filling my days with watching over Lucy when her mother, despite her fine intentions, keeps falling asleep.

Apart from Joshua's mother and one or two others, I note there are few visitors to our tent. Perhaps some are just embarrassed, not knowing what to say, or are held back by fear of their own children falling sick.

Those faithful friends who do visit bring food, full of apologies for its poor quality. They sometimes sit for hours to share stories of their previous lives. All have their tales of hardship, persecution, troubles with the law, with incurable illness, violence and death; our stories explain very well why we're here, looking for something better at the end of the Earth.

The young priest comes several times, intending comfort. But when he reminds us that soon it will be Christmas, which should be a joyful occasion even here, even now, I can see that Mrs Roberton is more offended than comforted.

As am I, reminded of what I have lost. Christmas Eve meant a roaring fire, a mother busy in the kitchen, her cheeks flushed. Dinner of roasted turkey stuffed with chestnuts, plum pudding with brandy sauce and silver coins buried inside. The joy of things red: berries on the holly trees, red-breasted robins in the snow, empty stockings made of scarlet felt, embroidered with gold thread and hung from the fire mantelpiece, to be filled by Saint Nicholas while we slept.

Outside, it could be snowing, great fluffy flakes, but still the carollers might be heard in the distance. *Hark! The herald angels sing* . . . Nearing midnight, the bells would ring out and we'd don our heaviest capes and carry lanterns to walk across the crunching snow to the stone church.

The whole village would be there, well wrapped up; every pew would be full, the singing lusty, the organist in his element. *While shepherds watched their flocks by night* . . . Our greetings of good will at the church door would be heartfelt; I might even be polite to my brother. In the morning, we'd gather before the fireplace to open our presents.

Here, a world without Christmas. No fire in a polished cast-iron grate, no plum pudding, no church, no carol singers, no snow, no presents. Nothing of cheerful scarlet: my favourite tree above Store Bay will probably have dropped most of its crimson needles by then, leaving only the usual dark green foliage.

For all those men labouring around in Store Bay and their

hungry families in draughty tents, Christmas Eve will likely pass without comment or joy.

Gifts of food for Tillie's grieving family come from another source. The day after the priest's visit, a canoe arrives on the high tide.

We're used to canoes bringing the hut-builders and supplies, but this one is different. It's plainer and smaller than any we've seen, needing only four paddlers, but carrying two passengers.

Being curious, I wander down to the beach. The passengers are two women, the first time I've seen females travelling in a canoe. The older in her toga blanket I recognise as the singer with the chin tattoo, the younger is the bare-chested girl, but today wearing some sort of flax cape over her shoulders. Both are carrying baskets, also woven of flax.

They stand in the shallows, running their eyes over our motley collection of tents, the stacked-up boxes and untidy piles of timber, the drab clothes hung on lines, the children playing.

I call out, hesitantly, 'Kia ora, wahine!' This makes them smile, and, encouraged, they start up the beach. The older, so powerful when singing, now seems tentative and anxious.

My guess that this visit is somehow connected to the burial proves correct, as the younger woman uses her forefingers to close her eyelids, then the older makes a gesture of rocking a baby. I beckon them to follow me, conscious of being watched from every part of our encampment.

'You have visitors.'

Mrs Roberton looks up from the mattress where — even though it is high noon — she's drowsing alongside a sleeping Lucy, stroking back the gingery hair. The fondling stops as she slowly registers what she is seeing: two silent, barefoot and bare-legged native women, to our eyes scantily dressed. At the back of their heads, two feathers are held upright by the thick tangle of black hair. Between the breasts of the older lies a pendant of a deep green stone. The day is overcast, but even so their smooth skin gleams like polished copper.

'I think they've come to pay their respects,' I say quickly, to forestall any unfriendliness. Behind us has now gathered a small retinue of silent, curious onlookers, wives and children. I have good reason to think some might see this visit as unwelcome, an intrusion.

But any fears I have are proved — so far — groundless. The natives kneel to place their baskets on the ground, pulling back the woven flax-leaf covers to reveal in one several large fish, and in the other the shells of scallops twice the size of any I ever saw in Sussex. They then stand for a brief moment, heads bowed, their fingertips quivering, before silently backing away. The English wives and children part for them to walk back down to the waiting canoe.

Not a word has been spoken; Mrs Roberton seems dumbstruck. But the faces around me are stony, bemused. And all I can feel, as I had at the hillside funeral, is shame and an uncontainable anger.

'Someone caught those fish and dug up those scallops,' I say just loud enough to be heard by them all. 'Someone made those beautiful baskets. Two women had a kind thought and took the trouble to find four paddlers and get in a canoe and bring us their gift' — by now I'm speaking so they can all hear — 'to show they understand what it is to lose a child. They might have taken hours to get here. And we can't even say thank you.'

Mrs Roberton at least has the decency to drop her head and remain silent, but not the rest of them. I'm informed I am an uppity, annoying, impertinent and unlikeable child, a troublemaker who has far too high an opinion of herself, forgets her station and talks far too much.

To justify their ingratitude, some of them start on the visitors: how dare they show their brown faces in our bay . . . bring their heathen ways to our shore . . .

I can't believe their malice.

The funeral had been bad enough, but this is inexcusable. My voice trembles as I try to find words to match my fury.

'Back at home you wouldn't dare treat a visitor bearing gifts like you just did. They meant well. They brought a gift . . . they showed respect . . . I cannot believe you . . . Oh, shame on you all! Shame!' — before turning to see the two women now seated in the canoe and one of the paddlers about to push off.

'Wait!' I shout, running helter-skelter down the beach in the hope of saying, at the very least, thank you. Showing by whatever means I can that at least one person in this bay appreciates their gesture of sympathy and kindness. 'Please, wait!'

Then, as I pull up just short of the water's edge, the young man pushing off the canoe turns around.

I'm in no doubt, as I watch the paddlers settle into a steady rhythm and turn the canoe to the direction of the Orakei beach, that it's him. The same handsome youth from that race three months ago, his black hair now loose rather than caught up in a knot. But never in a million moons could I have imagined what happens next.

When he turns, curious, to see who is delaying their departure, I nearly forget why I'm standing here, flushed and agitated. Up close, his beauty is greater than I remember. I'm reminded of those Greek statues in the big museum in London. He's not yet tattooed. The amusement in the brown eyes is the same, with that look of wonder, even though it's only me.

I stutter something about wanting to thank the women, and to cover my whirling emotions bend down to take off my boots. A male voice says, in English, thank you, miss, we wait, and I look up puzzled, to see him smiling. His expression says, yes, you heard right!

He holds the canoe steady while I pull off my boots, hitch up my skirts and wade out in my bare feet sufficiently close to say what I need to say. It comes out in a tumble: thank you for the gift, thank you for your kind thoughts, for coming all this way, thank you so much.

Behind me, he must be translating, as the women are smiling and pleased. They both climb nimbly out of the canoe — not needing to be concerned about getting silly long skirts wet — and splash through the shallows to clasp my arms and touch their noses against mine. We share our breathing. I know it's well meant.

His English is sufficient, along with gestures, for me to gather that they'll leave the canoe at the Orakei village. After that they'll walk over the hills to— But the other paddlers are calling him, impatient to leave, and the chance to know more is gone.

As I watch them pull away from the beach, I wonder whether I'd heard correctly: did he really say 'Maraetai'?

April–July 1840

AFTER I WAS RETURNED to Cascades, and as winter set in, I only ever saw Martha in the distance, at mealtimes, so supposed she had lost any interest she might have had in me. But one morning — I think it was now July — there she was in the laundry, on a new shift of wardens overseeing our labours. She kept her distance, but I had the uneasy feeling I was being watched. I couldn't imagine why. I'd done nothing wrong lately.

A few days later I was roused from my daydreams of home. Martha was standing close and whispering: 'You, Harriet, are too young and too clever for an early grave. And nothing surer, within a year you will be dead. So, listen.'

She waited while some women passed by, bearing more huge loads for washing.

'On my shift at midnight, I will wake you. You will creep silent as a ghost down to the front yard. The main door will be open. There will be a horse and cart at the gate, loading bags of clean laundry to deliver back to the town. The driver is my son.'

Another long pause, so she could continue safely.

The cart, she said, would leave with the bags piled on top of me. They would be heavy, press the breath out of my thin little body, but it was only for the two miles into town. After that I was on my own, free to survive how best I could.

She finished: 'I have faith that you will survive. You are resourceful and don't want for courage. I will pray for you. But be mindful, I am offering you only this one chance. Whether you take it or not — the choice is yours alone.'

I was too astonished and fearful to nod, overwhelmed by her bravery. I risked a quick glance at her face, much-lined, remembering her many other small acts of kindness. She must have been planning all this for quite some time. I risked squeezing her small knobbly hand.

That night I lay in my hammock shivering with excitement and no little fear. The punishment if I was caught would be cruel beyond anything I could imagine.

Martha had offered me the chance of escape, and I never

doubted, as I waited for midnight, that I would take it. Yes, it was foolhardy, hazardous, utterly mad. Especially risky in the dead of winter. But at Hobart, or some other port, I'd find a ship to take me home. I'd stow away if necessary.

As midnight crept closer, I could hear singing. I wonder if Martha had known that the Flash Mob would be having one of its rowdy parties in another dormitory, the constables looking elsewhere.

I had my burlap bag packed, my boots on. I was ready as I ever would be.

16. Outcast

IF IT IS CHRISTMAS EVE as the sun rises behind Rangi-toto — and I think I've counted off the days correctly — no one else seems to realise or care.

The men have left at daybreak as usual for Store Bay. The cows at the back of our encampment are mooing, the hens clucking. Seagulls scream, babies wail. The wives emerge yawning and bedraggled from their drooping tents or raupo huts to light fires for a billy of tea. Mechanics Bay has now become the only home they know, for better or for worse.

Except for me. Things have changed in the days since the Maoris came with their gifts of condolence: I've cooked my goose, been sent to Coventry. My last outburst has been one too many for the good wives of Mechanics Bay. They quickly decided to brand me an outcast, a pariah to be shunned, a leper cast into the wilderness.

They look away when I come anywhere near, clutch their children to their skirts to protect them from my evil influence. Not even the cows' slow-poke owner will serve me when I go to fetch the daily can of milk. Mrs Harris from the next-door tent has to get the milk for Lucy instead. I've become invisible. Me and my improper views are not to be tolerated any longer.

Of course this hadn't stopped Mrs Roberton from relishing the rich stew she cooked up with those fresh fish and plump scallops. Her husband likewise enjoyed the stew. Even I was grudgingly given a small helping.

I try to be helpful, and considerate of their grief, but there is a chill in the air. Tillie's absence doesn't help. One night, I hear the Robertons talking, and the next morning before he leaves for work he gives instruction that by his return I am to be gone. For once out of bed before he goes, Mrs Roberton tells me I am no longer welcome in their tent.

Embarrassment makes her spiteful. Perhaps, since I think so highly of them, I can go and live with the natives around in Orakei? Or with my youthful charms I might find some — she hesitates only a moment, but her meaning is clear — some *consolation* among the men working in Store Bay? She doesn't need my money any longer, or my help minding only the one child.

Although surprised by her heartless remarks, I have been expecting this moment. In fact, I'd already decided for myself that I could no longer stay in Mechanics Bay. So before she's even finished speaking, I have my meagre belongings all packed.

I'm going anyway, I say loftily, ignoring her hateful slurs. She falls silent as I produce the coins to offer as final payment for my food, which for all her fine words she is quick enough to accept. She doesn't prevent me from giving Lucy a brief hug goodbye.

But as I turn to leave, she delivers a parting shot, declaring in a shrill voice that I'm not to go anywhere near her precious Tillie around in Official Bay: *Do you hear me, Harriet? You keep away from her!* — Well, I beg her pardon, but that's a step too far.

You cannot stop me, I say quietly, holding back my anger. You're not my parent or my guardian. And Tillie can decide for herself who her friends are.

Taken aback by my vehemence, she makes no answer.

I am about to thank her for her initial kindness to me, but Lucy chooses this moment to spit out the porridge that's being carelessly spooned into her little pink mouth.

As I leave the camp, head held high and ignoring the turned backs, I'm feeling yet again that curious mixture of freedom, defiance and dread. The tide is too high to walk around the rocks to the next bay, so I have to take the track up to the ridge.

I should be used to it by now: not knowing when darkness falls where I'll lay my head; no idea where my next meal is coming from.

Fleeing from Cascades, a vagrant in Hobart, again in Port Nicholson. And here, yet again cast adrift, with added problems. My one pair of boots won't last much longer, my underwear is nearly rags. Hunger is constant, but strangely I sometimes feel bloated, as I would after a decent meal. Of late my breasts are often tender, almost sore to the touch — why is that?

And day after day has been passing with no big, beautiful ship arriving in the harbour to disembark immigrants and take on passengers for the Horn. In truth, it is of little matter: I cannot pay for a passage on even a smaller vessel to Sydney, a busier port where I might find a ship bound for England.

Am I desperate enough to revert to Harry, increasing my chances of getting work? With hair curling down to my ears I could still pass as an unkempt boy, but now don't too many people know me as Harriet? And the one certain way a girl can keep from starving — even a plain Jane like me — is too horrible to contemplate.

Now here's an even more outrageous thought. I can become one of those Pakeha-Maoris the young priest told us about. Sailors who jumped ship to live with a tribe, marry a native, get tattooed, learn the language. I've not heard tell of a white girl becoming Pakeha-Maori, but I could love a kind and handsome young Maori who loved me, and once I learned the language I could be useful as an interpreter like Mr Williams . . .

Arriving wearily on the top of the ridge, looking out over water glittering in the morning sun, I suddenly remember where I've heard the name of Maraetai. It was Mrs Mathew talking about her visit to the mission station there, the native children singing their A-B-C to the tune of 'God Save the Queen'.

The paddler must be connected in some way with the mission station. How else would he have learned some English?

A call to Official Bay might answer some of the new questions now filling my mind.

Mrs Mathew's visitor, evidently just taking her leave, has her back to me, but I know who it is.

'Harriet, my dear.' Mrs Mathew's greeting is civil, indicating that gossip of my banishment from Mechanics Bay has not yet reached her. 'Mrs Godfrey, this is Tillie's young friend Harriet. She also arrived in September, on the other ship. The *Platina*, if I remember correctly, from Hobart and Port Nicholson.'

Mrs Godfrey turns and of course immediately recognises me. She manages a tiny knowing smile, not enough to reveal those awful teeth, but in her eyes I see fear as well as cunning. Yes, you'd do well to take care, Violet, I think nastily; should our secrets become known, you have rather more to lose than me.

Ever the hostess, Mrs Mathew fills the silence.

'Mrs Godfrey is a recent arrival from New South Wales. Her husband is in the military, but they're intending to buy land when Mr Mathew's survey for the township is ready.'

She beckons for Tillie to come and take the tea things away. 'He is hopeful, a month or so, even though the governor has provided him with very little help in the field. All those measurements! And my goodness, the paperwork!'

Violet makes sympathetic noises as Mrs Mathew goes on: 'The people here are very critical of my dear husband. They simply have no idea how hard he works. But the land sales will be soon, and in six months, mark my words, Store Bay will be quite the little seaside village.'

'My husband also hopes for government work,' says Violet primly. 'And soon I intend to start my own little business, selling ribbons and threads, wools, drapery items. I had such a place in Sydney Town. I was doing quite well.'

'How enterprising,' says Mrs Mathew, appraising her visitor's ensemble, the skirt and jacket a checked pattern of yellowish-brown, the ornate bonnet a sickly lemon, the gloves a bright lime green. She had clearly made some effort to impress. 'You have a fine eye for such things, Mrs Godfrey. There'll be grateful customers, I'm sure, keen to add some colour to this rather drab place.'

From behind Violet, I catch Tillie's mocking glance. We both know that Violet's gaudy choice of dress to pay a social call on the wife of the surveyor-general is far removed from Mrs Mathew's more sombre taste. Today she is in the same dark burgundy with a collar of white lace that she'd worn the first time we'd met.

Violet turns to me, her eyes glinting with malice. 'And how did you come to be in Australia, Harriet?'

'My parents decided there was no future for us in England. We went to Hobart, but it's a harsh place. There were . . . accidents. My mother had to sell my hair for wigs so we could eat. Then she died.'

'My dear girl,' Violet simpers, 'how terrible for you, and so young. To lose your mother in a strange country . . . *and* lose your beautiful hair! That explains why you have no plait, like pretty little Tillie here.'

This is a dangerous game we're playing. I untie my cap and shake out the curls, trying not to look gleeful. 'It's growing again, see? Thicker than before!'

'But how are you managing here, with no family?'

'Tillie's family and Mrs Mathew have been very kind. I try to make myself useful.' Under the circumstances, Harriet, these are brave words.

Mrs Mathew again politely breaks the silence. Would Mrs Godfrey like Harriet to accompany her up the track? She is sure Harriet would be pleased to do so.

'Thank you kindly, Mrs Mathew, but that won't be necessary,' says Violet, to my great relief. A haughty gesture summons a young boy, I'd guess about twelve, from where the track starts. Maori, but in shabby English breeches and shirt. 'My dear husband is most thoughtful. I have my native guide. The boy will get a small purse when he sees me safely back.'

Lord, I think, it's only up a hill and down to the next bay, not exploring the wilds of Africa! How quickly she's learned to play the genteel wife, drinking tea so daintily, ordering around the natives and taking her leave like a duchess.

As I watch her stumble across the sand, hitch up her skirts and begin climbing awkwardly up the first steps of the track, I remember the feel of her bony left hand clamped on my skull to hold it steady, while her right hand drew the razor — with that curious scraping noise — over my scalp.

I remember the look of pleasure on her face when later I slunk into the hall for some food and a few of the nastier inmates tore off my cap. How they laughed and giggled and jeered at the grotesque object I'd become: a bald freak who wouldn't be amiss in a travelling circus.

Since I was first here, Official Bay has certainly grown. The Mathews are now resident in one of the first raupo huts to be completed, with their raupo kitchen, restored after that little fire, alongside the big marquee dining tent. Their hut even has a door and windows, not glass, but oiled calico. Tillie's cot and boxes of stores are accommodated in a smaller tent. Framing is up for the first wooden structures. The carpenters are a mix of native and settler, sawing and hammering away side-by-side, occasionally sharing a laugh.

'I didn't like her,' Tillie says bluntly, returning to the marquee with the tray to take away the last of the tea things. 'She's not as grand as she makes out. Something about her makes my skin crawl.'

'Mind your tongue, child,' snaps Mrs Mathew, but I think her remonstrance half-hearted. 'We should not judge prematurely. Anyone starting a business in Store Bay needs our support.'

'She has shifty eyes,' says Tillie. 'And those awful stained teeth.'

'A little kindness goes a long way, Tillie. When she begins trading I daresay I'll find something suitable. She must have premises being built, and goods coming from Sydney.'

Tillie, undeterred, mutters in my ear, 'That dreadful bonnet!'

Mrs Mathew pretends not to hear. 'My father, bless his dear heart, is a mercer in Oxford Street, considered the best in the whole of London. He sells Indian silks, the finest Irish linen. Lace from Brussels, all kinds of haberdashery items. Sometimes I helped him unwrap the consignments from India. They smelled so exotic, of spices warmed by the hot sun. Cinnamon perhaps, nutmeg, or cloves. And the saris and drapes, their colours so daring and bright we would gasp in amazement.'

'Well, *her* shop won't be so wonderful,' says Tillie. 'Not in a wooden shack, and certainly not if that bonnet is any indication.'

'Shush, girl!' says Mrs Mathew. 'You have potatoes to scrape for dinner. Harriet can help you.' She sniffs the air. 'Rain and wind coming, I think. We've guests expected: two missionaries from the north. Today or — in this weather — more likely a day or two.'

'Not from around these parts?' I ask, all innocence.

'The only mission station hereabouts is the Fairburns' at Maraetai, around the coast.'

'How far is that?'

'Maybe half a day's sailing. On foot, at least a full day. The countryside is difficult, bracken and forest. Though there are probably some native tracks.'

'Didn't you visit there once?'

'Oh yes, twice, last year when Mr Mathew and I were aboard the *Ranger* exploring the harbours south of Kororareka. She's a government cutter, sent over from Australia.'

She stares out at Rangi-toto and the channel beyond. Today it's overcast, the sea a muddy green.

'That voyage was hard. We set off from Paihia in early winter and were away two months. We climbed many steep hills, hacked our way through dense forests. And there were gales aplenty — on five or six occasions I was certain my last hour had come. I've never overcome my tendency to *mal de mer*.'

'It sounds like an absolute nightmare,' says Tillie, dumping the bag of potatoes on the big table.

'I had very little privacy. Our crew were eight convicts, young men mostly from various parts of Britain, victims of great injustice. But I assure you, they were civil enough. And grateful to be out at sea with a measure of freedom, rather than chained by leg irons, breaking up rocks.'

'What happens to the women who get transported?' asks Tillie, inspecting each potato as she takes it from the bag.

'Surely they don't break rocks or go as crew on ships?'

'Living in Sydney I knew something of the Female Factory at Parramatta,' says Mrs Mathew. 'There are others in Van Diemen's Land. One near Hobart is called Cascades. I believe the governor's wife Lady Jane Franklin takes a great personal interest in it.'

Yes, I'm thinking, the sort of interest that had her recommending the Crime Class inmates be put to breaking up rocks for roads, down to the size of an egg, because picking oakum was too lenient a punishment. Picking apart the strands of dirty old ropes from dawn to dusk only ruined your hands.

'Factory?' says Tillie. 'Why do they say "factory"?' I join her at the table to help sort the potatoes, very keen to put a stop to this conversation.

'The women were expected to work. They took in laundry, did weaving or sewed clothes. It was a harsh life, mostly for very minor crimes. Some finished their sentences and married, a few even did well. But many were broken physically and in spirit. In Sydney I belonged to a church group that tried to help some of those poor girls.'

'Girls?' asks Tillie. 'How young were they?'

'Oh, the youngest only twelve or so—'

'Mrs Mathew,' I interrupt, 'how many potatoes do you want done for supper?'

I have to tell Tillie why I can't stay here any longer than one night. The reasons for my exile from Mechanics Bay will reach Mrs Mathew soon enough. I can spare myself further humiliation when she finds out. And avoid any more talk about female factories.

As I help her wash the dishes after supper, Tillie is scornful of my inability to hold my tongue, just look where it has got me!

But don't you think I'm right, Tillie, I cry, when people are so rude and offensive to the natives, just because they're a different colour?

'Of course you're right, you silly goose,' she says, 'but you scolding them won't change anything. People are what they are. And now, foolish girl, I can't be your friend anymore. I'm trapped here, and Lord knows what you'll do over in Store Bay waiting for a ship going to England. Quite why you're so determined to go back, I'll never fathom.'

Disappointed at so little sympathy, I curtly tell her I'll not sleep in her cot for this last night, but in the unfinished hut, so I can creep away silently in the morning.

'As you wish,' she shrugs, but she does offer me a mattress and a blanket for the night.

Despite those, I'm cold and restless. Searching around for good memories to pass the hours, I imagine myself walking along Oxford Street. I'm about nine, holding my father's hand, and we're going to a certain shop to buy some cloth as a present for my mother, for a new gown. Equally to spend a pleasant afternoon admiring the Indian silks, the Brussels lace and Irish linens and all the other pretty items.

The weather outside is miserable, but the premises are spacious, warm and sweet-scented, the other customers noticeably well dressed. My father murmurs his appreciation of the way the wares are carefully displayed with an eye for beauty and order.

In pride of place are the Indian silks. They're costly, of course, far beyond our purse, but we ask to see the superior cottons and take many minutes to decide between a soft blue to match Mother's eyes, or a glowing emerald for something more exciting. In the end, we buy both. And then my father asks me to choose a length for myself. He approves of the lovely deep turquoise that is cut and wrapped with great care, just for me.

I leave that shop feeling like a princess.

I don't know why I didn't want to share with Mrs Mathew earlier that I'd once visited her father's beautiful shop. It would have given her great pleasure. Perhaps simply because it was my own happy memory, so precious to me.

And I have little else other than good memories to hold onto, as outside the wind gets up, the little native owl, the morepork, hoots, and the waves crash onto the beach.

July 1840

JUST AS MARTHA HAD promised, the cart was waiting in the yard. I didn't see the face of the man who helped me onto the cart and piled the laundry bags over me. Clip-clop out through the gate, the rattle of keys, a curt goodnight to the constable on watch and we were off down the track. The weight of the bags pressed nearly all the life out of me. I tried not to gag and cough on the dust and strong smell of carbolic soap.

Finally, the cart stopped. As I climbed down, a soft canvas bag was pressed into my hand with a whisper. 'My mother says, open this up before it gets light. Macquarie Street is that way, close by. Port a quarter-mile. God speed you, girl.'

I stood blinking, with no idea what I should do now, where to go. The sky was pitch black. If this was a street of cottages, it was still too early for the first candles or fires to be lit.

Some rat-like instinct made me scurry to what I thought was a hedge, wrap my arms around my two bags and curl up into the smallest possible ball. Lord, it was cold, the silence terrifying. More worrying again was the realisation that I was now utterly on my own. Since that day in the market, I'd been surrounded by people day and night, jostled by them, threatened by them, ordered around and bullied by them.

Now it was just me alone in all the world, and I was shaking with the pure horror of it.

One mistake . . . If caught, there would be no mercy at the prison up the hill. I'd be dead in a year, Martha had said.

I was startled out of my trance by a cock crow, close by. The light was turning from black to grey, enough to see that I was indeed in a street of cottages. Not those with pretty picket fences, but the cheaply built houses of poorer people. Carts stood in the puddles, ready for the horse and the day's work to begin. Behind some windows candles were being lit. The black shape of the mountain behind Cascades loomed above.

Open the parcel before it gets light, he'd said. Yes, and what then? I must find food, become the thief the judge said I was, but in my tell-tale grey shift I wouldn't last half a day . . .

The cock crowed again, like a trumpet waking up soldiers, waking up me. The bag I'd been given held something soft. Clothing? I drew it out, puzzled by the rough texture. It wasn't bulky enough for a proper long dress, or a skirt, or a jacket, or a shawl. The smell was different, not female.

Oh, Martha, you are clever! And you have such faith and trust in me.

What I was looking at, holding up, smiling at, amazed by, were the keys to my survival.

17. Again Harry

IN THE BLACK HOUR before dawn, I decide on my plan to ensure a place on a ship to take me home. It's risky, yet I can't think of anything better.

But I haven't bargained on the pale glimmer of a candle approaching the hut, nor Tillie's peaky face appearing ghost-like in the space where the wooden door will go. Tillie, servant girl out of her cot before anyone else to light a fire, boil water, set some bread dough to rise.

'Harriet?' she says sleepily. 'I'm sorry about our disagreement last night. Here, I've brought you some tea. There's bread you can take, two days old, but it's better than nothing, and cold potatoes—' And then, glimpsing a figure buttoning up his breeches, blurts out: 'Who are you? What are you doing here? Where's Harriet?'

In her agitation she drops the candle. I hear muttered curses as she stamps out the little flame, then: 'Who are you, boy? You've no right to be here! *Where's Harriet?*'

Oh, I wish I could see her face.

'This bay is no place for urchins,' she goes on, quite bravely I think, since the candlelight has provided only a fleeting glimpse of this gypsy boy who is taller and probably stronger than her. And who might not be alone. But what's done is done. Some explaining will be necessary, dammit.

'You need to leave — this minute,' she declares.

'Tillie, you sound just like Mrs Mathew,' I say, angry with her spoiling my plan for Harry to creep quietly away from Official Bay before dawn. 'You think Store Bay's the only proper place for the likes of me.'

'That's right. Be gone! Back to wherever you came from. And I do *not* sound like Mrs Mathew. Mr Mathew, perhaps . . . How do you know about them, anyways? How do you know my name? *And where's Harriet?*'

'Harriet is right here, standing in front of you.'

'Where? Where is she? What have you done with her?'

'Packed her into a bag,' I say, stupidly unable to resist a little joke.

I hear her gasp, probably thinking that only corpses, possibly without their limbs, get packed into bags, before she starts to cry out, 'Mrs Math—'

In a flash I'm across the hut, grabbing her, a hand cupping her chin to clamp her mouth shut before she can make another sound. If either of the Mathews appear on the scene, I'll be undone. In our scuffling, we both fall heavily to the sodden dirt floor. Very hot tea splashes onto my bare ankles.

'Shush!' I hiss. 'It's me — Harriet.' I don't dare take my hand away until I've convinced her not to scream for help. In the pitch blackness, still making muffled noises as she struggles to wrench herself free, she'll not be easily convinced.

'Listen, it's me, Harriet, your friend. Can't you tell my voice? Yesterday we listened to Mrs Mathew's stories about the *Ranger* and the mission station at Maraetai. Isn't that so! Then we scraped a mountain of potatoes, remember? And you told me how stupid I was not to keep my silly opinions to myself.'

During this garbled recital she has gradually relaxed, but I dare not take my hand away just yet.

'I am Harriet, cross my heart. So promise you won't call out. There's no need for help. Nod if you promise.'

I feel her head nodding, so cautiously release my grip from her chin. I need to be certain that her cry hasn't woken Mrs Mathew, or that she won't cry out again, so the only sound for a few moments as we climb to our feet is us both breathing heavily and brushing the dirt off our clothes. Licking my palm, my tongue registers the salty taste of blood.

'The Mathews sleep soundly,' she mutters.

'For your sake, just as well.'

'You hurt me.'

'You bit me!' I reply. 'Drew blood.'

'Serve you right. Why are you wearing boys' clothes? Where did you get them from?'

I sigh, trying to remember what lies I've already told her and must now be cautious. 'It's a long story. In Hobart I found some boys' clothes and stowed away on the *Platina* . . .'

'You didn't!'

'I was desperate. Then in Port Nicholson a kind sailor helped me stay on the ship, as a passenger. He told them some story about a rich uncle wanting to get rid of me.'

'How did you come to be in Hobart in the first place?'

Ah, my dear friend, it's not the time or place to tell you more about the horrors of female factories. Just the one word *convict* would be fatal; it would change everything. I ignore her question.

'I knew if I was discovered as a girl . . . Well, people take less notice of skinny, poor-looking boys.'

'But how did you eat?'

'Hunger makes you cunning. You learn where to look, you become invisible.'

'Why now?'

'Think, Tillie. All those rough men around in Store Bay? Oh, not the honest mechanics like your father doing his job, I mean the fortune-hunters and ruffians hanging about. Drunk half the time, playing cards, picking fights. All the time looking up and down anyone in skirts, wondering if . . . well, you know.'

'Wondering what?'

Can she really be so innocent, so unworldly? It's too dark to read her face, and I don't have time to explain.

'Look, I need money for a passage home. I need work. My name's Harry. People in Store Bay are more likely to give a job to Harry.'

'You can be a maidservant like me.'

I snort at this suggestion. 'No toffs around there wanting servant girls, just a few miserable hard-up wives and men who'd treat me like scum.' I can't help the trace of envy that makes me say, 'You've got it sweet with Mrs Mathew.'

'There's Mrs Godfrey, she might—'

I'm glad that the first hint of dawn behind Rangi-toto still isn't enough for her to see my face. 'I'd sooner jump off a ship and be swallowed whole by a whale. Crunched up by a shark!'

Perhaps my vehemence sets her thinking back to Violet's social call. There's a long pause before she says, 'Have you met her before?'

'Vi— Mrs Godfrey? Of course not! How can I?'

'I just thought . . .'

This conversation needs to end, now. 'I have to go.'

'Oh, Harriet. You're so brave. I could never be so brave.'

'That's because you have parents and a safe position here. You would be brave, too, if your life depended on it.'

'I wish I could see you, being a boy.' I hear her giggle a little. 'It must be quite fun, in breeches. And boys don't bleed, do they?'

'Have you started?'

'A few days ago. I felt all bloated, before. My breasts were tender. I stole two little cloths from Mrs Mathew. You haven't . . . you know, begun?'

'No.' My mind flashes back to the stained squares of cloth hanging to dry under the hammocks at Cascades, the trails of blood on the floor. 'No, I haven't, not yet.' But she has solved the mystery of my tender breasts, that slight ache deep in my belly.

'You will sometime. I was a bit scared, but it's not so bad.' After a pause, she adds: 'Sorry about the tea. Let's find that food bag I dropped.'

Scrabbling around in the dirt, I feel her arms going around me, hugging me tight for a long moment. 'Good luck,' she says. 'Just be more careful what you say. Better, say nothing at all!'

Picking up my bag, I suddenly realise that if a ship comes to take me home, I might never see her again, but I can't find adequate words of thanks or farewell.

I feel her ruffle my hair. 'You need— Wait there.'

Against the pink of the shy dawn, I see her turn towards the direction of the tents. A few moments later she is back. 'Scissors,' she whispers. 'Stand still.'

'Make it quick,' I say, recognising the rasping sound of hair being roughly cut. I push away the memory of hearing Violet's big shears doing the same work before she got out the razor.

Tillie gives me a last hug. 'Farewell . . . Harry. Oh, do remember to rub a little dirt on your face. Hands and knees, too. You're much too clean for a boy.'

And that is how I start up the track from Official Bay, slightly tearful, with my hair in an unruly crop, altogether grubby, my disguise complete.

July 1840

IT WAS SUCH A simple solution. Clever Martha had worked out that the only way I was going to survive in Hobart was if I wasn't a girl in a grey shift. In fact, not a girl at all.

I held up the clothes from the bag: two pairs of boys' breeches, two coarse shirts, a brown jerkin, and a boy's cap. Yes, from the smell they'd been worn before. Her grandson, perhaps. Garments her family could ill-afford to give away.

Instead of a Cascades girl out walking to fetch water, I would be just another boy. The sort who hung idly around markets and wharves looking for work or favours or pockets to pick.

I needed to change while it was still half-light and safe. These clothes would certainly be warmer than those I was wearing. The breeches fitted well when I tightened the belt. They came to halfway down my calves. I threw off the hated shift, pulled on the faded blue shirt and the tweedy jerkin. Off with the bonnet, running my hands through the short stubble that covered my scalp, and on with the baker boy's cap.

I'm not a girl, I'm . . . What about . . . Harry? A little nod to my Grandfather Harrington, perhaps. It felt right.

Martha's surprises were not yet over. There were other items in the bag. My fingers closed over a pouch which I could tell from its weight held coins, along with a little parcel of brown bread and a large wedge of yellow cheese nicer than was ever served to the inmates.

I repacked the bag, wiped away tears, and set off. The narrow street was slowly coming to life: men well wrapped up against the chill hitching horses to the carts, others striding off for a day's work. Smoke drifting from chimney pots, dogs barking, birds singing.

I turned as instructed into Macquarie Street, which I knew

from my water-carrying days led to the wharves. Already a few early ghosts in grey were scurrying with their pails towards the water taps, past the shops selling liquor and the grocery stores and several cheap-looking hotels.

As I got closer to where I could see ships' masts sticking up above the waterfront buildings, I recognised the church we'd marched past on the day we arrived here, all that time ago. And the courthouse and — look — the gardens and white façade of Government House. Lady Jane Franklin and her husband were probably still fast asleep in their four-poster bed.

I'd walked only half a mile, maybe, but enough to wonder at the difference it makes being freed from long skirts. And to think of just how boys *were* different. At home I knew only the village boys. My brother was three years older, nearly a man. Since that day in the market, I'd been surrounded mostly by women.

Martha's bread and cheese had satisfied my hunger, but as I ambled along, trying to appear nonchalant rather than furtive, I decided to spend some time at the wharves. I'd watch and listen, learn how to steal food and how to be a boy.

18. Invasion?

IT TAKES ME THREE days to get the short distance around to Store Bay.

Halfway up the track the heavens open. With no large trees nearby I'm forced to take shelter under a low shrub. The Guernsey and fearnought dragged from my bag keep my clothes mostly dry, and I coil up into a ball with the Cascades shift as a blanket. The track a few feet away is soon a muddy torrent, washing small rocks and debris down to Official Bay.

As the rain pelts down and the hours drag past, my spirits fall into a deep, dark pit of despair, the worst — if that is possible — since I stumbled, iron chains around my ankles, onto the ship at London docks, or during the very worst periods at Cascades. At least on the *Platina* and at Cascades I had a place to sleep and food to eat, although hardly fit for animals. Between bouts of fitful sleep, I begin to think how much better never to wake up, just . . . give up the struggle . . . just . . . drift away . . .

The third afternoon the rain eases to a light drizzle. I've eaten the last of Tillie's bread and potatoes, and sucked water from the bigger leaves of the dripping undergrowth. Stiff, cold and very hungry, I make myself stand up and get my legs working. As for boy-like grime on my face and elsewhere: after three days in the bush I must already be unclean. I feel dirty, all over.

Arriving on the ridge I see the carpenters have returned to work on the government house, now with its roof on and the long veranda half-built. I stop to watch, and am also ignored by several groups of men dawdling on the path down to Store Bay. No one gives this slouching, scruffy boy a second glance, or even a first one. I've already packed away the fearnought as it would mark me as a seafarer, so I am relieved when the rain finally stops.

Bigger strides, lower voice, keep eyes downcast and say little — these I must remember, always, as I stow my bag among the trunks of my magic tree (its fallen scarlet needles now all washed down the track) and arrive at the hellhole that is Store Bay.

Hellhole too strong? Many people — Mrs Mathew for one — have talked about the hellhole of Kororareka in the north. She'd lived there when she first came to this country, and Tillie had many times heard her tell visitors how glad she was to leave that rough, lawless place, 'full of whalemen, seal hunters, riff-raff and reprobates of the worst kind. And groups of wretched Maoris, sitting around, dressed in rags, begging.'

But to me, as I pass (bigger strides, eyes down, slouch and kick at stones like a boy) through the first group of raupo huts, Store Bay seems its own kind of hellhole. On my previous visit, the men — native and settler — had all been busy with hammers and saws, carting goods ashore from the canoes and small trading schooners, haggling over pigs and potatoes in return for blankets and nails and tobacco.

Now, besides many more tents and untidy piles of sawn timber, there are bigger groups of white men not working but drinking, playing cards, having arguments that sometimes lead to angry pushing and shoving. These must be more of the land-jobbers coming in from New South Wales, here only to buy lots at the first land sales, sell them on quickly and return to Sydney. I hear them boasting, shamelessly, about the fat profits to be made.

And they're seemingly blind to the rubbish lying everywhere: potato skins, pork bones cooked and uncooked, timber chippings, paper wrappings, ends of rope, discarded boxes, broken tools, rags — all strewn about, stinking and sodden from the rain. It seems likely, when I see a man pissing against a pile of scrap timber, that still no one's thought to have a latrine dug.

As I carefully pick my way down towards the canoes and boats, no one takes the slightest notice. I'm just another grubby urchin, probably a cabin boy off a Sydney vessel, waiting for his ship to leave. But all the time I'm noting the tents where bread is being sold, and where camp ovens are sitting beneath tent flaps, cooking up stews. I can drink water from the stream, but for food I'll have to wait until dark.

I learn a lot over the next few days, just listening and watching, keeping my distance from people I recognise. There's Mr Mathew, looking harassed, checking his measurements, sometimes with a boy helping to carry his instruments and heavy brass chains.

And here's Dr Campbell, busy with hammer and saw putting up a sturdy fence so that people walking up the track can't peer inside his tent. He seems to be good friends with another tall, important-looking man, Captain Symonds. I know him as one of the official party from the *Anna Watson*.

Several times I spy Violet outside her tent, cooking or playing cards with her husband. Her bright clothes make her conspicuous, even more so than the few other females wandering around with dulled, desperate eyes, dressed to attract attention.

Every day the canoes come in laden with firewood, pork meat, bags of potatoes and kumaras, sometimes melons, pumpkins, maize and small peaches. Schooners drop anchor to deliver boatloads of new arrivals from Sydney or Melbourne.

Occasionally the traders send ashore timber constructions that look like half-finished parts of houses.

Listening in to conversations without being noticed is easy, especially if drink makes the talk loud and careless. I quickly become an expert eavesdropper.

I hear the timbers are coming down from Kororareka, kitset houses to be erected in the new capital. I hear the land-jobbers complaining about the delay of the first land sales, and others who grumble that the delays mean yet more land-sharks arriving, who surely will, come March, cause the prices to go sky-high.

And I hear Dr Campbell complaining to Captain Symonds and other gentlemen about that officious idiot Mr Mathew — 'Master Red Tape Himself' — and how it's almost come to needing the surveyor-general's stamp on a passport before daring to put a foot in Official Bay.

And Store Bay itself is no longer — they're calling it Commercial Bay.

Now expert at recognising opportunities, I scavenge for food at night. From pork and potato stews left in billies, hunks torn off loaves of bread. But it's never enough, and more difficult now that they're keeping small fires alight all night long, I suppose to discourage thieves. I sleep under bushes where and when I can.

The morning that I'm so hungry I know it's time to act, I'm on the beach watching yet another boatload of Sydney land-jobbers wade ashore. My plan is to offer, for a few coins, to help with their luggage. Then I'll suggest that choosing a site and putting up a tent in this fresh northerly will be tricky, and I'm the man for the job.

A canoe pulls in close by. It's one of those with a small sail.

One of the paddlers jumps out and I'm instantly curious. He is most oddly dressed: ragged sailor's blouse and short breeches, but over them a native flax skirt and cape. Fair-skinned, but on his ruddy cheeks and forehead some tattooing. Long grey hair straggles out from underneath his cap. Once a sailor, now one of those Pakeha-Maori?

He looks around, agitated, and his eyes fall on me.

'Dr Campbell, boy? Hae this letter for 'im. Quick aboot it now!'

'I know his tent, sir.'

He follows me on his bare feet past the Government Store and up to the grassed area where Dr Campbell's tent is pitched. The new fence means I can linger unseen and overhear the reason for the visitor's haste.

The capital is about to be invaded! He's come from Waiheke island. His own wife has heard that a war party is on its way from the Bay of Islands to attack and destroy the capital. On God's honour, this is true!

But, Dr Campbell replies, this letter you bring me comes from my business partner, Mr Brown, and he tells me not to believe a word of it.

Now it sounds more like an argument, with the messenger becoming louder and more insistent and the doctor informing him testily it's all hearsay, just gossip. He should quietly go back home to Waiheke. Finally, after much shouting, the doctor loses patience.

'If you must, man, go see Captain Symonds up at his cottage. He's the police magistrate — it's him you need to convince. I'm just a trader here. I've no official status.'

I'm by the gate when the Pakeha-Maori emerges, looking wildly around. 'That man mebbe doctor,' he mutters, 'but he's an arrogant fool. He'll rue the day.'

'I know Captain Symonds' cottage, sir.'

He nods. 'Come to warn you folks, and what thanks I get? Hah! P'haps Cap'n has more sense.' Some more angry mutterings follow in the native language.

I say, to get back his attention: 'The cottage, it's up on the point, sir.'

We set off, him walking quickly and his bare feet not troubled by the small rocks and spikey branches left by the storm. His soles must be like the thick leather my father uses for his saddles.

Reaching the captain's one-room cottage, the seaman pushes past me and hurriedly knocks on the door, then enters without waiting for a reply. From outside I hear another loud conversation. The captain is inclined to agree with the doctor. It isn't long before both men appear at the cottage door. The visitor, dismissed with thanks for his concern, turns with an expression of disgust and lopes off down the hill. As he turns, the captain catches sight of me, and I am summoned.

'Boy, come here. You can find the surveyor-general, Mr Felton Mathew? Maybe at home in Official Bay?'

'Yes, I can, sir.'

'Go there. Even if he is out and about doing fieldwork, Mrs Mathew should know where he is.'

'Yes, sir. Think I saw him this morning, sir, by the Government Store, measuring with his chains. Sir.'

'Good. Wait here.' A few minutes later, he reappears from the cottage and hands me two letters: the original one, and the other, one I guess he has just written. 'Careful of this, the ink is still damp. It's vital he gets it without delay. If you can't find Mr Mathew, seek out one of the other officials, Lieutenant Shortland or Captain Rough. You know them?'

'Yes, sir, I do.'

'Are you trustworthy?'

'Yes, sir. I am, sir. Very.'

'Then off with you.' I resist the urge to give him a cheeky salute. He calls after me: 'Name?'

'Harry, sir.'

Messenger boy, that's me! If there's now a need for urgent messages to be passed between all of these important men, I can see opportunities ahead. A few coins here, a few there — when that ship leaves for the Horn, I'll be ready.

But as I run helter-skelter down the track, I'm not worrying about money or even my empty belly. Instead I'm picturing a fleet of war canoes out in the harbour, coming our way.

On the beach there'll be Captain Symonds shouting orders, urging the men to get the muskets out from the Government Store. Grab whatever weapons and ammunition they can find, form into squads and post sentries to defend the capital to the last man.

Tattooed warriors will storm ashore, their clubs and spears ready to massacre all those defenceless wives and little children around in Mechanics Bay. Tillie and Mrs Mathew in Official Bay. Me in Commercial Bay.

There'll be savage fighting, hand to hand. The natives might have muskets themselves, some might get injured, but they will do what they came to do. Most of the white men here aren't soldiers, probably have only ever used their fists in tavern brawls. None will be spared, they'll either be killed or taken as slaves. I don't want to think about the women and children.

Or perhaps the canoes will land — unnoticed by us — around at the Orakei beach, where other warriors living inland will join them. One or two days later they'll attack, come down from the hillsides. If night-time, those asleep in their tents will be the lucky ones. Anyone taking refuge in the Government Store will be routed out. The doctor's fence will prove useless. The Mathews' precious horses around in Official Bay will be hacked to death where they stand or let loose or ridden away as spoils of war. The tents and raupo huts might be set alight.

Why are the doctor and the captain so certain that the message from Waiheke is nothing but a silly rumour, idle gossip not to be taken seriously? Why is that Pakeha-Maori man so certain that it is true and we're all in peril of our lives? He trusts his native wife, enough to paddle all that way from the island to warn us. Shouldn't we rather trust him?

As I run down the track, pass my magic tree and come into the wide view of the beach, my stomach is knotted up with fear and confusion. Images of my kite friend, of the handsome paddler who speaks English, of all those canoes bringing us food and firewood, their help building huts, their singing and guffaws of laughter — these don't match with the image of fierce warriors rampaging through our tents and huts.

Mrs Mathew has told us we are here legally, we bought the land from the chiefs. There was a Deed of Purchase, we paid six gold sovereigns, also blankets, pots, hatchets, tobacco and pipes and clothing. We could only offer what we had brought on the two ships. They are glad for us to settle on this harbour, she'd said, as protection from other more warlike tribes. The governor's treaty of goodwill has been signed by many chiefs — Mr Mathew was there himself at Waitangi on the very day — so why should any tribe want to do us harm?

Maybe they are a totally different tribe from the north? We've heard plenty of gruesome sailors' stories of the chief Hongi Hika, and his terrible musket raids on other tribes up north and the Auckland area and down further south.

My task is to find Mr Mathew, give him Captain Symonds'

letter, but I'm confused — and if I'm honest, also very afraid for my life.

There are no canoes out there in the harbour or coming around the north head — not yet.

August 1840

I SPENT A USEFUL few days at the Hobart wharves, sitting for hours on an empty crate for a good view of the activity. Two ships were being loaded with timber, bales of wool, and cattle. Boats were bringing in crates and boxes from three others at anchor out in the harbour.

I watched the boys on their own, passing the time kicking stones or throwing them at seagulls and swans, running sticks along a stretch of iron railings to produce a clattering sound. They walked differently to girls — more of a swagger; and sat differently — legs sprawled, often jiggling. They picked their noses, and carelessly spat out phlegm. With no women about, they — and the older men — relieved themselves without shame against buildings or into the water.

Only one boy seemed to be working, as a messenger darting around between the ships, the wharf-side offices and the agents in their stiff black coats. When carts and coaches pulled up on the wharf he greeted the arrivals, gave them directions. That was a job I could do.

Feeling hungry and restive, I followed one boy down an alleyway to the back of a hotel. Above the clutter of bins and broken furniture a long brown skirt was hung out to dry. I muttered *sorry* to the owner, probably a scullery maid, as I thrust it deep into my bag. One day I might get to be a girl again, and

I'd prefer to wear anything other than that horrible grey shift.

From behind a fence I watched the boy, how he rummaged in the rubbish bins and ate what he found. When he'd gone, I did the same: the remains of an apple pie, roasted turnips, a chewable bone. For water, I'd have to go back to the wharf, where I'd seen a cask. Around it, the workers stopped for a few minutes to drink and smoke.

Kicking stones near to a group of black-coated agents, I overheard that one of the ships ex London was leaving in a few hours on the ebb, for Port Nicholson. A new settlement in New Zealand. She had a government house kitset in her holds. *Platina* she was called. Cap'n Wycherley, master.

I stared out at the two anchored ships. With their three masts, they looked much the same, but one was my prison ship of three years ago! If I was going to stow away on any ship it would not be her, with so many ghosts, such terrible memories. I'd been thinking of one of the ships tied up alongside, going to Sydney. Come nightfall . . .

But then another odd thing. One of the agents was calling: Hey boy, come here! I checked behind, but it was me he was beckoning. Some extra papers needed to be taken out to the *Platina*'s master. The dratted messenger boy had disappeared. You look trustworthy enough — here, take this satchel and get yerself on the next boat going out to the *Platina*.

He added, with a chuckle: And make sure you come back ashore, young man. Cap'ns don't like nasty surprises on their ships.

19. Readiness

I AM QUICKLY LEARNING what it is to be a trusted messenger. From Captain Symonds' cottage on the headland down to Commercial Bay, splashing through the low tide around to Mechanics, back up to the headland, down again. Up again to the point to warn the workers on the governor's house, back down again. I'm learning how to linger, to suggest by a hesitation or a look that for my trouble a coin or two might be offered.

All that running, thankful to be in breeches and not holding up my skirts — but then a girl wouldn't be asked to run messages in the first place. Even though back at home in races across the village green I used to beat nearly all the boys.

Those two fine gentlemen might have dismissed the message from the Pakeha-Maori man as just native chatter, but what if they prove to be wrong?

When eventually I find Mr Mathew in Commercial Bay, I can tell that he's much alarmed by Captain Symonds' note. His face, normally ruddy from the sun, turns pale.

'You must find Captain Rough,' he says, his voice trembling, 'and press him to read these notes. Also Lieutenant Shortland, and Dr Johnson. They must assemble here by the Government Store to organise our defences. Go, boy, on your way. Make all haste!'

While I'm dashing between the bays the word must have got out, because when I return to Commercial Bay none of the men are working, but are standing around in groups, much excited. Lieutenant Shortland and Captain Symonds seem to have taken charge, and I make sure that they know I'm on hand for running messages.

I hear orders being given to get the muskets from the store — not many are kept there, and probably rusty but better than nothing — be sure to check the ammunition, too!

Sentries are to be posted in all three bays, five sharp-eyed men to go up on the headland to scan the harbour entrance. The Maori carpenters coming down from the point and the traders on the beach are told to stop work — though not the reason why — and to take their canoes and return to their villages.

The land-jobbers look mostly bewildered and are taking refuge in drink, no doubt wishing they'd stayed in Australia.

To my great relief, one of the younger carpenters is sent to Official Bay to inform Mrs Mathew, but I'm to run over to Mechanics Bay and tell the women to gather up their children and enough food and bedding for two days and proceed with all haste up the track to the flagstaff. I'm given Captain Symonds' letter to produce if necessary.

In my role as obliging and reliable messenger boy, I can hardly refuse to go on this errand. And I don't relish telling the women of our danger. They would know, as well as anyone, that the capital would not survive a serious attack. We've not many soldiers and few muskets. There's nowhere to go, except flee up into the bracken, only to be hunted down by warriors who know the bush and tracks better than we do. Women and children will not be spared.

Mechanics Bay looks much the same as when I was banished — children playing in the stream, the washing hung on lines, perhaps a few more raupo huts being built. I skirt around the tent where Mrs Roberton is sitting with little Lucy, and find an older woman I know to be sensible and unlikely to recognise me. Message delivered, satisfied that she will organise the others, I start quickly back up the track.

Already some women have begun wailing that they should never have come to this godforsaken heathen place, scooping up the babies and little ones, shouting at their older children to gather up their warm jackets, take a blanket, pocket that half-eaten bread, hurry, make haste, for pity's sake *hurry*!

It's a long night. Harry the messenger boy retreats to his usual nest in the bracken, but I can still hear men's low, urgent voices. The usual lanterns and cooking fires are banned, so everyone is starving hungry.

We wait — and wait — and wait some more — through the night, all the long hours of the next day, another endless, restless night. Someone like Captain Symonds must have decided around noon that enough time — and therefore the danger — has passed, because I'm sent up to the point to tell the subdued groups of women and children that they should return to their tents. He even gives me a few extra coins for my good work.

All the sentries are stood down, the muskets put back in the store. The carpenters and sawyers resume their work. The land-jobbers have never stopped drinking or playing cards, but now noisily let loose their relief and frustrations.

Lingering by the doctor's fence, I hear him welcome Captain Symonds to his tent, with much laughter and congratulating each other on their cleverness, how much better they two understand the Maori mind than 'Master Red Tape' and those other over-excitable and pompous officials. There was no invasion planned, the emergency was quite unnecessary.

'Tis a shame for the women and children to have been so alarmed. That tattooed Pakeha-Maori fellow shouldn't have listened to his native wife.

If I thought that Harry, again confined to Commercial Bay, can resume his searching for food and earning money, with Violet as the only threat, I've been too optimistic.

Yes, I'm constantly looking out for anyone dressed in skirts amongst all the hustle and bustle of men. The prostitutes are easily identified. When I spy Mrs Godfrey in the distance, usually draped on the arm of her short-legged soldier, I keep well clear. I'm running some errands, earning a few coins, and eating what I can find at night — usually not enough, because the light from the fires means I must be much more careful.

I'm also using the cover of darkness to steal ends of timber long enough to build myself a makeshift hut well hidden up in the bracken. It isn't yet weatherproof, but it's better than nothing, and it is mine.

But a few mornings after our 'invasion scare', I am down by the high-tide mark, watching yet another small schooner drop anchor and a boatload of scruffy-looking men trudge ashore through the wet mud.

I've had some success with my offers to help newcomers pitch their tents in fresh winds, but today it's calm, so I'm not hopeful. Still, I'm hungry enough to know I must make the effort.

At the high-tide mark, the four men drop their bags onto the dry sand and raise bloodshot eyes to survey the scene.

'Behold the capital!' an older one says. 'Heaven help us!'

By now I've got used to this reaction of new arrivals, dirty and bone-weary and stumbling around on the sand after twelve, maybe even twenty, days at sea.

I see how they silently take in the hastily built weatherboard store, the randomly pitched tents and the raupo huts, the heaps of sawn timber, the men working and the men idling. How they stare for some time at the canoes lying on the mud waiting for the tide and the small knot of Maoris and settlers noisily trading pigs.

'Told us 'twere bad, but . . . Who be all them May-oris? How do they get here?'

I step forward. 'You from New South Wales, good sirs?'

'Nay, Victoria. Melbourne. Nineteen 'orrible days and nights at sea.'

'Once across Tasman 'twere bad enough,' mutters another, stretching his arms to the sky, 'but *twice*, needs must for returnin' . . . Still, right now ne'er so glad to find meself on dry land.'

'I know a good place for tents,' I say boldly.

'You here with family, boy?' says a third, the youngest, the least disreputable of the four and the only one who's taken the trouble to come ashore with his beard neatly trimmed.

'Yes, sir.' This question, and the smile that goes with it, is odd, but I give it no thought. 'Nigh on four months here, I know the good places still. And where to get water fit for drinking.'

'Proper li'l Samaritan,' says the first, swaying as people do when first stepping on land after time at sea. Their scraggy beards, hair and outer clothes are all encrusted with salt.

'And firewood,' I add. 'And where to buy bread. Come!'

They all nod wearily, and I set off to a level grassy spot I know to be available. I point out the raupo hut where noon tomorrow they can buy bread and potatoes, and, if they're lucky, pork meat. Over there is the stream fit for drinking. Care needs to be taken with cooking fires, this being high summer and winds often onshore. There are no snakes or nasty spiders and snarling animals. The natives are friendly.

I linger just long enough for two of them to rummage in their pockets for coins to press into my hand.

'Thankee, sirs,' I say, suitably obliged. 'You want messages, or to find acquaintances, I can help. I know the officials here.' They're all too weary even to mumble any thanks. 'I'll check with you morning-time.'

That might be the only contact I'll have with any of that particular group, as they pitch their tents and blend in among all the land-jobbers. I guess two hundred or more are now whiling away the days until the land sales. Complaints about the delays are loud and constant, criticism of the Governor and surveyor nasty and often foul-mouthed.

For the officials who trusted me with messages during the days of the invasion alarm, I'm now their regular messenger boy, spending much of my time running up and down between Commercial Bay and the activity up around Government House.

If sent over to Official Bay, I take care to avoid the Mathews' raupo hut and the marquee where Mrs Mathew might be preparing food, and only once have found myself unable to avoid coming face-to-face with Tillie. After she has got over her surprise and some amusement at my transformation, we talk only briefly. She seems low in spirits, barely interested in my secret life and grumbling that her workdays are long and tiring, the bread-making now almost daily.

Lucky you, all that freedom, she says, you run where you like. No one expects you to knead bread dough for hours on end, sweep out all the huts and tents every day and wash up dozens of dirty pots and pans.

Hardly free, I think sourly. I'm bound hand and foot to the guise of Harry, all my plans dependent on remaining undetected, and avoiding Violet at all costs.

With the tide out, I am able to splash in my bare feet around to Commercial Bay, carrying a small bag of instruments that in his haste Mr Mathew had left behind this morning. I am about to approach Mr Mathew where he has set up a writing table and stool in the shelter of the Government Store, but he's being waylaid by someone who looks familiar. Of course, it's that youngest man of the four I'd shown to a tent site a few days ago, the one with the neatly trimmed beard.

Waiting nearby, unseen behind a pile of wood, it's easy for me to overhear most of the conversation. This I discover: the newcomer is here to buy land, being tired of life at sea and especially the ill-run ship called the *Platina.* Mr Mathew of course would remember the vessel in the harbour, that day they ran up the Royal Standard and fired salutes. The *Platina* had returned to Sydney for stores and cargo, but the master is an incompetent bully — *what*?! — and he didn't fancy rounding the Horn with such a despot. So in Sydney he'd signed off, gladly.

I fight back the urge to reveal myself and passionately defend Captain Wycherley as a kindly, wise man, a proper captain and no tyrant. My restraint is rewarded. The young man seems anxious for Mr Mathew to know that he comes from a good land-owning family in Dorset, that, being a third son without hope of inheritance but a free spirit, he has defied his strict parents and run away to sea, quickly reaching the rank of second mate.

He's come here, with some family promissory notes, to buy land and perhaps could be apprenticed to Mr Mathew as a surveyor? It's a profession he's keen to learn and for which this new colony will present many opportunities.

His is not a seaman's rough voice. From my father's well-off customers, I know the voice of an educated man when I hear it. And lies when I hear them. Second mate indeed! Promissory notes! He is shameless.

So hearing his name is no surprise. It explains the smirk and the odd question of me when first he came ashore. He knew very well that I was Harry, that odd unattached boy who had joined the *Platina* in Port Nicholson.

And now I know his name: Albert, of course.

I have tried so hard to put this person out of my mind — and, until now, succeeded. But creeping away from my hiding place, with Albert's smooth lies ringing in my ears, I'm remembering a brief conversation with Pigtail Paddy.

I'm not going to tell you which of the seamen is Albert, he is saying. There's no need for you to know. He'll not trouble you again. But how can you be sure? I ask. He tried twice to molest me, why would he not try again?

Paddy was silent for a few moments. One night, he said, Albert got into his cups and in a fit of self-pity spilled much of his story. He was born into a wealthy West Country family and when only eighteen was blamed for the abuse and unpleasant deaths of two farm boys. He denied everything, of course, but his reputation was ruined. As a third son he might have been packed off into the military, but this being out of the question, now shamed, disowned and cast out, he ran away to sea.

Not navy ships, of course, Paddy went on, that door was forever closed, but rough merchantmen, convict ships, colliers and the like, where his accent and manner marked him as an odd fish. He was tolerated on the *Platina* as a competent enough seaman, though inclined to be insolent and lazy. Capable of tormenting farm boys and murder? Very likely!

So some part of that fanciful story spun to Mr Mathew is true. And the reason that Pigtail Paddy could assure me I was safe from further interference was simple: Albert was told that his shady past might become common knowledge if he so much as laid a hand, even his little finger, on the boy Harry.

So here is Albert in the capital, finished, he says, with the sea, seeking his luck in the colony and toadying up to any official who might prove useful. Yet another misfit with secrets to hide, sharing that dread of betrayal leading to banishment, becoming homeless, hungry and forever lonely.

I wonder anew, how much does it take to decide that the future is so bleak, so full of anger and hate and deceit and struggle, so bereft of hope, that to fill one's pockets with gravel and just walk into the sea seems the only sensible option?

I remember the first sight from the ship of those three pretty bays, three unspoiled beaches. Clean sands, overhanging trees, birdsong, peace and stillness.

Over the spring and summer, we've turned them into dirty, squabbling villages of too many frightened, suspicious and greedy people with something to hide and nowhere to go.

August 1840

THE IMPATIENT OARSMAN TAKING me out to the *Platina* wanted me to just throw the satchel up to the sailor looking down from the rails, but I had other ideas.

Too risky, I said firmly, standing up and grabbing at the rope ladder hanging over the side. Take it to the cap'n meself, want to have a look around, never been on a big ship like this before. The oarsman muttered something about getting myself back ashore, and pulled away.

Climbing over the rail, I found myself breathing hard, as though I'd been running. Fighting down a feeling of panic, as all those memories flood back — of chains, vomit, terror, vermin, sick children, storms, the smell. The sailor looked at me oddly as I handed over the satchel. Just want a look, sir, I said. Be quick 'bout it, he snarled.

Left alone, I tried to think of a plan. Nip below, hide in a cupboard until dark, then creep up to the main deck, skirt past the pens holding the sheep, goats and chickens and clamber into one of the small boats kept on deck. Hope that the sailor by the rails forgets that the messenger boy has not returned to shore as they pull up the anchor. It's worth a try; it's the only plan I've got.

After what seemed an age crouched in a tiny, dark space behind a ladder, I finally heard the anchor being raised, barked orders, the pounding footfalls of sailors raising sail, the cook clanking pans in the nearby galley. The slapping sounds of waves against the hull getting louder.

Many hours passed before most of the noises subsided and I felt brave enough to sneak up to the main deck. It was nearly night-time by then.

Land lay behind us, just dark smudges on the horizon, so we were well out to sea. Farewell, Hobart! Martha, you would be proud of me — this far at least.

Hiding under the boat's canvas cover was like being in a shallow, dark cave. I could only lie with the wooden ribs sticking into my back. My bag made a lumpy pillow. Like it or not, eventually I'd have to pull down my breeches and pee into the bottom of the boat.

I settled myself to the only thing I could do, for however long it took. I was dreaming about that warm, bright shop in Oxford Street when I heard footfalls. They stopped close by.

A voice said check the small boats, Paddy.

20. An unwelcome visitor

DURING THE NEXT FEW days after overhearing that conversation with Mr Mathew, I begin to suspect that Albert is following me. Maybe he just happens to be nearby, bent on making the acquaintance of important men who can be useful. Or maybe he's watching and waiting for his chance to make my better acquaintance?

Sleepless in my makeshift hut, I realise that, yes, although he knows me from the *Platina*, he's unlikely to be aware that I know of his shady past. Here, he's merely a handsome gentleman speculator with a polished manner, looking for land and a new life.

Late one afternoon, the slopes above the beach already in shadow, I've just reached my hut and sat down wearily on the scraps of old canvas that cover the ground, when I become aware of cracking and rustling noises. Someone is approaching, pushing aside the bracken, treading on broken-off branches.

I freeze as the snapping sounds grow louder, vainly hoping that it's just someone idly exploring the area, who won't stumble across my hideaway, who'll soon go away.

'Nice place you have here,' says Albert, looming over me. His smile is triumphant. 'Aren't you going to welcome me in?'

'No, I am not.'

'I brought you some stew. Look.'

'Go away.' Ah, how my belly rumbles, my mouth longs for the salty taste of meat. He holds out a billy-can.

'It's still warm from the fire. Pork, potatoes, bread, too. Enough for us to share.'

'I don't want your food. Go *away*.'

He puts down the can, and crouches beside me. I note that he might be keeping his beard neatly trimmed, but his breath stinks and his voice is oily. He has a pronounced Adam's apple, which, once you notice it, goes disconcertingly up and down in his throat.

'That's no way to treat a gentleman, Harry.'

'*Gentleman?* You're not even a remittance man.' It's rash, but I can't contain myself. 'Your family cast you out for unnatural acts, and the only job you're fit for is common sailor. Not even that — I'd wager ten pounds that in Sydney they threw you off the *Platina*. Is that why you're telling such lies about it — and maligning the captain?'

His smirking silence tells me I'm right. I go on: 'You might have deceived Mr Mathew into thinking you a gentleman, but I know—'

'I'm thinking perhaps your hunger is making you feverish,' he says evenly. He picks up the can. 'Here. Take some. I brought a spoon, too.'

'I don't want your spoon or your food.'

'It's delicious. Good as any pork you can buy in England.'

My arm shoots out and the tin can goes flying. A tempting aroma fills the small space.

'Oh dear me,' he says. 'All over your sleeping accommodation, what a shame. P'haps you can salvage some from the dirt. The black Maori potatoes look strange but are actually quite delicious.'

'Get out!' I rage, brushing away the pork pieces from where

they've landed across my breeches, resisting the temptation to put them straight into my mouth. 'Get OUT!'

He laughs. 'Or what? Report me to that pompous police magistrate?'

I discover all my running of messages and the earlier carrying of *Platina*'s cargo have made me stronger than I realise, for when he comes at me, I'm able to push him back and scramble to my feet to look him in the eye.

'I'll do more than report you,' I warn him. 'Those officials trust me. They'll believe me.'

'Come now, Harry — a good boy like you wouldn't tell on a mate.'

'Wouldn't I? You're no mate of mine.'

'And just when he's about to offer you a regular place to sleep in his comfortable tent.'

His grip is stronger this time, and to my horror, despite all my frantic struggling, I feel the length of my body pinned against his body and one hand is trying to reach down inside my breeches. I register his smell — is that tobacco? — his nasty smile, so certain of victory. Then there's a sort of gasp and the hand is exploring elsewhere and finding something unexpected. My breasts are fondled, squeezed hard, fondled again. Grunting like an animal, he tears aside my shirt.

'Good God!' he whispers in my ear, still holding me tight against him. 'You're a girl! A girl, as I live and breathe. Well, well, well — quite the little thespian. Congratulations on your subterfuge, my pretty one.'

'So of course you're not interested,' I shoot back.

'I'm not fussy. I've bedded the odd kitchen maid in my time. Plainer ones than you. But yes, I prefer boys.'

His grip has relaxed, presumably because he reckons a slip of a girl will be more easily subdued for what he now has in mind.

'You're a monster!'

As he stands chuckling, marvelling at his discovery, he doesn't notice me picking up one of the lengths of timber. I bring up my knee sharply to where it hurts and swing the piece of wood in the general direction of his head. A cracking sound confirms it has connected.

He collapses against the stand of bracken like a puppet whose strings have been cut. Or — my mind flashes back to the marketplace — like one of Mr Punch's victims! But then Mr Punch used that stick for laughs and to bully people, not to save his honour and his life.

Albert is only out for a few minutes, long enough for me to transfer all the pieces of meat and potatoes from the floor of the hut to my mouth. Despite some grittiness, it's been a long time since I have enjoyed such a feast, easily enough for two.

When his eyes flicker, and he's able to pull himself to his feet, I say my piece.

'You will walk away from here, Albert, and you will keep my secret. If you don't, I will shout across all Commercial Bay that you're a pervert and probably a murderer, disowned by his family, a disgrace to his class. You'll be finished here.'

I pause for him to take this in — and for me to restrain an urge to belch.

'But if the truth does come out,' I continue, 'I have less to lose. Let's face it, I'm just a foolish weak girl; no one cares about me. People will soon forget about that boy who ran messages, and I can always get work as a scullery maid. For you, though? Not so easy, I expect. So, that's my deal. Do you agree to it?'

He nods, still unsteady on his feet.

'Say "Yes, I agree".'

'I agree.'

'Say it: "My word is as good as my bond".'

I've been told that between gentlemen this is a binding declaration of good faith, so when he hesitates, I add: 'I know it was you on the *Platina* who twice tried to molest me. Not until later, but I did find out. *So say it!* Loud and clear.'

'My word is as good as my bond.'

'Now leave.'

He straightens up and brushes the dirt and bracken twigs off his clothes. A trickle of blood is running down his forehead.

'I see you ate all the food,' he complains, as I watch him stumble out of my hut and out of my sight.

Yes, I have eaten my fill and more, and as darkness falls and the night wears on, and I toss and turn on the scraps of canvas that pass for a bed, I become increasingly uncomfortable. It's not just feeling shaken by Albert's assault, and the violence of my reaction. Used to much smaller quantities of food, my stomach is rebelling with a prolonged attack of hiccups.

I try sitting up, holding my breath, deep-breathing, to no avail. I have an unwelcome vision of my horrible brother trying to cure his regular attacks — in his case, caused by regular over-eating and too much strong ale — by standing on his head against a wall. But since I've no wall available, I pull on my Guernsey and scramble through the bracken onto the track. Perhaps a walk down to the beach will cure me. Water from the stream might help.

I'm so intent on taking safe steps down the uneven track, then skirting around the bulk of the tents and huts where small fires are still burning, that I don't raise my eyes until I've reached the water's edge. Automatically I assess the tide; from the high watermark of seaweed and driftwood it looks not long past full. Some riding lights indicate a number of small vessels anchored out in the harbour.

Then I look upwards. I remember the blazing stars the night Paddy rowed me away from the *Platina*, but the Milky Way across this clear, moonless sky is even brighter. The bigger stars twinkle and dance. There's the Southern Cross!

Down this end of the beach, there are usually some small boats pulled up safely above the high tide, but in the glow of that dazzling night sky I see something unusual: close by, a dinghy that's bumping gently against the sand. The oars have been left in, a rope dangles from its bow. Someone has tied a knot badly.

It feels like a gift from the gods smiling down at me from the starry heavens. I take off my boots, push the little craft out a yard or two and clamber in. I've never had the chance to actually row before, but since leaving England I've often watched the sailors and I know the rhythm. It comes easily, after I discover it helps to brace my feet against the stern — I'm glad not to be doing this in skirts — and *voilà!* my hiccups and tummy-ache are gone.

I'm skimming over shining black glass, with a canopy of twinkling stars above and below, where every splash of the oars creates a trailing mirror-image of tiny lights, just as they had that night with Paddy. Some tiny sea creature, he'd said.

Surprisingly soon, reckless with pleasure and warmed up by the exertion, I'm passing the rocks below the flagstaff point, and recognising the little fires of Official Bay, the familiar outlines of the black hills behind.

But when I pass what I know to be the fires among the tents of Mechanics Bay, I hear a small voice of caution.

You've stolen a boat, Harriet. You're probably being swept

along faster than you think by an outgoing tide. And you're lightly clad for the cold hours before dawn.

And now take care, for you've gone beyond your known limits. You've not seen the bays and headlands of the south Waitemata shores beyond Mechanics Bay since your arrival, standing with Paddy on the deck of the *Platina*. You can get swept out of the harbour, to the wide, open sea, and not be strong enough . . . you can't swim . . .

My foolish curiosity wins the day. I've heard people talk of a native village and gardens at Orakei, on the slopes leading up to the mountain Mr Mathew has named for the governor, Mount Hobson. If I hug the shoreline closely, I'm probably halfway there already.

The night deepens and still I row, getting weary now, until I recognise that I've come around a point and am now at the mouth of a wide bay. Looming over it is the rounded bulk of the mountain. I experiment with the oars to turn the dinghy towards where there's probably a beach, and immediately know that the tide is flowing out of this bay. Making headway against the current is harder.

Time passes. Above Rangi-toto a shooting star flares briefly, a single heavenly firework. I settle into a slow rhythm, breathing in harmony with the steady pull and splash, watching the starry night slowly fade and the eastern sky behind Rangi-toto turn from palest silvery-grey to a soft apricot then the brightest imaginable orange, more intense even than the displays of Spanish oranges sometimes seen piled high in markets at home. With my gypsy life, I've seen some gorgeous sunsets here, but this glow is reflected in the dinghy's glittering wake, giving twice the pleasure.

As the sun rises, I can make out a beach, and soon, a little way inland, some raupo huts. The dinghy grounds itself on soft mud, which I estimate to be about half-tide, so there's a walk ahead. Do I trouble myself to think, as I pull the dinghy a little further up the mud and secure the oars, that I'm being unwise? That I'm trespassing, and might not be welcome?

Only momentarily. I tie up my boots and stand.

It's certainly a small village, but no one is stirring, no one comes forward to challenge me. The huts, randomly spaced quite close together, are mostly bigger than those they've built for us. I recognise the way the reeds are bundled and tied to make the walls, also the rough thatching of the roof. In front of some huts are heaped rocks, perhaps for cooking fires. Large fish are hanging to dry from regularly spaced racks.

But where are the people? I remember being told that most natives in this area live in a bigger village, they call a 'pah', beside the other harbour to the south. They come over here only occasionally, to tend the gardens and fish.

How to explain, then, this uncanny feeling that I'm being watched?

With the full glare of the rising sun, I now find an answer to one question, anyway: where do all those potatoes come from, the flax bags-full that they bring to we settlers almost daily? Behind the village are green potato plants, fenced off in sections. I know what a modest potato patch looks like, but nothing on this scale, with plants stretching right up to the lower slopes of the mountain. Not all are in neat rows — some are in flower, making a white carpet, others seemed bushier. So they cleverly plant and harvest at different seasons.

And not only potatoes. I've only to wander a little way to come across pumpkins, maybe onions, and a small orchard of peach trees, but alas the fruit is not ripe enough to eat. Perhaps this is just as well, considering the night's hiccups and general discomfort.

The mountain rises enticingly above the gardens, but for once I'm sensible enough to restrain myself from setting out for the summit. I know enough about the harbour to estimate that the tide will be fully out during the morning hours and return in the afternoon. I need to be back at Commercial Bay before the owner finds his dinghy gone. And I don't fancy being obliged to stay here for another tidal cycle, where even in daylight ghosts might roam. Or try to walk back to Commercial Bay through the bracken.

Meantime . . . in this deserted village I have a rare chance to explore, be at nobody's beck and call, encounter no unfriendly faces. I can relax, examine the huts more closely, find the stream where they get their water, imagine a life which must be, compared to what I know, so simple.

That young girl I'd seen at Thomas's funeral: she'd not been taught that a bare breast, or even a bare ankle, is sinful and must be kept hidden from men under many yards of heavy clothing. Does she sleep in one of these huts, curling up nearly naked and uncovered on the bare ground? Has she already lain with a young man? Is she already aware, like me, that one day she will bleed in harmony with the moon? She's probably seen babies born and aged chiefs or injured warriors take their last breaths.

With the sun now rising overhead, I decide that, in the absence of people and any of their belongings, there is little more to see. Back on the beach, I note my boat is still stranded on the mud, but surely the tide is returning?

I'm sitting, almost asleep, under a tree, when something — a cough? a rustle of flax? — urges me awake.

Before me stands the same native woman who had surprised me bathing naked in the waterfall above Official Bay, all those many moons ago. Or if not her, a wrinkled old woman with a mass of tangled grey hair and drooping bare breasts very like her. Through blinking eyes, I can see she is offering me something: a flax basket.

It's time to try out my three words of Maori.

'Ah — kia ora,' I say, smiling nervously. 'Kia ora, wahine.'

Encouraged, smiling shyly, she takes a step further and lays the basket on the ground. A broader smile shows me that she has few if any teeth. Her gestures make it clear, these potatoes overflowing from the basket are freshly dug and are for me.

Truly, I'm amazed how much can be shared even without words, just by miming and suitable noises. It's just like the games of charades my mother loved for us to play at home. Gummy smiles are flashed and her little breasts shake with laughter as moments of understanding are reached.

She'd watched me come ashore, put on my boots, go up into the gardens. I'd pulled up a plant to check the roots were indeed white potatoes, looked around guiltily. At the stream I'd drunk a good deal of water and looked longingly at the peach trees.

I understand that she has given birth to two boys with much pain, one has died. The others of her tribe are over the hills to the south. She seems intrigued that I've come from far over the sea.

Whether she's a slave — as I guessed at our first encounter — I can't decide. That, and why she's here alone, perhaps as the village's guardian — questions like those need words.

I'm sufficiently engrossed in this strange encounter not to notice the dinghy is afloat, until I catch its movement out of the corner of my eye.

'Oh Lordy, I must go!' I cry, pulling off my boots and gathering up all the spilled potatoes into the basket once more. Unsure of an acceptable farewell, I settle for a hug. How thin she is, how strong her hair smells. But halfway across the shining mud, I realise she's following me, and once at the boat she makes it clear that she'll hold it steady while I stow my boots and the basket of potatoes in the bow and climb in.

She then pushes me off with surprising vigour, and, as my oars find their rhythm, stands knee-deep in water waving until I have rounded the point.

Back in the harbour proper, it crosses my mind that if I turn east and keep rowing I might eventually reach Maraetai. But it is 'half a day's sail', Mrs Mathew said, and I am dog-tired and sore from all this rowing. So I become just another small craft heading towards Commercial Bay. The usual afternoon breezes have arrived, so up by Rangi-toto two coastal vessels are making the most of the north-easterly to reach the harbour before nightfall. They will be from the Bay of Islands, or maybe New South Wales. Canoes coming from Commercial Bay are heading towards me, having swapped their cargoes of potatoes and pork, fish and firewood for the usual blankets, tobacco, clothes and nails.

I've timed it well, now being helped by the tide flowing into the harbour. Even so, it's taken some determined rowing to reach Mechanics Bay, and more to round the flagstaff point to where the Commercial Bay beach opens up. My plan is to ignore any other boats or idle person watching from the shore. I'll just jump out with my boots and my basket, pull up the boat and quickly blend in with the general activity of the Commercial Bay foreshore. I'm just another cabin boy from one of the small ships on some errand.

Thank you, someone, for the loan of your dinghy. I didn't steal it.

My return goes without a hitch, and, reaching my hut, collapsing down on the hard ground, I ponder the strange beauty of these past hours. From the need to find relief from hiccups, I've learned to row under the wondrous Milky Way, lit by a golden sunrise. I've explored a native village and marvelled at their gardens, and made a friend who may have taken me in my breeches for a boy, or maybe not. At the time it didn't matter. We connected, without words, just as two lonely human beings finding each other by chance on an empty beach.

Yet here I am, alone in this makeshift hut, longing with all my heart for the one thing that would make this day perfect: to share my wonder with one other person, ideally dear Father or Mother of course, or friends like Paddy and Tillie, even Mrs Mathew. Just one person. What is the point of beauty if it can't be shared?

As the light fades, I fight back tears. I've never felt more alone.

August 1840

I WAS EXPECTING, when the boat cover was lifted, to be met by a pair of wide eyes, then a shout, crew come rushing, me hauled roughly out, put in chains, taken below, the ship turned back to Hobart and me walked in disgrace through jeering onlookers back to Cascades.

Instead, the wide-eyed look was followed by a chuckle. Well, well, what we got here! A cuckoo in the nest. What's your name, lad? What you runnin' from, then?

I managed to whisper: Harry, sir. My mother's just died and my father don't want me.

A little more of the cover was pulled back, so I could see the amused expression on a weather-beaten face. Let's see now, he said chattily, Port Nicholson be a wee town about a thousand mile to the east, eight days' sail, but I'll bring you tucker. A tin to pee into and a couple of rags to scoop up t'other stuff and throw over the side. Oh, and they call me Paddy. But take care, boyo. The Old Man is one of the better, but no master takes kindly to finding a stranger aboard his ship.

About the second day in my hideaway, the canvas flap was lifted. I was brusquely ordered to climb out, get below. Bad weather comin', Paddy said, you can't stay here. My protest was ignored. It's not safe. We're a store ship, there are spare berths below. Trust me, boy.

Getting below was tricky as it was nearly dark, with wind screaming across the deck, the animals complaining loudly, and the ship already rocking side to side and pitching up and down like a corkscrew, a mad thing.

Awful memories of my earlier long voyage on this ship came unbidden. The dark, narrow berth Paddy led me to was tucked away on the lower deck, but mercifully not the orlop where three years earlier we had endured such misery.

It's only a ship, I told myself. Banish the ghosts! At least I was out of the wind, and, after Paddy provided a blanket, even warm. But seven more days of this . . .

21. Something must change

THE NEXT DAY I go over to Official Bay and give the old woman's potatoes to Tillie. I have no way of cooking them. She eyes the basket suspiciously. 'Where did you get these?' I reply 'Never you mind. They're freshly dug, so just enjoy them', and leave her to her interminable kneading.

The summer days come and go. I rebuild my ruined hut further up the slope, thoroughly well hidden, in case Albert again comes snooping around with evil intent. If he's killed once, perhaps twice, he can again.

Overhearing Dr Campbell boast of how he and Mr Brown lived for a time with the natives, sleeping soundly on fronds cut from big ferns, I go exploring. In a pretty gully some way inland, I find ferns like giant green umbrellas growing beneath huge trees. The doctor was right — the six fronds I drag back to my hut, plus a layer of bracken, make a far more comfortable mattress than a few rags of old canvas on the hard ground.

But I know I can't sustain this gypsy life forever. Something must change. I'm earning enough pennies to buy some food and still keep money aside for my passage home, but I'm always hungry, and have to steal a length of thin rope to keep my breeches up around my waist.

And where will I get new boots when my only pair finally fall to pieces? It might be months before a cobbler sets up shop, or boots are imported from Sydney. Please, God, before winter.

I miss the company of Tillie and, just as much, the children around in Mechanics Bay.

There is also the risk of coming unexpectedly upon my tormentors, Violet and now Albert. Gossip can start with just a whisper. Without my ever knowing, Violet might quietly hint to an official over a cup of tea that there is a young girl here in the capital who's an escaped convict from Hobart, who should be found and brought to justice. Or Albert suggest to mates over a mug of ale there is something unnaturally girlish about that messenger boy.

Besides, Commercial Bay itself has become a place of rumour and discontent. Running my errands between the bay and the headland, I hear endless complaints and criticisms.

The natives are charging too much for their produce, they're getting cheeky, their work on the raupo huts is far too slow. The sun is too hot, the nights too humid, the onshore winds too often blow out cooking fires. There is no shade, the harbour is too tidal, the delay putting in a wharf is intolerable.

Further: the allocation of the raupo huts is unfair when those arriving with abundant cash can get priority and demand a wooden floor and windows made of oiled calico or, even better, the panes of glass coming from Sydney. The camp sites are over-crowded, the rubbish and flotsam are everywhere, the drying seaweed and fish spines along the high-tide line — all stink to high heaven.

As for the officials disporting themselves around in Official Bay, what in God's name are they all doing?! That very proper and pompous surveyor-general, Mr Mathew, why is his precious town plan still not ready? Is he the reason why the land sales are now being postponed yet again, not now March but the middle of April?

After the recent threat of invasion, why are there still so few soldiers here to protect the settlement, armed with muskets that can actually be fired? Where is the governor?

Nearly every day a small vessel arrives in the harbour with more land-jobbers from Sydney and other ports in Australia, ensuring the lot prices will rise to the heavens, and increasing the fury of those already here who just want to buy a little land and settle in the new capital.

Although I enquire at every opportunity, none of the Sydney vessels want to hire a cabin boy for the return passage to New South Wales; they'll take me only if I can pay, which I can't, yet. Their vessels are too small for stowing away.

So my frustrations increase, too. Every day I also scan the canoes coming into the bay in the vain hope that one of the paddlers will be the boy from the Maraetai mission station who knows some English.

And every day I scan the harbour entrance in vain for the beautiful tall ship that will take me around the Horn and home.

I know something is afoot when my errands to and from the governor's house on the point greatly increase. The track has become smoother from its constant use by the carpenters and gardeners, but it's still a steep climb.

And now, Mr Mathew tells me one day while handing over yet another message for Captain Symonds, the track is in future to be called Shortland Crescent, after the governor's esteemed police magistrate. He has marked it on the plan he's preparing for the land sales.

'Shortland Crescent will be the capital's main thoroughfare,' he says, 'linking Commercial Bay with the governor's house, the barracks and the Trafalgar Circus. Well named, don't you think, after Nelson's famous battle? You know about that?'

'Yes, sir, I do.'

'For the circus, I have in mind the elegant curving streets of Bath, in England. Did you ever go there, boy?'

'No sir. My home is in Sussex.'

'One day you must tell me how you came to be here. Your family is around in Mechanics Bay?'

'Yes, sir.'

'Well now, off you go, lad. This message is important. We'll be welcoming the governor and his family any day now. All must be made ready.'

'Yes, sir. Are you all right, sir?'

He has risen from his stool and is coughing and swaying alarmingly.

'Yes, yes. Just tired.' Between coughs, he confides: 'I'm just weary of being confronted, day and night, often quite aggressively. "When are the land sales, Mr Mathew?" "Why taking so damn long, Mr Mathew?" "We didn't come across the friggin' Tasman — beg pardon, boy — to sit around idle, Mr Mathew!" None of them know or care that Sydney's rules require us to give three months' notice of any auction. And the governor has provided me with next to no help. I'm doing my best, y'know.'

'Of course, sir.'

After this coughing fit subsides, he adds: 'A young man who has offered assistance may be educated, but he's turning out to be rather lazy and unreliable.'

I hide a smile. That will be Albert.

He rouses himself. 'Mine is a precise calling, Harry. It requires diligence, a good head for figures. Equally, an appetite for climbing over hills and battling through thick undergrowth. I did ten years of it in New South Wales before coming here.

Mrs Mathew often came with me. She's a remarkable woman.'

'Yes, sir,' I agree.

'You would be well suited for this life, boy. You're healthy. You can read and write. What about mathematics?'

'I have some, sir.' Again, I keep a straight face. Girls doing mathematics! I'm lucky that my father taught me to read and write, and shared with me his favourite books. And I can count to a hundred.

'Well, run on now. We can talk more another time.'

I take the note, recalling how Mrs Mathew has spoken of him burying two tiny stillborn babies under a willow tree. They had no children after that. This might explain his fatherly kindness, his sad, tired eyes.

As I approach the beginning of the track, near my magic tree, I hear some shouting from up on the point.

'Look, look! Ahoy, the governor's ship!'

Arriving out of breath at the flagstaff, I can see the two-masted ship just rounding the north head of the harbour. The flag above me flies to a north-easterly, so her sails are full.

It will be a while before she anchors and a boat is lowered, so I run back to Captain Symonds' cottage to deliver my note. He's nowhere to be seen, so I try the governor's new mansion, where I find him busily instructing the remaining workers to get on tidying up the garden area, and chivvying along others who are still carrying in small items of furniture, candlesticks and boxes.

The governor's brig wasn't expected quite so soon, the captain tells me. He's puffing at a large cigar and seems, for him, unusually anxious.

'Still, we're fortunate it's such a beautiful day and all will be ready. Run down to the beach, boy, and tell Mr Mathew I'm on my way. We must give our governor the best welcome we can muster.'

But the arrival takes longer than expected. We see the brig drop anchor further down the harbour and a boat set out for the Orakei shore. From a distant chorus of men's voices carried to us on the wind, the governor must be visiting the native village there first.

Down on the beach the official party of Captain Symonds, Mr Mathew and Captain Rough waits . . . and waits — along with some new officials and their wives who arrived some days earlier, and some others I recognise as Mechanics Bay families. Quite a few natives have gathered here, too, perhaps fifty or more, men, women and some children.

Finally, the governor's boat appears and is brought alongside the reef exposed at low tide. The sailors ship their oars in smart naval style, straight upwards. The governor's slow and awkward climb from the boat reminds me of the rumours that he's a mortally sick man. Mrs Hobson in pretty bonnet, green skirt and fine boots is lifted onto the dry sand by one of the oarsmen; the four children, too. I'm surprised how young Mrs Hobson looks beside her husband.

As the official party starts up the beach towards the Shortland Crescent rise, I decide that I've seen enough saluting, bowing and handshaking for one day. Uniformed soldiers are forming a guard of honour while two of the oarsmen gamely provide a march, one banging on a small drum, the other playing a fife, but to no great effect. Nothing like the military band I once saw with my father in Hyde Park, with trumpeters, drummers and fife-players in rows abreast and one man carrying a big bass drum, all in splendid red — but I suppose it's something, the best that can be done.

Captain Hobson, in full uniform and a plumed hat, leads the way, Mrs Hobson and the children close behind, and the gentlemen and families and soldiers following. Trailing at the rear, the assembled Maoris.

I note with disgust that both Albert and Violet — with her stout little husband in tow — have positioned themselves towards the front of the procession. No doubt they're hoping for introductions and early acceptance into the governor's inner circle. Balls at government house, receptions for visiting missionaries and ships' captains. Tea with Mrs Hobson and her coterie.

But I'm soon regretting my decision not to walk with the procession. Not long after they have disappeared up the track, those of us still on the beach are alerted to the sounds of men's voices, a long chanting chorus being carried by the wind down from the flagstaff hill.

It has no melody that I can make out, but I can sense its raw power. I overhear a nearby sailor inform his mate that they're giving the governor a haka . . . explaining that it's a sort of war dance with much stomping of feet and rolling of eyes and protruding of tongues. He'd once seen it performed, up near Kororareka — and feckin' terrifying it was, too!

Annoyed to have missed this spectacle, I busy myself scavenging more scraps of wood for my hut, looking for pieces that will make the roof more water-tight. Best not to have a leaking roof when the autumn rains come. And with many of Commercial Bay's residents gone up the hill with the governor's party, my quest for food is more successful than usual.

August 1840

SEVERAL DAYS AND NIGHTS went by, I lost count. Mouse-like, I chose my moments to creep to the water closets at the dead of night; but the days dragged on interminably in my enforced confinement. Paddy brought me food for the seven days of gales it took to cross the Tasman Sea. A nasty piece o' water, he growled, but it's a westerly so makin' good time. One day more! Port Nicholson was said to be a grand wee harbour but no finger wharves yet, so we'd be puttin' down anchor.

He'd get me ashore somehow. I must be patient.

My patience was to be sorely tested. To get off this ship I was at Paddy's mercy.

Then, just as Paddy had predicted, the next day I began to recognise the routine of a ship coming to anchor: curt orders, swearing, footfalls pounding on the decks above, pots and pans clanking, always the watch bells, eventually the anchor chain. At last! Soon I would be free and back on land.

But several days passed with no sign of my being allowed ashore.

When Paddy brought me food, he never seemed to have time to stop and talk. Things clearly were not going as planned. Swinging between frustration and worry, I had no choice but to wait and trust.

Then one morning I heard something unusual — a woman's voice, then a baby's cry — and not long after there was Paddy crouching by my little nest.

We're takin' on passengers for the Waitemata, he said. About forty settlers and families who hate the never-endin' wind and the rains that kept floodin' their land. The Maoris causin' troubles.

Also, cap'n is weary of endless bitter arguments with the New

Zealand Company officials about unloading the governor's house here. We're leavin' for the Waitemata on the next tide.

But what about me? I need to get ashore, I cried. I swear I'll go mad if I have to stay cooped up here any longer.

Better idea, said Paddy, you be just one of the payin' passengers. Everyone, cap'n down, will assume you're just one of them joined to go north. I'll see you get food. And you can use the water closets anytime you like. Won't tha' be sometin now!

22. A tangled web

OFTEN IN THE DAYS leading to the land sales I have cause to wonder: do all these oh-so-important men think that a messenger boy has no ears? Nor might have quite a good memory?

On Mr Mathew's recommendation, I've become messenger boy for the governor as well as all the officials in Commercial or Official Bay. Always 'with urgency now, boy', I'm up and down Shortland Crescent several times a day, much like that yo-yo in my old toy box.

Frequently, I'm kept waiting while they finish a conversation, or hastily write a note, or sometimes even want to have a brief chat with me, usually to vent some immediate frustration or annoyance. I'm often amazed by what they tell me. I also loiter around the noisy groups of men here to buy land, all of them certain that the first sales are developing into a complete farce.

So day by day I'm probably hearing more current gossip than any one other person in the capital.

I know that some people have seen Mr Mathew's town plan. He might have had Bath in mind, but the comments being made are not charitable. Ridiculous, hasty, fanciful, ill suited to the terrain, that cobweb of streets around the Trafalgar Circus just plain silly. 'The man is a fool, a pretentious, pompous idiot.' Yet I know him to be kind, conscientious and well meaning — all this nastiness is not fair.

But the people who genuinely do want to settle here are anxious and afraid they won't be able to afford to buy their dreamed-of plot of land, because of the speculators with their deep pockets and easy credit. The land-sharks are telling each other they only need a ten percent deposit, then the trick is to divide and resell the lots quickly to find the balance and make a nice little profit on the side. Then you board the first ship leaving for Australia — that's just the ticket!

I also learn that Dr Campbell is so confident of buying a particular prime lot fronting onto Shortland Crescent that he's already building a cottage on it.

And settlers and speculators alike are all furious that the governor is allowing the government officials to secure prime lots before anyone else. There will be only a hundred and sixteen lots for sale — to an eager crowd of perhaps five or six hundred!

Of course the prices are going to be pushed up to the sky and beyond. Even a messenger boy can see that.

The preparations for the great day intensify. I'm kept running nearly from dawn to dusk, always on the lookout for Violet, Albert and now also Mr Edward Williams, the tall and handsome interpreter who I spied in the governor's party when they came ashore.

But there are some rewards: my savings are building up and I'm often offered a crust of bread. One day, while waiting for the governor's message, I'm called up to the government house veranda where Mrs Hobson is sitting with two of her children. The boy is younger than me, maybe ten or eleven and rather stout. On Mrs Hobson's lap is a child, perhaps twelve months old, although wearing that baby's frilly white dress and bonnet whether a boy or girl I can't tell.

I stop beneath the veranda and pull my cap down over my eyes. From listening to my father talk with his customers I know that English gentlewomen, although they say little when with their husbands, are often quite talkative when alone, quick-witted and sharp-eyed. Mrs Hobson, for all her amiable manner, might well discern that there's something strange about the boy on the grass below her.

So when she holds out two pairs of boys' breeches and a jacket, neatly folded, I don't immediately step forward. These are no longer needed by her son William, she says. Perhaps I'll be able to use them?

I mumble my awkward thanks, grateful beyond words. Surely, anything will be better than those I'm wearing, now grimy, the hems ragged and buttons missing?

'You're only a little older,' she says kindly, 'so they should be amply big enough. There's some wear left in them yet.'

I nod; a bashful boy wouldn't do much more than that, and nod again dutifully when she tells me how she loves this veranda, with its fine view of the harbour. And now she is settled here in the capital, she's so looking forward to receiving some hives from a mission sister in the Hokianga, to begin her very great interest in bee-keeping.

And was I present at their official arrival in the capital a few weeks back? She had not herself gone ashore for the big native welcome at Orakei, where there's a village and many hundred Maoris had gathered to perform their ritual war dance, the haka. But she hoped I'd seen the two hakas danced in their honour that day as they approached this house.

I replied no, I was detained down at the beach.

'Oh, a great pity,' she says. 'It's astonishing, the way the men chant in perfect unison, all the time jumping around with their spears, but my husband assures me the haka can also be a ritual of welcome. The missionaries have apparently been trying for many years to persuade the natives to put aside their hakas and sing hymns instead.'

'I should like to have seen the haka, ma'am,' I say, refraining from adding that I would have found the haka rather more exciting than any of the hymns I knew sung in my village church back in Sussex, endless dull verses, over and over.

'Another time perhaps,' she says. 'Is your family intent on settling here in the capital?'

'Yes, ma'am.'

'I'm pleased to hear so. My husband desires a good class of settler to help the development of a fine port and township. He says this beautiful harbour deserves no less.'

She pauses for some moments to dandle the child on her lap, but when she speaks again her voice is sombre.

'I heard . . . there's been an invasion scare in the capital? You were here? It must have been very frightening for you and your family?'

'Yes, ma'am, for a few days.' She waits for me to tell her more. 'We were told canoes and warriors might arrive any moment. The women and children all came up here on the point for two nights. Everyone was very anxious.'

She nods thoughtfully. I wonder whether, with the governor being away so much, she might be a rather lonely person, so is enjoying the chance just to sit in the sun and talk, even if only to me.

'I must confess,' she says, 'I'm taking comfort in the arrival of Major Bunbury with eighty soldiers. I believe they come from the 80th Regiment in Sydney.'

She waves at the small collection of tents that has sprung up further down the point, closer to the flagstaff. 'Soon they will build themselves a barracks and we shall all feel a little more secure. Tell me, what brought your family— Ah, here he is now!'

I'm greatly relieved that the governor has suddenly appeared, to say that his message for Mr Mathew is now ready and I should make haste. I will find the surveyor-general down in Official Bay, preoccupied with drawing up lists in preparation for the land sales. There is a surprising amount of paperwork involved.

Official Bay! Of course my heart sank, for I'm beginning to think it's only a matter of time before some incident or carelessness will lead to my undoing.

So I run down the Official Bay track — first stowing Mrs Hobson's gift under a tree root to collect later — and step out onto the sands with a great degree of wariness.

The tableau before me is my worst dream come true: from his desk strewn with papers Mr Mathew is engaged in a lively conversation with none other than Mr Williams, with Mrs Mathew nearby along with a scowling Tillie. Also present, sitting casually on the sand examining shells, is Albert, the surveyor's would-be apprentice.

I can't approach Mr Mathew without disturbing all five of the group, each with their own particular — but only partial — knowledge of the girl Harriet and the boy Harry.

At a loss, I linger at some distance, hoping that Mr Mathew will notice me and come over to receive his message. But no, when he sees me he beckons me into the circle, and I've no choice but to step forward.

'This is Harry, our excellent messenger,' he says cheerfully, addressing Mr Williams. 'With so much activity before the sales, he's doing a grand job running hither and yon. Aren't you, boy? Fleet of foot, polite and reliable.'

I hear a splutter from Tillie, turned quickly into a cough. From the corner of my eye, I see Albert alter his lounging position to stare directly up at me, an insolent grin on his face.

'From the governor, sir,' I mutter, expecting that the note will be taken and I can quickly flee from here. But Mr Mathew is more interested in continuing his exchange with the interpreter.

'I suppose there will be natives attending the sales?' he asks.

'That's very likely,' Mr Williams replies. 'They're certainly curious. Of course you're already aware, the Maoris have no concept of one person's sole ownership of land to do with as he chooses. The tribes constantly negotiate rights to fish or grow food.'

'I am aware,' says Mr Mathew stiffly, slightly offended. We all know that he was up at Waitangi last year when they signed the treaty, and would have heard all the debating about land that went on for several days.

'But you saw how many came to greet the governor,' says Mr Williams. 'He's well liked among the Maoris. Before his official arrival here, something like a thousand gathered at the Orakei beach to welcome him. He was honoured with a great haka.'

'They can't be . . . dissuaded?' asks Mr Mathew. 'There are some rough elements among the arrivals in Commercial Bay. On the day, they might not appreciate a native presence.'

'But there must also be some better-class arrivals?' enquires Mr Williams. I note that he doesn't answer Mr Mathew's absurd question; surely the natives can't be 'dissuaded' from attending the sales? Why should they be?

'I ask,' Mr Williams continues, 'because I've heard that the Fairburns want to expand their native school at the Maraetai mission.'

'Mr Mathew and I have been there twice,' says Mrs Mathew, a touch smugly. 'Last year, on our voyage around the gulf on the *Ranger*. I well remember Miss Fairburn's little school. The native children were singing their A B C to "God Save the Queen". One doesn't forget that in a hurry!'

Mr Williams smiles, humouring her. 'The Fairburns are wondering, when the land sales are over, if there might be one or two younger Christian men agreeable to remaining here. With them, I mean, at Maraetai, to teach English at their native school.'

'We can always ask,' says Mr Mathew, a touch dubiously. He looks down at Albert.

'Albert, would you consider doing this important work? It's highly desirable that the native population acquires some knowledge of English. But of course,' he adds hastily, 'that's only if you find land surveying not to your liking.'

Albert is quick to reply. 'Alas, good sir, not cut out to be a missionary. Nor a teacher, God help me. I've no great sympathy for children and their perverse and grubby ways. I'm the third son of a large and disorderly family, with far too many younger siblings. I'm not over-endowed with patience.'

He languidly throws shells into the water, hoping to make them bounce along the surface.

After a pause, Mr Williams says, 'There is also . . . No, it's of no importance. A long shot.'

'Continue please, Mr Williams.' I'm longing to hand over my note and swiftly leave, but Mr Mathew is determined to hear the interpreter out.

'They've been told of a young English girl, around fourteen or so who . . . well, you might say has shown unusual interest in the natives here, building huts and so on. A female teacher would be just as welcome.'

'That young English girl would be Harriet,' says Mrs Mathew briskly. 'She may be found in Commercial Bay, or perhaps has left the capital altogether. I wouldn't know. She's rather . . . forward.'

I dare not look at either Tillie or Albert, both no doubt enjoying this scene and, especially, my discomfort. I'm not having to *act* the part of a gawky boy not knowing where to put his feet.

'Come to think of it, I might have met her myself,' says Mr Williams. 'A lively lass. We were watching Dr Campbell and the natives trading pigs. She wanted me to ask him how she could earn some money.'

'That would be her,' sniffs Mrs Mathew. 'We knew Harriet for only a short time. She's not well suited to colonial life. Frankly, I wasn't sorry to see her go.'

I interrupt in my deepest voice. 'Please, sir, Mr Mathew, is there any message for the governor in return?'

He now takes the note from me and quickly scans it. 'No, just tell him I'll be at the Government Store soon after daybreak tomorrow.'

'Yes, sir. G'day, sir. Thankee, sir.'

I'm off up the track like a streak of lightning.

Later, needing to rest my aching legs, I'm nestled comfortably between the gnarled trunks of my favourite tree, the Christmas one. I can't be seen from the track below, but I have a clear view of the whole sweep of Commercial Bay.

It's the eve of the land sales, therefore the beach and foreshore are crowded with land-jobbers' tents, hundreds of noisy, eager men gossiping, shouting, singing, probably drunk. Smaller boats from all of the vessels anchored out in the stream are lined up along the shoreline. The house builders and sawyers haven't yet stopped work for the night.

Tomorrow the auctions will begin. I know from Mr Mathew

that a man from Sydney has put himself forward as an experienced auctioneer. It will all be done calmly, properly, with decorum, befittingly from the front veranda of government house.

The light is fading. I should get down from here and find my shelter. It's so well hidden that I must find it before nightfall. Lanterns and fires are being lit on the beach below. It looks quite festive, a carnival even.

But I don't think I'm imagining the tension in the air. Men down there are dreaming of sudden riches. How many of them, I ponder, would Mr Williams describe as 'better-class', good Christian men suitable as mission teachers?

And here's the puzzle: who told the Fairburns about the 'young English girl' who would be welcome at their mission station? On the strength of that single meeting on the beach when those native women brought fish, was it the paddler who speaks English?

Wouldn't it actually be quite an adventure, teaching in a native school, learning their language and their songs, paddling a canoe, making friends — one in particular?

But as I climb down, hungry and weary, another day escaping detection, I know there's only one life I truly want, and it's not here.

If I can find a ship soon, I'll be close to sixteen when I arrive. It might be autumn, or the dead of winter and snow on the ground. Somehow I'll get myself to our village from wherever the ship docks, walk the whole way home in my bare and blistering feet if I have to. I'll pass the baker shop, the grocer, the butcher and the church, and turn onto the path lined with bushes of holly. I'll catch my breath a moment, then knock on the oak door.

I see her, the dawning recognition on her face, the disbelief, her outburst of joy and love, feel her arms around me. She smells sweetly, of the lavender water she likes to make. Her blue eyes are brimming over with tears. She gently pinches my cheeks to check that I am real. She has lost me for five years, now I am found. My precious wee Sparrow, she whispers.

She'll pull me into the warmth of the kitchen, and later sing me to sleep in my own bed in the tiny room at the top of the stairs.

Lavender's green, dilly dilly, lavender's blue . . .

September 1840

SO, LIKE IT OR NOT, I was now a passenger on the *Platina* bound for the Waitemata.

After so many days hidden away, I climbed on deck to a whole new world of sunshine, fluffy clouds against blue skies, circling birds. We were leaving a wide harbour enclosed by many hills, with a small island in the middle. Even in sunlight, it was a bleak place, the heights practically bare of trees. Ahead, waves broke over a reef guarding a narrow passage to the open sea.

Oh, the sweet feeling of release: fresh, clean air, sun on my cheeks, lightness of spirit, even if the wind had a cutting edge to it.

But this was different to our miserable arrival in Hobart. For the first time since leaving London, I was actually free! No chains around my ankles, no prospect of being locked up and my body and spirit broken. I had no further plan, but once we got to the Waitemata I did have a choice. As long as no one ever recognised me from Cascades, I could begin again.

Meantime all I had to do was remember I'm Harry, I joined in Port Nicholson, I'm not a talkative sort. And best keep out of the way of the sailor who saw a boy climb aboard in Hobart with a satchel.

But of course I was curious to meet my protector, Paddy. Around noon, when we had cleared the high headlands guarding the harbour, an older sailor came to lean alongside me on the railings. Grey hair in a pigtail, well-worn clothes, calloused hands, bare feet. Those kindly eyes.

For a while we watched the birds and the rocky coast slide past. He was but fifteen, he began, when he also stowed away. On a collier, Belfast to London, desperate to escape a brutal father and not a penny to his name. He'd hid in the anchor chain locker, and feckin' 'orrible it was, too. The Irish Sea in middle of winter was no place to be. No one knew he was there. He didn't eat for a week. But it was worth it — he got a job in a shipyard soon after, and married a black-haired colleen the year after that.

Harriet would have given him a huge hug, but Harry can't, can only stammer out his thanks.

You can keep the same berth, he said. All is above-board now. Cap'n reckons about eight days up the coast to the Waitemata. He thinks this good weather will hold.

23. Foolishness

SOMETHING IS DIFFERENT WHEN I wake the next morning. Curled up in my makeshift shelter, I've grown used to the night-time noises of twigs snapping, a bird that might be an owl, gusts of wind whistling through the bracken. Occasionally, in a northerly, I'll hear men's shouts or singing carried up from the beach camp or anchored ships.

But these voices are quite close, and continuous. My hut, though well hidden, is maybe only fifty yards in a direct line from the track. I realise that these are the sounds of the men trudging up Shortland Crescent, dozens of them.

Of course, they're gathering for the land sales, early birds anticipating front-row places for the thrilling prospect of becoming rich land-owners — and the sun not even risen over Rangi-toto.

As I chew on the piece of dry bread kept for breakfast, I decide there'll be no work for me today. Everybody will be up at government house. But definitely, I'm not going to miss out on the excitement; I might even change into William Hobson's cast-off breeches and jacket in honour of the occasion. I'll need to be extra careful, though, not get too close to certain people among the crowd.

'Ahoy, Harry! There you are!' I've been hoping to slip unnoticed into the procession winding up the track, but my luck is out.

I turn to see the trim figure of Captain Rough behind me. Even at this hour of the morning he's wearing his usual white kid gloves.

'Mornin', Cap'n.'

'Mr Mathew wants to see you on the governor's veranda. He was looking for you yesterday, all afternoon.'

In truth, after my close shave at Official Bay, I'd been kept waiting most of the afternoon, with a manservant appearing at intervals to say His Excellency was feeling poorly, but I was to remain at my post. A housemaid came out onto the veranda with the three younger Hobson children, but, with a sharp glance in my direction, made it clear that they were not to talk to the lowly messenger boy. I didn't mind, but took pleasure in listening to their singing games about oranges and lemons, London Bridge falling down and the like, imagining myself back playing with friends on the village green.

'Well, m'lad, get yourself up to the house at the double. I think he has a job for you.'

A job! Today, it won't be panting up and down the tracks, for sure. I quicken my pace, darting between the groups of hopeful buyers.

On the crest of the ridge, I stop, noting that the column of men is winding around to the front of the governor's house. There, they stand shoulder to shoulder, an expectant, jostling mob keen for action. I have never seen such a crowd, not even in London — perhaps nine hundred, not counting a large group of natives, mostly men, who must have come up the Official and Mechanics Bay tracks, or taken an inland path.

No familiar faces among them that I can see. They stand behind the picket fence, leaning on sticks, still and silent, just watching. Who knows what they're making of this unruly scene.

Up on the veranda, I spy Mr Mathew leaning over the railing, scanning the crowd, looking anxious. Behind him is a knot of men, talking with much waving of hands. Several tables have been placed, chairs, carafes of drinking water, and an easel with a large-scale plan showing the lots to be auctioned. I guess the portly giant with the black top hat and imposing side whiskers to be the auctioneer from Sydney. He looks impatient to get started.

'You wanted to see me, Mr Mathew.'

'Harry! Yes, yes, come up here. I've work for you today.'

'Yes, sir,' I reply, stepping up to the veranda to await instructions. The large easel provides a convenient screen between me and any interested parties among the throng below.

'You see this crowd!' he says. 'You say you can write?'

'Yes, sir, I can.'

'So listen carefully. As each lot is sold, you will go promptly to the successful bidder and write his name carefully on this sheet. Check the spelling, of course, and remind him that the sale is null and void unless he reports immediately, that's *immediately* at close of day to the official record-keeper seated over there. Failure to report, his bid will be forfeit and the lot put back into the auction for the morrow.'

He waves a hand at a scribe seated at a table. 'This is government work. It is important that we keep the most meticulous records.'

'Me, sir?' I'm not keen on this prospect, having to push through crowds that will surely somewhere contain Albert, Violet and her little husband, Mr Williams, and most likely Mrs Mathew, too. 'Can't you ask your assistant Albert to do this, sir?'

'Albert? That lazy and arrogant dandy is no longer my assistant. No, I trust you, Harry. And there'll be a small purse for your efforts.' Behind us, from one of the inner rooms comes a peal of laughter, a woman's. Turning, I get a glimpse of a figure in lavender silk. 'By the way, if one of the lots is sold to a woman, no need to get her name. She's Lady Franklin, Lady Jane, visiting us from Van Diemen's Land. Her husband, Sir John, is the governor there. She told Mrs Mathew she is desirous of purchasing a lot or two. Apparently she is a keen buyer of real estate in and around Hobart.'

Lowering his voice, he adds: 'She must be fifty or so, but we've found her *très formidable*. Very, well, particular! She's just back from a trip into the Waikato with Captain Hobson, carried a good deal of the way on a sedan chair. An injured foot, I believe. She's said to be a most determined traveller. As is my dear wife . . . Ah, I forget myself. Off you go, Harry, I trust you to do your part well.'

I'm grateful, of course, for his trust and his money, but the very mention of Van Diemen's Land and Lady Franklin has sent a shiver down my spine. I'm filled with foreboding. Mr Mathew has no idea of the risks he's asking me to take.

By the time the sun is high in the sky, I have identified where each of my 'friends' are standing, and it's obvious the auctions are not going to Mr Mathew's plan, calmly and with decorum.

They start smoothly enough. In his booming voice the auctioneer calls out each lot number and its dimensions, pointing with a stick to the site on the town plan.

The initial figures, yelled out from the crowd before the auctioneer has even stopped speaking, quickly rise, and rise, and continue rising, until one by one bidders fall away, two or three are left, finally only one — then the big man's gavel comes down on the table — *WHACK* — so hard it makes the scribe's ink bottles and glasses of water jump about.

'Sold to the gentleman in the brown cap!'

'Sold to the gentleman in the straw hat with the fancy red ribbon!'

'Sold to the gentleman holding aloft a crooked walking stick!'

But what I hear as I slip like a pickpocket through the crush to list each buyer's name are not cries of victory nor respectful clapping. Instead, there's a low rumble of discontent pierced by louder shouts of dismay and protest. I'm aware of scuffles, threats being made, people talking and gesturing angrily at each other, while others form clusters around them to show support or opposition.

Still more others are complaining that with all this racket the auctioneer and the bids can't be heard.

'Harry!' I'm standing on the veranda as the auctioneer turns his back on the crowd to take a long swig from a silver hip flask, probably whisky. He looks flustered, his cheeks rosy and the papers in his hands shaking. Captain Symonds is beckoning me. 'Harry, come here!'

I slink over to his desk. He's also looking uneasy. 'Tell me, boy. What are they saying down there? What's all this noise about?'

I'm surprised he has to ask. 'Sir, the prices are much too high. Everyone knows that the Australian people only want to re-sell for a big, fat profit. They're winning the bids. Some people are buying two or even three lots.'

'There's not much we can—'

'The people who want to settle here, sir, they haven't got that sort of money. They're missing out and getting very angry.'

'What about the scuffles? What's causing those?'

'They're saying there aren't enough lots for sale. And Mr Mathew has made them far too big—'

'But he's very—'

'—big enough to be cut in half. So the unhappy settlers who've missed out are pressing the sharks to sell them half, right now, on the spot.'

Captain Symonds looks thoughtful. 'God knows, we can do with the money. London has kept us woefully short of funds. The governor will no doubt be pleased.'

'Then he's—' I stop myself from saying then he's a fool, but decide there is something more the captain needs to know.

'And some people are also really angry that the government officials are bidding. There's Lieutenant Shortland, Mr Mason, Dr Johnson. Mr Mathew, too. They're saying land's already been put aside for them. Prime land, in the best spots, like Official Bay. And getting it cheap.'

'Well, yes, that was the governor's doing.'

Again I bite my tongue. How can grown men with fancy titles and plumed hats be so *stupid*! So blind and unaware and uncaring of how ordinary people think. And I'm giving Captain Symonds only the polite version. The language down among the crowd is terrible.

'Even Dr Campbell is upset,' I continue, since he has asked for my opinion. 'More than upset. He was outbid for the land he's already put a house on.'

'Well to do that was probably unwise, don't you think?'

'Sir, not my place.'

Thankfully, our increasingly uncomfortable conversation is brought to an end. The auctioneer has stopped wiping his moist lips and put away his kerchief, ready for the next round.

As the final lots come up, the frenzy gathers pace, as does the discontent. When the last bid for a prime lot halfway up Shortland Crescent is called, the outcry from the crowd is louder than ever.

'Sir, that price is outrageous!'

'Yer ain't got the money!'

'Ya greedy bastard!'

As the top-hatted giant bellows the customary words — 'Going once . . . going twice . . . *sold* — to the big man in the tartan tam-o'-shanter, thank you, thank you, thank you, most generous sir!' — I note to my dismay that he's pointing to the area of the crowd where I know both Violet and Albert are standing, and which up until now I've managed to avoid.

WHACK! Down comes the gavel, bouncing the water carafe right off the desk to shatter on the wooden decking. Doing my job, I leap off the veranda in search of the man with the tartan tam-o'-shanter.

He's not hard to find among the crush. Clearly he's not popular among the Commercial Bay crowd.

'Friggin' Scotsman!' 'Mind yer purses, lads!' 'Already a bankrupt, don't ya know!' And another Scot yelling 'Yer bum's oot the windae, ya friggin' bampot!' Meaning, I'm guessing, he's a half-wit, an idiot.

When I reach the object of derision, two things are obvious. One, the Scot has already had a drink or two — enough to now be dancing a triumphant highland fling, jumping up and down like a jack-in-the-box, arms curved upwards, toes pointed, sporran jingling in time, whooping with joy.

'Och aye — a braw day! I say, a bonnie braw day for the Scots!' He's a Scottish version of the grinning and nasty Mr Punch I remember at the market.

And second, the natives standing behind the picket fence are trying to hold back their giggles, but not very successfully. Their bare chests are rippling with supressed laughter, and I hear a few snorts of mirth.

I begin 'Please sir, your name, for the record', but Mr Tam-o'-Shanter's attention appears to have shifted from the auction to elsewhere. He's still dancing, but moving purposefully, aggressively, towards the nearest Maoris, his voice rising as he gets closer.

Why is this odious savage laughing, how dare he mock and laugh and sneer at a white man? Similar challenges and insults follow, about his flat nose and fat lips, his stupid tattoos, his unwashed smell, his grass skirts and gobbledook language and his stone-age dumb violence — until I can stand it no longer.

Mr Tam-o'-Shanter is twice my size and the native being insulted is equally burly, but as I jump between them I don't care.

'You can't talk to him or anyone like that. It's not right! He's a father, a good, kind man!' For I have recognised one of them as the native who had brought a kite for little Thomas, shown him how to fly it. At Thomas's burial he had pressed noses with the boy's father.

Not only that. A younger man has pushed to the front of the group and caught my eye — and, glory be, it's the paddler who speaks some English, and probably enough to now know how offensive and nasty these words are.

'Show some *respect*!' I yell, aware I'm blushing scarlet.

'So, respect, is it? Kowtowing, is it? And who sez, yer feckin' wee pipsqueak?' The Scotsman stops his dancing up and down and looks around for support. 'We got ourselves a nigger-lover 'ere, folks, 'ave we not? Who needs some educatin'!'

The first blow lands on my cheekbone, the second on my chest, sending me staggering. I think I hear a few cheers, the uppity boy being taught a lesson. I try to duck, but despite being tipsy he's surprisingly nimble for his size. As a third punch lands heavily on my nose, I register that the paddler and the kite man and other grim-faced natives are halfway over the picket fence and that behind his shaggy gingery beard my assailant is smiling with glee, fists up like a boxer as I take the blow and fall to the ground.

Blood is pouring from my nose, my head is spinning, and I brace myself for a vicious kick to my curled-up body.

It never comes.

'Stop that, you mad Scottish bully!' cries a voice I vaguely know. 'Stop it now! That's a girl! You can't beat up a slip of a girl like that!'

And another voice I know rather better, singing out over the crowd noises in triumphant malice. She's been waiting, longing for her opportunity — and now it has arrived.

'And not just any girl. That's Harriet, a convict. She's an escaped convict from Hobart!'

It's quite odd, but as I lie on the rough grass curled up like a broad bean, I'm thinking about boots. My father's voice is saying 'Always note a person's footwear. New or down-at-heel, plain or fancy, polished or scuffed — they tell you something.'

Through swollen eyes I can make out many legs and all types of boots, mostly plain, mostly well worn. I think the shiny brand-new black ones closest to me with the higher heels are the Scotsman's — ah yes, a vain man wanting to appear taller.

And look there, a pair of women's boots, bright red, pointed and showy. And over there, by the picket fence, the natives' brawny calves and wide, bare feet, those leathery heels planted into the ground.

And the noise, that general rumble of angry male voices, numbers being shouted, back and forth. Ah yes, it's an auction and I have a job; I'm supposed to be writing down names. The crowd won't yet be aware of the incident taking place towards the back, close to the picket fence. They don't yet realise a riot is about to break out, if the Scotsman keeps mouthing his vile insults and the paddler and the kite man and their friends choose to take offence. There could well be a nasty brawl or even a war, and it will be all my fault.

I must get up, stop my nose bleeding, confront the man who has betrayed Harry but probably also saved him from being killed or crippled for life. And confront the woman who has told the world Harriet's darkest secret, which in this entire country only she knows. She and perhaps that bandy-legged wee husband with his waxed moustache and chest full of medals.

But as I raise my head to look them both in face, I find I'm actually smiling. What I'm feeling at this moment is mostly sheer relief.

Now I'm freed of the need for pretence, daily living an untruth, always fearful of betrayal and the shame and fury that comes with it. I'm Harriet, female and proud of it. I did a boy's work, day in and day out, rain or shine, and no one suspected. I did it better than a boy. The 'weaker sex'? Whichever pompous male said that can't have been more wrong.

And as for being a convict, I dare anyone to stand here and say that seven years for taking an apple is fair and just.

As I stagger to my feet, I'm suddenly feeling foolish in William Hobson's cast-off breeches. I'm just acting in one of the parlour games my mother delighted in us playing on cosy winter nights. Yet my battered body is telling my logical mind that there's an easy way to stop the pretence, the humiliation and the pain.

Harriet, you must run like the wind down to the end of the point where the British flag is flying, spread your arms out wide and just keep going. The cliff there is high enough.

September 1840

ON THE SECOND DAY out, the *Platina* turned north and I began to understand why sailors endure the storms and bad times at sea.

These were the good times. A south-westerly was blowing us fast up the coast. The sails were full, the ship humming. The decks were quite stable, so for most the nausea lasted only a day. The crew seemed relaxed, the families happy to sit on deck. Some of the wives brought up knitting and sewing to do, the men chatted in groups or played cards. The children looked mostly subdued, bewildered, although two boys, rascals a bit younger than me, delighted in chasing each other and teasing the girls. None of them was curious about me.

I spent most of the daylight hours alone on deck, watching how the ship cut a glittering white bow-wave through the blue ocean. Birds wheeled overhead, various sorts of gulls and cormorants. Groups of dolphins appeared from time to time, and once I heard the lookout shouting 'Whales! Lookee thar, whales to starboard!' Maybe four, they were close enough for us to see their curving mottled grey backs and how their flukes cut so cleanly through the water when they dived.

I worked out that the sailor who might connect me with the messenger boy who'd delivered a satchel in Hobart was the cook's mate, so he was nearly always down in the galley.

Don't worry, Paddy said when I told him. He owes me a favour. He won't blab.

24. Flight

THE CROWD HAS BACKED away, leaving me swaying on my feet, facing Albert, Violet and the Scotsman. My kite friend and the paddler, no doubt mystified by this turn of events, have retreated back into the protection of their silent and watchful group.

The auction goes on around us, while we four stare at each other, trying to make sense of the deceits that have just been laid bare. Albert is the first to find his voice.

'See here, Harry, or whatever your name is,' he says, 'it was either I tell your secret or watch that obnoxious Scotsman kill you. I've no stomach for seeing a girl being assaulted, damn it.'

He turns to my assailant, who is being restrained by four or five other men. 'You're a drunken brute, sir, a bully with a nasty and ignorant tongue on you. Even if the kid was a boy . . . You are despicable!'

I gape at him, astonished. I, and only I, know that this is a smooth-talking dandy, a pervert who has fled England suspected of two murders, now gallantly rescuing a 'boy' he has himself tried several times to molest.

'Here, take this,' he continues, holding out a kerchief. 'That's a nasty nose-bleed. Your nose might be broken.' Turning back to the bearded Scotsman, he snarls, 'Shame on you, sir! You are no gentleman.'

Violet is not to be outdone. Today it seems so apt that, to match those flashy boots, she has chosen to wear a dress of bright red, the colour of fire and danger. At her most strident, she tells the circle: 'Not him. Save your breath — he's not the villain here. That girl had it coming. She deserves no sympathy. She's not just an imposter.'

Dramatically pointing at me with a bony finger, she looks more than ever like a pantomime witch.

'A convict is what she really is! Escaped from the Cascades Female Factory near Hobart Town.'

Her audience of men — the Scotsman and those trying to restrain him, even Albert — gasp and recoil as one. Horror of horrors, a convict! Worse, an *escaped* convict! A wretched degenerate child found guilty of an unspeakable crime, thrown out of Mother England to rot and hopefully die in a distant colony. No matter her age: a bad egg, a vixen, and probably now and always a whore.

'And how do you know this, Mrs Godfrey?' I ask, willing myself to stay calm, even though my heart is pounding in my chest and my cheeks are crimson with shame.

Her smug reply is addressed not to me, but to the whole group of fascinated onlookers.

'Hah, only too well!'

'Oh? Please tell us, how well?' Caught up in the pleasure she is taking in publicly denouncing me, she seems to have forgotten I still hold a card in this trading of secrets. Or perhaps she knows that any accusation I make she can simply deny. Her word, and that of the puffed-up corporal, against mine.

'My good husband, the corporal here — when we lived in Hobart, he had dealings with Cascades. He supervised the soldiers sent to work there.'

'Oh my word!' I manage a crooked smile and a small bow in his direction.

'You were serving a seven-year sentence. You escaped, somehow. It reflected badly on him.'

She tugs at her husband's arm, urging his nod of agreement.

'It wasn't hard,' I say, to annoy them both.

'But, madam, she had you fooled here, too,' chuckles Albert, 'what with her running around in boys' attire for weeks and weeks.'

Violet retorts, 'As she equally fooled you, sir, about her criminal past.'

'I just didn't mention it,' I say. 'Why would I? Why would anyone? . . . Why would *you*, Violet?' But in her determination to make the most of her moment, Violet doesn't register the threat, barely pauses for breath.

'Cascades knew you as a troublemaker, an insolent and cunning child. God knows how you've survived this long, but mark my words, missie, your luck ends here. Corporal Godfrey, do your—'

She is interrupted by a sudden roar from the crowd. The auctioneer's voice strains to be heard over the din.

'Lot Ten, going once . . . nineteen perches, at three hundred and fifteen pounds, thirteen shillings . . . going once . . . going twice . . . GONE! To Lieutenant Willoughby Shortland!' The conclusion of this sale elicits an even louder roar of protest.

I welcome the Scotsman's attention going elsewhere. 'Ya greedy walloper, Shortland!' he bellows. 'A fuckin' scandal! Should'na be allowed!'

Freed from restraint he begins to leap about and shake his fist in the direction of the government house veranda.

But I'm barely registering any of this. As Corporal Godfrey moves purposefully towards me, and Violet folds her arms and smirks, I know I have only one option.

Fear gives me the wings to leap clear over the picket fence. And oh, during my short career as a messenger boy how well I've learned to dart and dodge my way through crowds.

I reckon on Albert not bothering to come after me, nor Violet in her silly red-heeled boots, nor the drunken Scotsman who can barely stand up. Only Corporal Godfrey with his short little legs might set off in pursuit.

Besides, I know the tracks between the bays better than anyone. As I run across the roughly cleared ground, a glance behind tells me that I've already outrun him, and can turn without being seen onto the second pathway down to Official Bay. No one ever seems to use it but me. It is narrow, rocky and steep in places, criss-crossed by tangled tree roots, but I fly downwards over all obstacles.

I know Mr Mathew will be all day at the auction, and all the other officials, too, along with the native group. And I'd spotted Mrs Mathew with Lady Franklin on the veranda looking down on the proceedings, a pair of pretty birds in their fine gowns and bonnets.

That leaves my last hope, Tillie, in Official Bay. As usual, there she is, hunched over the big marquee table, kneading bread dough.

'Holy mother of God!' She backs away from the table, and I see her hand reaching behind her for a large kitchen knife. 'Be gone, boy! Scram!'

I realise she doesn't recognise me, and being alone in the bay feels threatened by this breathless apparition with its bloodied clothes, and swollen and bruised face. I'd fallen heavily against a sharp rock on the way down the track, so am now bleeding badly from one knee, too.

'I don't need a haircut today, thank you,' I say, taking off the cap which of late has become rather necessary to hide my curls. 'I'm growing it again.'

'What? What's this talk about haircuts?' She's found the knife and is brandishing it at me. 'Get ye gone, ragamuffin. There's nothing for you here. If you want food get it elsewhere.'

'Tillie, I'm . . . I'm Harriet . . . no more Har—'

I must have fainted onto the soft sand warmed by the afternoon sun. A hand is urgently patting my face, but I just want to sleep.

'Harriet? Oh, Harriet — wake up! Wake up! Oh Lordy, I thought you'd died.'

'Maybe better if I had,' I mumble.

'What nonsense! Don't say such things. What's happened to you?'

'You know Harry is me, Harriet.'

'I know a silly goose called Harriet who can't hold her tongue. "Not well suited to colonial life" Mrs Mathew says. So what have you done this time?'

'I can't stay here. I can't go back to . . .' I can't stop the tears nor say the word.

'Why not here? Why can't you stay? Back to where? Look, I don't care what Mrs Mathew says, you're injured and thin and dirty and you need proper, clean clothes. Girls' clothes! You need to stay here.'

'She won't let me. I'm being chased and sooner or later they'll find me. I'll be put back in leg irons and taken back to—'

'Oh, don't talk such nonsense. She mightn't like the way you talk about the natives, but—'

'It's not that.'

'What then?'

'I never told you.'

'Never told me what?' She is now quite cross with me. 'Told me *what*?'

'About . . . Cascades.' There, I've said it.

'What cascades? There's only one waterfall around here.'

'No, Cascades: a prison close to Hobart. For female convicts . . . sent from England. I'm . . .'

As I expect, she can't help herself. Just like the men reacting to Violet's proclamation earlier, she recoils. 'You're a *convict*? You?'

'Worse than that: I escaped. After that . . . I told you my mother sold my hair for wigs so we could eat . . . that she died in Hobart . . . It was all lies . . . My mother is back in Sussex—'

'Tillie!' We are both startled by a new voice from the direction of the track. 'Tillie? What's the matter? What are you doing?'

Tillie scrambles to her feet, leaving me again curled up and protecting my head, the bloody wound on my knee now thickly coated with sand.

'I thought you were attending the land sales, ma'am,' says Tillie curtly. She sounds aggrieved, but Mrs Mathew is too flustered to notice.

'I was indeed. But, dear me, with all those cunning speculators winning the bids, it's a calamity. The prices are outrageous — they're saying more expensive even than London, would you believe? — and Mr Mathew is being most unfairly blamed. Some terrible things are being shouted at him. At the other officials, too. I simply couldn't bear it any longer. What must Lady Franklin be thinking of us? And there was some sort of ugly disturbance at the back of the crowd, too.'

I hear the crunch of her boots coming closer. 'Who's this?'

'It's Harriet,' says Tillie.

'Harriet! What's she doing here? Curled up like that! Heavens above, dressed in short breeches?'

I find myself ignoring Mrs Mathew, instead pathetically clutching at Tillie's skirts.

'Tillie, you must listen, please. My wicked brother let me take the blame for stealing an apple from a cart. A judge sent me to Australia, for seven years. At the Cascades Female Factory there are three hundred convicts. I was the youngest there, barely eleven.'

I hear Mrs Mathew gasp, give a small cry, perhaps of distress.

'For being defiant, I got solitary confinement. Bread and water for weeks on end. They shaved my hair off and mocked me. I watched babies die, corpses thrown over the wall. I saw guards beat up women, call them foul names. Some lost their minds, even hurt themselves. I knew girls who were bullied and tortured in all sorts of ways. And some who were raped, many times over.'

They're both staring at me, horrified.

'An old warden called Martha took pity and helped me escape, gave me some money and some boys' clothes. I lived like a rat. In Hobart I stowed away on the same ship that took me away from England three years earlier . . . The *Platina* . . .'

They wait for me to compose myself sufficiently to continue.

'In Port Nicholson a kind sailor helped me. We arrived here just before your ship, remember? You know the rest. At least, you do, Tillie.'

They're still gazing at me, speechless, as my voice gets stronger.

'And now my secrets are out, which is actually quite a relief, but Corporal Godfrey doing his duty must put me in chains. I will be sent on a ship back to Cascades. I'd rather die.'

'Don't even—' begins Mrs Mathew, but I'm beyond comfort.

'I swear before God I will never *ever* be taken back to that place. If he catches me, as soon as the ship has left the harbour I'll throw myself over the side. I swear to God I will!'

I let Tillie's skirt fall, hoist myself upright and head unsteadily for the shoreline. It's high tide, and the harbour waters are calm, a glistening mirror of indigo. Small ships lie at anchor, and a few canoes paddle towards Commercial Bay with their produce. The peace and beauty of the scene and the futility of my life set me weeping afresh.

Where will — where can — I go? What will become of me? I've no future here, a stain on my name, and not enough money for a ship to take me home. And if by some miracle I do manage to get back to England? What then? To live in hiding, forever afraid of discovery . . . Surely best to just walk into the water now and finish it? Just let go . . .

I feel arms go around my waist, know that two figures are standing on either side of me, close by, propping me up.

Tillie says: 'What's happened? Why are you telling us this now?'

Mrs Mathew says: 'My poor child. Who has hurt you? And for pity's sake, why?'

'You'd have found out soon enough,' I say. 'The disturbance you heard, Mrs Mathew: that was a drunk Scotsman insulting some natives . . . Yes, I know what you're thinking: yes, I did . . . But then, that isn't the worst of it . . .'

'Go on, dear,' says Mrs Mathew softly, as tears overwhelm me.

'The Scotsman was hitting me, and two people there took their chances, and told my secrets. Albert was stopping him beating me, by protesting I'm a girl — he'd guessed . . .'

'I applaud him for that, even though my husband thought him unreliable and devious,' begins Mrs Mathew.

'Yes, but he's a sailor from the *Platina* who twice tried to molest me in my hammock, and another time, right here, he stalked me. It was night and . . . he would have . . .'

'When disguised as a boy?' exclaims Mrs Mathew. 'Dear God! And the other?'

'Violet — that's Mrs Godfrey, to you — she was at Cascades, too. Like me, a convict. But she was known as a bully and a snitch. When they ordered my hair shaved off, she offered to do it. She *enjoyed* doing it.'

I hear them both cry out with disgust. Tillie says, 'I knew that woman was nasty and mean, and dangerous, too. So she's known about you all along?'

'Yes, but she never guessed I was Harry the messenger boy. Until Albert . . . So you see, I can't stay here.'

'Nonsense,' says Mrs Mathew. 'You're safe here with us, for the time being. Not many people visit Official Bay these days. If they do, they need not see you. I can deal with Mr Mathew. Now, you must get out of those clothes . . .'

'Mrs Hobson gave them to me,' I sniff. 'Cast-offs, from William Hobson.'

'Gracious! Your story gets stranger by the minute,' she smiles.

'I thought you'd . . . I'm a convict. You sent me away once, I expected you'd . . . You don't like me. You hate me. You think I'm scum. And now you've been proven right: I'm a liar, a criminal.'

'My dear girl, your sympathy for the natives is one thing. Your story of injustice and extreme cruelty is quite another.'

They are escorting me across the sand towards the marquee when Tillie suddenly gives a cry and sprints ahead. She has forgotten about setting her bread dough to rise.

I think I've died and gone to heaven. Sharing Tillie's cot, I'm cosy and comfortable for the first time in months, snuggling into her warm back, two spoons again. I've had a decent supper, as much pork and potatoes as I can eat. And I can still taste the sweetness of my first fruit since leaving England, a ripe yellow peach picked from a native orchard, perhaps the Orakei gardens I visited under the Milky Way, a shooting star to guide me.

Towards the last of the daylight, sneaking over to Commercial Bay like two thieves, Tillie and I had retrieved my canvas bag from the shelter. All my precious possessions — Mrs Fry's Bible, the pouch of coins, Paddy's scrimshaw — are there.

So I'm back in skirts (to be sure warmer than short breeches), and I'm drifting off to sleep to the tinkling sound of Mrs Mathew's piano, the one I saw a long time ago being brought ashore by sailors from the *Anna Watson*. That's a Chopin prelude, murmurs Tillie. She plays Chopin when she's upset, to calm herself after an argument with Mr Mathew.

But that wasn't really an argument, I say; she was just angry and upset on his behalf, the way the land sales went, those awful people yelling at him and blaming him for everything. And especially how the folks who really wanted to settle here didn't stand a chance against the land-sharks. They even outbid that Very Important Person Lady Franklin. 'I saw her, Tillie, up at the governor's house; she has a very loud laugh and amazing tight ringlets all around her face. Mr Mathew said she is very grand, but *exhausting*—'

Tillie turns over on the cot to face me. 'Enough about her. She sounds tiresome. Tell me more about Albert and Violet.'

I think back to that scene by the picket fence and start to smile.

'Oh, Tillie, truly there is a funny side. There's Violet playing the lady, thinking she is talking to a handsome adventurer with a refined accent, when he's actually a very dubious character, probably a murderer banished from England. And there's Albert being so very polite and attentive to the corporal's charming wife, not knowing she's a convict and — even worse — a snitch, and before that was likely a prostitute.'

Tillie doesn't reply for a long moment, then says in her blunt manner: 'I see two nasty, worthless people who don't deserve to keep their secrets. The capital doesn't need people like them. They betrayed you. And you, my dear Harriet, must return the favour.'

We both think about this, then she continues. 'Albert might have saved you from a worse beating, but that doesn't make him a hero, any better than the scoundrel and imposter he is. Sooner or later respectable people will start to question all his stupid stories. Word will get around. Already I've heard Mr Mathew say that he's lazy and arrogant and will never make a surveyor. He'll soon run out of prospects. And as for that Violet, she can go and have the child somewhere else, and good riddance to her! Back in Australia would be a start.'

'Child?' I ask. 'What child? She's *pregnant*? How do you know about a child?'

'Servant girls have big ears,' she whispers. 'I overheard Mr Mathew about a week ago, telling Mrs Mathew he'd heard from one of the officials. Men are great gossips. I suppose today you were too . . . preoccupied to notice.'

Perhaps. But now, thinking back: yes, as Violet pointed accusingly at me, I did think she'd lost that gaunt look. So now, to go with the new life, a new baby to make up for the one that died in the Cascades nursery. Am I so heartless that I don't feel a flicker of sympathy? To Tillie, I can only murmur good night, turn over and try to quell my racing mind.

I'm just about asleep when the piano-playing abruptly stops. The Mathews' tent is only a few yards away, so their talk is easily heard. Sarah, he says, you'll be pleased to know the land sales finish tomorrow, thank the Lord.

I'm more than pleased, she begins. As your wife, I was horrified—

But she is interrupted.

'My dear, let us not dwell on what's happened. The capital will thrive, regardless. But hear me out: there's another excitement on the horizon, literally. I've just had word from Captain Rough that a ship has been sighted out in the gulf. Unless the wind swings round to the south-west, we should expect her arrival in three or four days.'

September 1840

AS THE *PLATINA* SAILED on north, I told myself to forget the grim past, not worry about the unknown future, just enjoy the swishing waves, the sunshine, the dolphins jumping alongside, the soaring birds.

When I noticed one of the settler boys get taken up the mast, I asked Paddy if I could go aloft, too.

'One hand for the ship, one hand for yourself,' he said as I pulled myself up from the railing onto the first rung of the rope ladder. It got narrower near the top, and then — the most terrifying moment — I had to swing outwards by just my arms to clamber onto the crow's nest where the lookout stood.

Paddy, climbing like a monkey behind me, joined us and grinned at my pleasure. I felt triumphant! And I laughed: where was that prim little girl, the saddler's daughter now?

We sailed past some high white cliffs that are marked on the charts, said Paddy, as Cape Kidnappers, but he didn't know why. Several days later, we passed between the mainland and an island with smoke belching from its peak: a volcano! White Island on the chart, named by Captain Cook seventy-odd years ago, I was told. Perhaps Cape Kidnappers had something to do with him, too?

Most interesting of all, we sighted numbers of long, thin native canoes, which Paddy had heard were carved from a single tree. Some had sails, others were being paddled. Local Maoris out fishing. But we were too far out from the coast to see any houses along the foreshore.

One night, Paddy woke me from a deep sleep. I should come up on deck, he said. A full moon was casting a beam of light across the sea, but he took me to the railings near the bow. Below, a group of dolphins, their bodies long, slender tubes of bright silver, were jumping so close to the ship I could almost have leant down and touched them. They were diving and swerving away, and returning to leap out of the water again for the pure playful pleasure of it. Sharing that pleasure with we humans.

Messengers of the sea gods, Paddy murmured. For mariners, and for you, Harry, 'tis a good omen.

25. Going home

OUR PATIENCE IS SORELY tested. Infuriatingly, the light winds settle into the south-west, meaning the ship sighted by Captain Rough takes a full six days to be seen off Rangi-toto.

I am of course confined to Tillie's tent, out of sight of the officials coming and going. Mostly they are all over in Commercial Bay from dawn to dusk, so I'm able to enjoy the autumn sunshine. I help Tillie knead the bread, scrape potatoes and collect driftwood. These days most of the Maori canoes are heading straight for the market at Commercial Bay.

But our frustration, in waiting for the ship to arrive, grows by the day. Everyone, reports Mrs Mathew, is speculating wildly about what she'll be carrying.

New settlers, surely? Mail, of course! Furniture? Dry goods of all kinds? Barrels of ale? French wine for the governor's cellar? Silk dresses from London for his wife? Sturdy calico for everyone else? Glass for windows? Tobacco, blankets and nails to trade with the natives? Tools? Plants, seeds, animals? Please God . . . boots!

Finally, around noon on the sixth day there she is, a fine three-master out by Rangi-toto, needing Captain Rough to row out and go aboard as pilot and order a few tacks to get her around the north head. We watch her drop anchor, all the sails come smartly down, always a sign of a well-run ship.

When she has discharged all her passengers and cargo, on the night before her departure, I'll be rowed out to climb up the rope ladder, step onto the deck and be shown below to where I'll sleep. I'll meet an older woman directed to care for me on the journey home, back to where I belong.

All this will happen because Mrs Mathew has somehow arranged it with her friend Captain Rough and the ship's captain. I'm promised a berth, and she will give me money to add to what I have saved from Martha's gift and my earnings.

Though it might be out of pity, she understands my yearning to go home. And I think she must now have decided that she actually quite likes me, after all!

The ship is called the *Saint George* and it's the most beautiful ship in the world. Every night I dream of home.

Perhaps it's a sign that my worst times might be over and better things to come that I now join Tillie as no longer a girl. One morning I wake to find blood on my bedding. Only a little, but surely it is the reason for those tender breasts and a feeling of having eaten too much.

This is quite different from all the females in Cascades for whom bleeding was a reason for shame and disgust. When I tell Tillie, she smiles and hugs me.

'Now all grown-up, a real lady,' she declares. 'I'll get you some rags. We can sponge off the blood with cold water. Are you sore?'

'Not really.'

'Don't worry if you are, it goes once you start. I've never had any of the stomach cramps Mother told me to expect.' Her comforting words are so utterly different from what I remembered at Cascades that I burst into tears. Mostly relief, but some sadness too — my dear mother would have wanted to share this moment with me. When I get home I'll tell her and we'll talk more about it.

Captain Rough's pilot boat brings back disquieting news from the *Saint George*. It spreads through the bays like wildfire.

I quickly learn from Tillie and Mrs Mathew's breathless narrative that these are not only ordinary settlers coming ashore. Oh, in no possible way are they 'ordinary'.

They are ex-prisoners, a hundred and twenty-eight of them, all boys from the Parkhurst Prison in England, mostly guilty of only minor offences, nicking watches and clothes and the like.

Mrs Mathew provides details. They have been pardoned on condition they stay in the colony, to live and work where they are told. In the prison they have been taught useful trades, to be shoemakers, tailors, carpenters, brick-layers. The youngest is twelve, the oldest twenty.

'They'll be trouble!' declares Tillie, tugging so sharply at the sheets we're folding that I lose my balance. 'A hundred and more boys milling around, getting into bad company with all those horrid Sydney land-jobbers still here.'

'We should impute virtue, Tillie,' says Mrs Mathew tartly. 'Let us give them at least a fair chance. Captain Rough has been put in charge. They've probably been just as harshly treated as our Harriet here.'

'Mmmm,' grunts Tillie. 'It's all right for her: she can't wait to get on that ship and sail away.'

'And she has her reasons — good reasons,' replies Mrs Mathew. 'You still have your loving family with you, close by. You've no ties pulling you back home.'

'Do you, Mrs Mathew?' I ask. She pauses for a long moment before replying.

'I miss my family, of course I do. I'm one of thirteen children, the fifth daughter. I correspond regularly with two or three of them.'

'Lordy!' says Tillie. 'Thirteen!'

'Mr Mathew and I want to settle here, but I worry for my husband. For all his conscientious hard work, his position as surveyor-general is not as secure as he would like. And his nasty cough also worries me.' She adds wistfully: 'One day we might go back.'

She picks up the pile of neatly folded sheets. 'Harriet, I do understand why you yearn more than anything to see your family again. It's a terrible thing for such a young child to be torn so cruelly away from everything that's loving and certain in her life.'

'Look!' says Tillie, pointing out to the ship. 'There's the first boat coming ashore. The first load of trouble-makers.'

'Tillie!' chides Mrs Mathew, but we both know she's teasing.

It takes two days to bring all the boys ashore to Commercial Bay. We hear that they are being housed with kind people until they find work and proper lodgings.

Confined to Official Bay, I watch the ship for many hours, the small boats coming and going with cargo, stores and animals. Sailors work for long periods up on the rigging and scrubbing the topsides, preparing the ship for the long voyage to Lima in Peru and then around the Horn.

I'm always very careful to remain unseen by anyone in Official Bay. My bag is ready for the call to board the *Saint George*.

I know Tillie is right to keep prompting me, at least once a day: Harriet, when are you going to make up your mind about Albert and Violet?

You can of course just sail away, she says, and they will heave a sigh of relief and life will go on. But for their sort of nastiness, surely there have to be consequences? Good people mustn't let bad people go on being cruel and evil. Otherwise they'll go on doing it, they'll never be stopped.

'And that is exactly,' I murmur one night as we cuddle like spoons in her cot, 'why I have decided to ask Mrs Mathew to tell her good husband what she already knows about Albert.'

'So, knowing how men love to gossip,' replies Tillie, 'he'll tell the other officials. I think the term is blacklisted.'

'He'll just go somewhere else,' I say. 'Join the scoundrels already down in Port Nicholson or the southern settlements. Go back to Australia. But he might now understand that his victims won't always remain silent.'

'You don't feel any remorse yourself about dobbing him in?' asked Tillie. 'Not after his one decent act of rescuing you from that assault?'

'None at all. That was mostly just instinct, from his nursery days. Can't you just see a stern governess buttoned up to the neck in black telling him, over and over, nice well-bred boys like you don't ever *ever* hit girls? No, there's no remorse — on either side.'

'Bravo!' whispers Tillie, giving me an extra-firm hug.

Mrs Mathew has told me to prepare for departure in five days' time, so I have to make up my mind about Violet.

Over the daily kneading of the bread dough, I say, 'Tillie, will you do something for me? Something you might find . . . well, a bit distasteful.'

'Yes?' she responds doubtfully.

'Will you go over to Commercial Bay and bring back Violet? I can send a message, but I need to talk to her directly. And most definitely *alone*! If you can find her apart from her husband, so much the better. Will you do that for me?'

She takes out her annoyance on slapping around the bread dough, but eventually says, 'If I must. I won't enjoy it, and I will curse you for asking me, but I'll go.'

'Thank you, my friend.' I lean over and give her a quick kiss on the cheek. 'Just tell her I want to see her — but please, don't breathe a word about me leaving. Just that I need to talk. She will come, I'm sure of it. Can you go this afternoon?'

'Get it over with?'

I nod. 'It'll be low tide. You can go around the rocks. And bring her back that way.'

'Oh dear, she'll have to take off her smart red boots. Get her dainty ankles wet!'

Our laughter dispels some of the tension, and we turn our attention back to our work.

Sure enough, sitting on the beach after lunch I spot two figures picking their way through the shallows, Tillie leading, with Violet trailing behind. Even from a distance, I can sense the older woman's reluctance. Today she's wearing a dress and bonnet of respectable dark grey — reminding me unpleasantly of Cascades.

As she approaches, I look for any tell-tale swelling but can see none. Tillie joins me on the washed-up log that often does duty as a bench, leaving Violet to stand before us, barefoot, restive, and clutching her boots to her chest. I let her remain so for a while, noting her increasing discomfort. Rarely have I felt such power, knowing that what I'm going to say is right and fair.

'Thank you for coming,' I say politely.

'You'll regret it,' she spits at me. 'Now we know where you've been hiding, my husband is following within the hour. He's determined you shall be taken into custody—'

'I think not, when he hears of our agreement.'

'I'm sorry, Harriet,' says Tillie. 'She wouldn't listen to me unless her husband was there, too.'

'Quite right. That girl is an aggressive little minx,' says Violet, pointing at Tillie. She takes a step towards me. 'What agreement?'

'In five days' time the corporal will watch me taken out to yon beautiful ship. See her, Violet,' I add chattily, 'the *Saint George* out there, bound for Lima, the Horn and the snowy white cliffs of Dover.'

'You'll never get away from here.'

'Five days is quite time enough for stories to spread.' I drop my voice to a whisper. 'Have you heard? The esteemed corporal's wife, that tall Mrs Violet Godfrey, well, she's not the fine lady she'd have us all believe. She's an ex-convict. From that place in Hobart. And before that, the reason for her sentence — you won't believe this, but . . .'

'They'll never believe you. Lies upon lies! A vindictive girl taking her revenge, a parting shot.'

'There'll be prattle. Oh yes, there'll be prattle. And prattle tends to get believed, in time.'

'Once you're gone,' she snarls, 'no one will care one jot about my time at Cascades. Those who do suspect, they'll forget soon enough.'

'Do you really believe that?'

'I finished my sentence; I'm pardoned! I'll start my business for the town's quality, and they'll be glad of it.' Despite her bluster, I can see fear in her eyes. 'But what's this you say about an agreement? What agreement? I've agreed nothing.'

Noting that she's getting tired of standing on the sand's

uneven surface, I take my time to answer.

'You'll instruct the corporal I'm to board the *Saint George* without hindrance.'

'I will not.'

'In return, I'll sail away from here keeping your secret to myself. The only people who know about you at Cascades, other than me, are Tillie and Mrs Felton Mathew. They're both sworn to secrecy.'

'Hah! Cascades taught me to trust no one.'

'That I do understand, but I trust them absolutely to keep their word — as I will — because of the child.'

'What child?'

Tillie and I look at each other. 'Oh Violet,' I say, 'just because you're maybe ten years older than us, don't think that we're naïve or stupid. Your husband has let it be known that you're with child, and besides, we already guessed, you look so well! Tillie, doesn't she look well?'

'Well enough,' says Tillie ungraciously. 'Fuller in the face, perhaps. But I don't think any quickening as yet. I hope everything is all right. There are no doctors here. Or midwives.'

Something in Violet snaps. She sags at the knees and sits down heavily on the sand. Now, I can see a very slight swelling beneath her skirts.

'My baby was born healthy but died in that terrible nursery,' she whimpers. 'He was starved to death.'

'You don't deserve my pity,' I say. 'You took pleasure in tormenting me, shaving my head with that blunt razor. You *offered* to do it, which makes it worse. And you enjoyed it. How could you, an inmate yourself? You watched me grow thin and gaunt, so far out of my mind I wanted only to die.'

Her hands are over her ears, vainly trying to shut my voice out.

'And here, out of pure malice, you betrayed me. You've made

it impossible for me to stay, even if I wanted to. So understand this, Mrs Godfrey: it's only for the baby's sake that I'm keeping quiet about Cascades. The child deserves to have some chance of making a good life here.'

'I'm trying to build a new life,' she cries. 'I've got a good husband. I've done my time. I shouldn't be punished forever.'

'And the child shouldn't be punished at all—'

'Harriet, look over there!' interrupts Tillie. Not one but three figures are splashing through the shallows towards us. 'Corporal Godfrey and the cavalry!'

'Help me, Tillie.' We pull Violet to her feet and brush the sand off her skirts.

'You may go,' I say. 'It's up to you to convince the corporal why he and his henchmen will return empty-handed to Commercial Bay. Go to him. There'll be no further discussion with me. Good day to you.'

I catch Tillie's eye as I turn my back on Violet, and together we trudge up the sand towards the marquee. Tillie's broad smile mirrors my own feelings of satisfaction.

Down by the waterline the mime show plays out. The corporal runs to his wife, and she sags into his arms. They talk, he starts up towards us, she pulls him back, urgently now. There is more talk, more entreating and crying and hugging, before they slowly turn, followed by the two men, to resume the walk back to Commercial Bay.

'You're too kind,' says Tillie. 'I wouldn't have been half so forgiving . . . But what does it matter? You're leaving anyway — you want to leave.'

'Oh yes, more than ever now.'

The *Saint George* sits tantalisingly out in the harbour, sailors as usual up on her rigging, ensign flying bravely. Rocking quietly, awaiting her departure. Five days to go.

'I'll miss you terribly,' Tillie says quietly, drawing my attention back on land, back to the present. 'Will you remember me, Harriet?'

'Always! Especially when I'm kneading bread—'

'Oh Lordy, thanks for reminding me! And the oven not even hot — there'll be no bread ready for supper.' She runs to attend to the bowl of risen dough.

The encounter with Violet leaves me feeling limp with relief. I slump down onto the sand with the log at my back and let the late afternoon sun warm me. With the five raupo huts completed, there are no native builders in the bay today.

I'd earlier taken Pigtail Paddy's piece of scrimshaw from my bag and placed it in my pocket. It now seems, as my fingers trace the tiny ship lovingly carved into the smooth surface, like a token of good luck, for better times. I can hear the ship's bells sounding a change of watch. I'm leaving the capital with a stain on my name, to be sure, but my conscience is clear.

I'm half-asleep, thinking of my mother's garden when her spring daffodils are pushing up into the light, when I hear voices.

'This is a nicer bay than the one over the hill.'

'The gov'mint officials live 'ere, that's why.'

'Look, two horses in that hut!'

'Don't get any ideas, boy!'

'Captain Rough says leave our bags in the tent nearest the big marquee.'

'Where we goin' sleep?'

Recognising that the voices come from unknown people walking down the track, I scramble to my feet, but am too late. Four young men have emerged from the trees and are taking in their surroundings. Of course, they're some of the Parkhurst boys from the *Saint George* being looked after by Captain Rough, probably here to bed down in his tent.

Some instinct tells me I should be on my guard, and I put my precious piece of scrimshaw deep into a pocket. Aware of being silently scrutinised, I meet their gaze more boldly than I feel.

The tall boy at the back of the group catches my eye. Something about him seems familiar, and in the time it takes me to be certain he has pushed through to the front.

There, just as shocked as me, stands my brother, the last person in the world I ever wished to see, ever again.

26. Jesse's news

'WELL, BUGGER ME!' EXCLAIMS Jesse. 'It's my precious sister, all grown up. Alive and well in the capital of New Zealand. Who would have thought! We reckoned you'd probably be dead 'n' buried by now.'

I gulp, determined to keep my voice even and myself from falling over. 'I'm very much alive, thank you, Jesse. I'm sorry to disappoint you.'

'We heard you were sent to Newgate and then Hobart.'

'It wasn't a nice place. I left. I had many adventures. I arrived here.' I take in his scruffy clothes, a deep scar across one cheek, and an unpleasant expression that manages to be both mocking and suspicious. 'And you? Surely not! A Parkhurst boy. How did that happen? Don't tell me you stole an apple!'

He sighs and, as bold as brass, trots across the sand to sit on the log. The three others have walked down to the waterline and started throwing shells. I know they're listening, though.

'Nice bay, this. Pretty. You know I like to fish.'

'Yes. When you should have been at work helping father.'

'Well, one day I didn't see the small sign saying *No Fishing, Keep Off, Private Property*. I didn't see the gamekeeper before he saw me. Such a pity, they were good-sized carp. Mother was frying them up for supper when the bobby came to take me away. We offered him some, but he refused.'

'So for the sake of a few carp, you broke our mother's heart.'

'I tell you, I didn't see the sign. It was an old one, half-hidden in the bushes and the paint flaking off. The fuckin' gamekeeper wasn't doing his job.'

'So, not your fault. Of course — it never is your fault. How can you have been so *stupid*!'

He looks up at me, frowning as if deciding what to say next. 'I didn't break our mother's heart. Well, she grieved, but only for a short time.'

'What do you mean? Grief doesn't get turned off like a tap.'

'It does if she . . . died. About a month after my trial. Remember she told you just before your trial that she was with child? She lost that baby.'

Oh, my dear sweet mother . . .

'But then there was some peculiar swelling in her belly, not a baby, something else, and she couldn't take food. I got a message from Father a few days before leaving. She just faded away in great pain and anguish. He blamed me for her suffering. That wasn't fair, you know!'

'Why didn't he write to tell me this?' I cry. 'I never got one letter in four years.'

'They did write,' says Jesse, 'but they said they never heard a word from you.'

Of course they didn't, I think bitterly, when we were not allowed pen and paper, and the wardens must have burned any letters that did find their way to Cascades. And now I'm realising that the letter Paddy promised to have written for me and delivered to my family must never have arrived. I would never know why, for what reason he didn't — or couldn't — keep his word.

'If anyone broke their hearts, it was *you*,' he continues. 'It was sickening, the way Father tried to get his rich friends to use their influence. Could they prevent your case from being heard? Get you out of Newgate? Even stop your transportation?

Lordy lordy, how he tried, day and night. But he was wasting his breath. From what I heard, that old magistrate at the Lewes Assizes was having none of it. He was determined to rid England of undesirables like you. "The law must take its course." So off went my sweet sister — their dear little Sparrow flew away . . .'

He leans down to pick up a rock from the sand and hurl it angrily towards the sea.

'For me, his only son, when I was hauled off to the Assizes and sent to Parkhurst, were similar efforts made?' He laughs, and for the first time looks up at me directly. I'm shocked by the hatred in his eyes. 'He didn't lift a finger. Did *nothing*.'

With that, my heartless brother stands up, indicating an end to this conversation, and goes to join his mates throwing shells into the water. I'm left slowly turning in a circle, seeking something, seeing nothing, my body and mind reeling at the cruelty of how he's conveyed this dreadful news about Mother and the depth of his animosity. He is consumed by envy, disappointment and rage; he is incapable of remorse, sympathy, compassion or love.

Rage boils up in me, hot and violent. I run down to the water, and spin him around by the shoulders to face me. Taken by surprise, he stumbles and falls full-length backwards into water about a foot deep.

'Why, you little vixen!'

Beyond just plain anger, beyond sense, I leap onto his chest, legs astride and my hands around his throat. His face isn't completely submerged under the water, but enough to have him spluttering for breath between a string of foul curses.

'Tell me . . .' I roar, '. . . *convince* me . . . that you didn't make up . . . the whole story . . . about the apple. To get rid of me!'

'Don't be absurd! Take your fucking—'

'No! You see, your sweet sister heard that row you had with Father, the morning we went to the market. I remember every word. Father was tired of your drinking, your insolence. You were so useless in the saddlery he was beginning to think your sister — me — had a better chance of running the business. Even though only ten, I was already — what was it he said? — "smarter, more industrious, dependable, and altogether better company". The saddlery would be in safer hands.'

As he struggles, water flying everywhere, I tighten my grip around his throat.

'And then you shouted back, "Of course — she's your darling little girl, your favourite wee Sparrow who gets excursions to London and pretty dresses and you take riding." And Father roared, "I gave you riding lessons when you were sober enough to sit on a horse. I taught you leatherwork when you turned up, which wasn't often. I made excuses when I heard village stories about your drinking and whoring and cheating at cards."'

'All lies! Lies!'

'And then you stormed out, bellowing, "You never loved me!"'

'Well, he didn't. He hated me! It was *you* he loved.'

'Because of you, I . . . You *planted* that apple.'

'It was meant to be a joke, a prank. Tom's idea—'

With my hand flat on his face, I hold his nose down under the water, while his hands vainly try to push away my shoulders and his legs flail in the air like an upturned sheep. As the seconds tick by I realise that I, fit from many months' running up and down hills and lifting things, am actually stronger than him, who's grown weak from five months at sea. But with his idle life at home, he was always soft, his muscles flabby, pot belly from too much ale already hanging, and him not yet fifteen when I left.

So I have the strength to hold his nose down. Drown him if I want. Revenge and justice for four years of misery.

But there are witnesses. So is he really worth the risk or even certainty of a hangman's noose? Or living the rest of my life as a fugitive, again?

Feeling I've sufficiently made my point, I release my clamp across his face. Now he knows my strength. With much gasping and spluttering and waving around of limbs, he struggles to throw me off.

Still astride his chest, I snarl: 'Listen to me, brother. See that fine ship out there? When she leaves in five days, I'll be on it — I'm going home.'

'Fine, good riddance,' he gasps, wiping the salt water from his eyes. 'I'll get work here—'

'What work — you don't know what a day's work is!'

'They taught us trades in Parkhurst. I'm a bootmaker.'

'Fancy that!'

'You could do with some new boots.'

'I'll buy my next pair in England. And take care of my father. I'll help him in the saddlery.'

At that, the monster actually chuckles, his confidence returning as he pushes me aside and sits up. 'Good luck to you, little sister. I've told you only the half of it.'

Can he inflict a worse blow? Yes, being Jesse and even half-drowned, he can.

'You know those fearsome big shears Father used to cut the leathers? Well, there was an accident.'

He pauses, the water lapping around him, suddenly reluctant to impart details that he knows will upset me.

'And?' I am standing at the edge of an abyss of despair I know is about to swallow me up. 'Were you involved?'

'I was there when it happened, yes. But he did it to himself.'

'Did what?'

'Got careless. The silly man was always lecturing me about

the safe use of tools . . . and he got careless. I've never seen so much blood.'

'Let me guess,' I cry. 'You'd been drinking, he was in a rage, you had words, you fought—'

'Such a clever sister!' sneers Jesse, hauling himself upright. 'Always has the answers. And before you ask: he damaged a thumb and two fingers so badly . . . the surgeon had to come and finish the job.'

I cry out, imagining the horror of the scene. The abyss closes over me.

'Now he can't handle the tools. Last I heard, the saddlery was being sold to the Master of the Hunt. You remember him? And his lisping daughter Mary? I secretly walked out with her for a while, but her father found out. She was forbidden to see me, only the saddler's son. No great loss — she was no beauty. I'd have done better.'

He smooths back his dripping wet hair, seemingly just enjoying a chatty conversation.

'God knows what Father does with himself all day now. He's gone wrinkled and grey rather quickly, poor old man. Has had to go live with his sister's family, the very fussy Aunt Dorothy — remember her? Barely talks to anyone. Now, tell me, which is Captain Rough's tent?'

Eventually, disgusted and left drained by his malice and utter lack of compassion, my skirt and jacket soaked, I get to my feet.

Only now does it occur to me that the other three Parkhurst boys haven't come to his aid. How very strange. The village boys I knew usually hunted in packs, and were quick to defend a friend under attack, no matter what stupidity or crime was being committed.

But when I look around, I see them sitting in a row together, a little way up the beach, and they are actually grinning broadly. Nothing has been said. They are looking down at Jesse as he stands there in his sodden clothes, shamed and humiliated for all his bravado, and they're laughing at him.

Whatever punishment I think I've inflicted on Jesse, this is an unexpected bonus. From all my time in men's company, I know how — more than anything — they hate to be scorned or ridiculed or — worst of all — openly laughed at.

By a woman is bad enough, but by a mere slip of a girl — it's the end of the world!

And there can be only one reason for them standing by, watching a feeble girl half-drown one of their mates, and with the further mortification of her then deliberately choosing to spare him. Two of them provide me with the answer.

'Serve 'im right, miss. You ain't only one wot 'ates 'is guts.'

''E's feckin' *scum.*'

27. Crossroads

THE TIDE IS COMING IN, enough now to deny any chance of going to sit on the rocks between here and Mechanics Bay. Blinded by tears and rage, I creep up the beach in my wet clothes, avoiding Captain Rough's tent, where Jesse and the rest of the Parkhurst boys have headed to make themselves at home.

The only quiet and remote place I know is the secret track up to the headland, the one that only I use. It runs parallel to the usual track. I can be safe there. I climb about halfway up, my mind numb, insensible to the sharp rocks and the knee-high slippery tree roots crossing the path.

A tui chuckles above me, right above the hollowed-out trunk of a fallen tree. It feels like a message to stop here, now, Harriet. Listen to my song. Let your tears go.

Crouching inside the trunk, hugging my knees, I can't help the noise I'm making, howling like an animal. Jesse might prick up his ears and then just shrug. He isn't his sister's keeper.

I can't stop weeping, for my mother in unbearable pain, her eyes closing forever, my father losing a thumb and fingers, that saddlery he was so proud of, gone. Weeping for my lost dreams of a welcoming path lined with holly bushes and pink hollyhocks, my mother's joyful smile, my own bed at the top of the stairs — the future swept away without mercy or hope.

Some time passes before I notice that the light, already dim under the trees, is fading. I hear the heavy flap of the tui's wings as it flies away. I can't stay here in my sodden clothes forever.

But I'm drained of the will to move, paralysed, and I can't stop crying.

'Harriet?' Someone, a woman, is fighting her way towards me. She must have been coming down the main track and heard my wailing. 'Harriet!'

Through the tangled undergrowth I see Mrs Mathew's burgundy skirt in the flickering glow of the lantern she's carrying. 'Harriet? Oh, my goodness, there you are!'

She doesn't ask me what has happened, or what I'm doing here crouched inside a hollowed-out tree trunk. Finding a comfortable place close by to sit, she waits for me to inch closer, and finally surrender to the consolation of her warm shoulder and soothing hands.

'My dear, you're all wet,' she murmurs, putting her woollen shawl around my shoulders and holding me tighter. 'You can tell me why, when you're ready. If you wish.' To Tillie, who is following, she calls, 'You go on. I'll bring her down soon.'

Haltingly, between renewed tears, I tell her of Jesse's news, so callously imparted. 'My poor dear father . . .'

Neither of us speaks for a long moment. She doesn't ask me why my clothes are soaked. When she moves, I hear the tinkle of her little charm bracelet, reminding me of her stillborn babies. That little owl called a morepork tells us it's perched nearby.

'Such a pretty sound,' sighs Mrs Mathew. 'And the tuis, that throaty chuckle. But I do miss our skylarks and blackbirds. And have you noticed, there are no house sparrows here?'

'I've always been fond of sparrows,' I say. 'If they think there's food around, they don't give up.'

Mrs Mathew laughs. 'Well now, Harriet, perhaps it's time we got you some dry clothes. You know, Official Bay has come to feel quite like home to me, despite the lack of sparrows. Today I've been over in Commercial Bay. Many of the land-sharks have left, praise the Lord. But some are still fighting over prices for the subdivided lots. There's much anger and drunkenness. So much bad feeling. I fear it'll be a long time before Auckland becomes a capital worthy of the name.'

She starts to gather up her skirts, a signal we need to go.

'Oh, and I must tell you, I was approached by the interpreter Mr Williams. Do you remember him?'

'Of course I do,' I say. 'Mr Edward, from the mission family up in Paihia. Young and handsome.'

'He watched the land sales with that native group by the picket fence. No doubt he was explaining to them what it was all about.'

I grunt, loath to recall even a moment of that ugly scene.

'They noticed that you ran off much distressed. Mr Williams says that one of them in particular, a youth from the mission station, was most concerned to know where you were. No one in Commercial Bay knows, of course.'

'Oh? The mission at Maraetai?'

'The message from Mr Williams was — now I must get this right, as it was a little cryptic — he said, if you find her, thank her for her courage and honesty and remind her about the native school.'

If I didn't have Tillie's warm back to hug, or take comfort in knowing that Mrs Mathew's raupo hut is only a few yards away, tonight I wouldn't be sleeping at all. To have my selfish, scheming, hateful brother in the same country, let alone snoring his head off in a tent in the same bay, is almost more than I can bear.

Kind and remarkably strong, Mrs Mathew had half-carried me down the track to the marquee, stripped off my wet clothes, found layers of warm clothing and blankets, and made me a hot drink. Eventually my teeth stopped chattering and I could stand without feeling dizzy.

After supper she summoned Captain Rough to her hut and told him that in the morning one of the Parkhurst boys — Jesse? — must be moved immediately to a more suitable lodging in Commercial Bay.

Captain Rough naturally pressed her for an explanation — from Tillie's cot I could hear them clearly — but she said please, David, just accept that I have my reasons and it's for the best. He can't stay here. Not now and not ever. Send him off to a farm somewhere. Or the settlements down in the south.

I also hear the captain say the *Saint George* is nearly ready for departure, and will be leaving earlier than originally envisaged. If the wind stays in the south-west, then either tomorrow or the day following. In the morning he must remind folk to be sure to hand over any letters and packets destined for Old Blighty. They will have until noon.

Tillie says sleepily, 'That's your ship. Are you still going back? After all you've told me?'

Getting no answer, she presses on.

'Your poor father will be overjoyed at first, but then what? You'd both live the rest of your days fearful of being hunted down, and you sent back to Australia. Harriet, it would break your father's heart all over again. Tell me I'm wrong!'

'Go to sleep, Tillie.'

'And if you go, that hateful brother will . . . I could kill him myself for what he's done to you. You should've drowned him when you had the chance.'

'Tillie!' I give her a good squeeze. 'Promise me you won't do anything silly. Just ignore him. You know the opposite of loving is not hating, it's just not caring a fig. Being indifferent.

Don't give him any chance of ruining your life, too. Promise me. *Promise!*

A grunt is the best she can offer.

With the dawn, I slip off the cot, take a warm blanket and go down on the beach. It's coming up to high tide. Behind Rangitoto and the twin green humps now being called North Head and Mount Victoria, the eastern sky glows a pale lime with streaks of cloud tinted rose-pink and gold. A few stars remain.

Out in the stream sits the *Saint George*, a riding light on her bow, the three masts black and sharp. Her long bowsprit points like a finger, beckoning me. Come aboard, Harriet. Let me take you home.

First Lima, then rounding the Horn . . . at sea a hundred days and more . . . my father's tears of joy . . .

Then what?

Earning a pittance as a scullery maid, maybe even a stable hand, later perhaps a governess? But only by changing my name, leaving my poor crippled father with his sister and moving myself to another part of the country, far away from everything once so familiar and secure.

I'm still an escaped convict. I'm not pardoned, not even possessed of a ticket-of-leave. I'll have to keep this secret from any good man who might see me as his wife, the mother of his children. A terrible secret and fear of betrayal for all my days. And for my father, for as long as he lives.

Across the still water, I hear the bells of the morning watch. No one in Official Bay is yet stirring. Looking down towards Brown's Island, I'm startled to see the sails of two native canoes, probably bringing produce to sell. This early? They must have set off well before daylight.

I remember that day they raised the flag, the pounding of the guns and the canoes racing around the stern of the *Platina*. That handsome and inquisitive paddler, who I later found out understands English. Can it be he who sent the message with Mr Williams? Could he care about me? Like me? Want to get to know me better?

Will living around the coast at Maraetai be far enough distant from those who would do me harm or lock me up again? That wretch Albert will soon be gone, also my brother if Mrs Mathew has her way, which she will; but Violet and her husband — and the baby — are likely to stay.

The canoes are nearer, although the light south-westerly is making it hard for them. I can see they're also paddling. I wonder if they've come from Brown's Island, or across the gulf, or further around the coast. What is it like to paddle in strict time and rhythm with all the others, careful not to miss a beat, to have the satisfaction of feeling the canoe surge forward through the water?

How many children are there at the native school? I know many more interesting and tuneful songs than 'God Save the Queen'. And they can teach me their songs and chants in return. I wonder what's the native word for song?

As the very tip of the sun gleams bright and golden above Rangi-toto and I feel the first warmth on my face, I know where my future lies.

Tillie is kneading bread dough as usual. Mr Mathew has just saddled up his horse. It's a beautiful, still morning, with much activity already on the harbour. On the *Saint George* I can see sailors out on the yards, readying the ship to leave with the afternoon sea breeze.

I'm sitting with Mrs Mathew at Mr Mathew's desk in the marquee. She has lent me two pages of her precious writing paper, her pen and ink, and is helping me with my letter.

To my dearest Father
Auckland, April 1841

Forgive me that I am writing this letter in haste, but the *Saint George* is leaving in a few hours. You will get another longer one from me on the next ship bound for England. (But, I must warn you, we don't get many big ships here.)

So much has happened since I left England, I hardly know where to start. The longer letter will tell you more of my adventures.

But please know that I am safe in Auckland, the new capital of New Zealand. It is being established beside a fine harbour. I have been here since last September. We are still living in tents, but huts are being built for us by the local natives. They have been very helpful, bringing food and firewood. They are such interesting people.

The recent arrival of the *Saint George* brought boys from the Parkhurst Prison. As you can imagine, this caused me much distress, when I found that Jesse was among them.

We have met just the once. He has told me of your accident and our mother's passing.

I have no words to describe my grief at hearing of her suffering. For you left alone and injured, your two children transported, and the saddlery sold. I pray for you and hope with all my heart that you are finding solace in the company of your dear sister Dorothy and her family.

I also learned from Jesse that you never received a letter from me, just as I had none from you. The wardens at the prison near Hobart took much pleasure ensuring convicts were properly punished for their crimes. It seems that denying us pen and paper and destroying our letters from home was one such amusement. However, I did try, as soon as I was able, to get word of my safety to you and Mother. I'm so very sorry that this letter, which I had thought faithfully delivered to you by a friendly sailor from a ship called the *Platina*, in fact never reached you.

Do believe me that since I have arrived in Auckland, I have longed for a ship to bring me back to England. And I have worked tirelessly towards earning a passage.

So forgive me, Father, that the *Saint George* will leave today without me. I have decided to stay in this new country, and become a teacher in a mission school not far from the capital. The longer letter will explain my reasons.

Of course I am experiencing some sharp regret and especially guilt, but I believe you will understand. This is a new colony with many opportunities for women, many more than in England. My convict past will be forgotten here, as it would not be back home. At the mission I will be with good people and will learn the native language, Maori. And here, I believe, the doors of opportunity closed to young women in England can be opened.

I must finish off now, in haste to catch the mail, but also because I see that a waka (Maori for canoe) is just pulling into our bay to take me to my new home at Maraetai. There are five paddlers on each side. I am hoping they might allow me a turn at being a kaihoe (paddler).

Would you please consider joining me in New Zealand? I would be overjoyed, and I think you would like the simple life being established here. There is a great need for leather workers, for saddles and belts and satchels. And just as much for skilled artisan teachers, to pass on their knowledge.

The voyage out is long and arduous, but the rewards great. The air is so clear, the Milky

Way and the stars shine so much brighter here. There are beautiful birds, and trees as grand as you ever saw. I would care for you, always.

I remain your loving Daughter

Harriet

Historical note

Many of the characters in this novel are imaginary — Harriet and her English family, her fellow convicts, the crew of the *Platina* and the settlers. Some, like Harriet's friend Tillie Roberton and the *Platina*'s captain, are loosely based on figures mentioned in accounts of early Auckland.

And some are recognisable historical identities: Sarah and Felton Mathew, Governor William Hobson and his wife Eliza, John Logan Campbell, Captain Symonds, and the interpreter Edward Williams. Their activities during the first few months of Capital Auckland closely follow the historical record. Once or twice dates have been slightly altered, notably the arrival of the Parkhurst boy convicts which was a little later than described, but never significantly.

Harriet's Auckland differs greatly from the downtown area of the city we know today. From the 1860s extensive reclamations re-shaped the harbour's southern shoreline, and headlands considered obstructive such as Point Britomart were gradually removed. The wide sweep of Commercial Bay, initially known as Store Bay, now lies under lower Queen Street; pretty little Official Bay is now buried beneath the main offices and container stacks of the Ports of Auckland; and Mechanics Bay was the beach that led up to the slopes of what is now the Auckland Domain. (It's pleasing that at least two of the names of these three original bays have survived.) Harriet's night-time adventure takes her to the Māori pā and gardens at Orakei, at the head of the deep inlet known as Hobson Bay; in the 1930s this bay was cut off from the harbour proper by the creation of Tamaki Drive.

In keeping with the period in which the story is set, macrons have not been applied to te reo Māori, and the anglicised plurals of te reo Māori then in use have likewise been retained. Similarly, some words and phrases now regarded as abhorrent have been kept, to reflect the views known by written records to be held by some at the time.

Acknowledgements

Re-imagining the past means a *lot* of reading. For personal on-the-spot accounts of the very earliest days of Auckland, there are only the writings of the Scot John Logan Campbell, Captain David Rough and the English adventurer Charles Terry, along with the invaluable journals and letters of the lesser-known Sarah Mathew, wife of the first surveyor, Felton Mathew, but very much an important historical figure in her own right. The research on her I did for my 2015 book *Sarah Mathew: explorer, journalist and Auckland's 'First Lady'* has provided much of the basis for *The Sparrow.*

To flesh out Harriet's story I then had to go to the works of historians like Russell Stone, emeritus professor of history at the University of Auckland and author of many classic books on early Auckland, and John Logan Campbell. To the Australian writers Elspeth Hardie and Deborah J. Swiss, whose recent research into the lives of female convicts in early 19th century Australia makes unforgettable if disturbing reading. To other essential works, by Governor Hobson's biographer, Paul Moon, and by art historian Una Platts. I am grateful to them all. A complete list of their books follows.

After the years of writing come the months of editing, and thanks are due to Harriet Allan and Kate Stone, who encouraged me to make more of Harriet's backstory as a convict transported to the Cascades Female Factory in Tasmania, while bringing their considerable experience editing historical fiction to bear on my narrative. Thank you both, also Stuart Lipshaw and Carla Sy, for your many skills and patience.

To my family, thanks are also due, especially for their support during Auckland's two lengthy Covid-19 lockdowns, in 2020 and 2021, when much of this book was written. Novelists are used to locking themselves down for long periods of solitude, but even so, those were uneasy and testing times, and with their help I remained Covid-free and able to concentrate on Harriet's story.

Bibliography

During the writing of this book, I consulted the following books on the earliest days of Capital Auckland:

Campbell, John Logan, *Poenamo*, 1881

Campbell, John Logan (edited by R.C.J. Stone), *Reminiscences of a long life*, David Ling Publishing, 2017

Duder, Tessa, *Sarah Mathew: Explorer, Journalist and Auckland's 'First Lady'*, David Ling Publishing, 2015

Hardie, Elspeth, *The Girl Who Stole Stockings: the true story of Susannah Noon and women of the convict ship* Friends, Australian Teachers of Media, 2015

Mathew, Sarah, *Extracts from autobiography of Mrs Felton Mathew*, Sir George Grey Special Collection, Auckland Libraries

Mathew, Sarah, *Journal*, 1840, Sir George Grey Special Collection, Auckland Libraries

Mathew, Sarah, *Letters*, 1858–61, Sir George Grey Special Collection, Auckland Libraries

Mathew, Sarah, *Scrapbook*, Sir George Grey Special Collection, Auckland Libraries

Moon, Paul, *Hobson: Governor of New Zealand, 1840–1842*, David Ling Publishing, 2009

Platts, Una, *The lively capital: Auckland 1840–1865*, Avon Fine Prints, 1971

Stone, R. C. J., *Young Logan Campbell*, Auckland University Press, 1982

Stone, R.C. J., *From Tamaki-makau-rau to Auckland*, Auckland University Press, 2001

Swiss, Deborah J., *The Tin Ticket: the heroic journey of Australia's convict women*, Berkley Publishing Corporation/Penguin, 2011

Terry, Charles, *New Zealand, its advantages and prospects as a British Colony*, T. & W. Boone, 1842

Trubuhovich, Ronald V., *Governor William Hobson: his health problems and final illness*, monograph, 2015

Also by Tessa Duder

Young adult and junior fiction

Night Race to Kawau
Jellybean
Alex
Alex in Winter
Alessandra: Alex in Rome
Songs for Alex
Mercury Beach
Hot Mail (with William Taylor)
The Tiggie Tompson Show
Tiggie Tompson All at Sea
Tiggie Tompson's Longest Journey
Alex the Quartet

Short story collections

Too close to the wind and other stories
Out on the water: twelve tales of the sea
Is she still alive? Scintillating stories for women of a certain age (adult)

Picture books and readers

Play it again Sam (reader)
Carpet of Dreams
Restoring Tissot

Non-fiction

Journey to Olympia: the story of the Olympic Games
Spirit of Adventure: the story of New Zealand's sail training ship
The Making of Alex the Movie
The Story of Peter Blake
Margaret Mahy: a writer's life
Sarah Mathew: explorer, journalist and Auckland's 'First Lady'
First Map: how James Cook charted Aotearoa New Zealand

Plays

The Warrior Virgin, Joan of Arc (with Martin Baynton)

For a complete list including anthologies, go to www.tessaduder.co.nz